Pride Publishing b

All on t
Brought b

C000134003

All on the Line

BROUGHT BY THE STORM

GARETH CHRIS

Brought by the Storm
ISBN # 978-1-80250-772-0
©Copyright Gareth Chris 2024
Cover Art by Erin Dameron-Hill ©Copyright April 2024
Interior text design by Claire Siemaszkiewicz
Pride Publishing

Published in 2024 by Pride Publishing, United Kingdom.

BROUGHT BY THE STORM

Dedication

I would like to thank the Totally Entwined –
Pride Publishing team members who helped
make this book possible. Their expertise, faith in
my work, and guidance every step of the way
meant so much to me.
A special thanks to my readers. I hope you'll
enjoy reading the story of Eric and Carrington as
much as I loved writing it.

Chapter One

Eric

"This storm could have a catastrophic impact," the radio station's meteorologist warned for what seemed the hundredth time today. "People should take appropriate precautions. There will be power outages from downed trees, extensive property damage from wind and flooding and possible loss of life. It's shaping up to be the storm of the century."

Although the forecasters had been watching the hurricane for over a week, it had only been in the last couple of days they had started betting on a Northeastern track that would bring New England's worst disaster in decades. I should have stocked up supplies when the storm's path was becoming clearer, but long days at work had me procrastinating. Now, with one day before impact, I was waiting in a line of cars just to enter the grocery store parking lot. It would be a miracle if there were still non-perishable items and supplies available.

After gaining lot access and driving around it more than a dozen times, I spotted a car backing from its spot. I eyed a woman in an over-sized SUV approaching from the other direction, beginning to speed up to claim the space. I pulled up to the exiting car just enough to allow them room to leave, then started nosing my Audi in just as the female competitor tried to do the same. I beat her by about two feet, and she gave me the finger and leaned on her horn. When she saw I wasn't backing out, she did so, then sped down the lane in a huff. Once I had gotten parked, my body was tense to the point of aching.

Someone was exiting the store and abandoning a shopping cart just as I approached the entrance. Since no other carts were in sight, I grabbed it, knowing I would need more than I could carry in my hands. I maneuvered through the store's crowd, securing items without checking prices or searching for favored brands. Every grab felt like a victory.

Although non-perishables were preferred, since I had invested in an all-house generator a year earlier, I took the chance of purchasing milk, eggs and butter as well. The deli counter wasn't as crowded as other parts of the store, and I guessed it was because many other people didn't have functioning appliances during a power outage. I stood behind a man who I thought would, like me, order large quantities of meats. Instead, I heard him ordering deli sandwiches. Armageddon was upon us, and he was ordering lunch? He was out of place—wearing a nice tailored suit and speaking with an unfamiliar European-sounding accent. It made me wonder if he had been transported from another country without means of communication, oblivious to the fact that he'd be starving the next day if he didn't stock up.

As if to satisfy my curiosity, a heavyset man who had been standing nearby approached the guy in front of me and through his conversation, began to make sense of the situation.

"Mr. Howard, I'm going to need to leave you and your companions here. I can't drive you to Newark Airport at this point. I just checked the news on my phone and reports are indicating flights are already canceled because of wind and rain conditions," the man informed him. "The roads are becoming too dangerous for me to drive you the rest of the way to New Jersey."

The handsome man in front of me turned to look at the driver, concern and annoyance on his face. "That won't do," the irritated man protested. "My mother, assistant and I must return to my country today. It is of the utmost importance."

The driver shook his head. "Sorry. I told you it was a gamble when we started this trek. The cards didn't play out. The storm is accelerating, and I'm not risking my life to get you there. Even if we made it, there's a good chance that your flight will be canceled. And how am I supposed to drive back to my family in Massachusetts at that point? The storm will be strengthening and conditions will continue to deteriorate northward."

"I'll pay you double," the foreigner offered, panic in his voice.

"Mr. Howard, it isn't about money. It's about safety—mine and yours. I'm sorry, but I'm heading back to Boston while I still have a chance of getting there. If you want to return with me, you're welcome.

Otherwise, I'll make sure the agency credits you. You should try to find a hotel here in Connecticut to shelter during the storm. I'd pick one away from the shore to avoid flood zones."

Mr. Howard sighed, running a hand over his face. "Please. It is imperative that I return to my country today."

The driver shrugged. "I left your luggage with your assistant in front of the store," he said before leaving for the exit. Mr. Howard looked crestfallen, not even hearing the deli manager call for him to take the sandwiches that he'd made.

"Um, excuse me," I ventured. "I'm sorry. I wasn't trying to eavesdrop, but I heard everything since you're right in front of me. Do you need a ride to a hotel?" I had never offered to chauffeur strangers in my car, but the situation seemed to warrant an exception. Though it wasn't rational, his attractiveness lowered my apprehension. I had heard enough to doubt the guy was a murderer—someone who'd be killing people while traveling with his mother.

Mr. Howard looked at me as if just realizing there were other people in the store. I thought my offer would elicit a small smile, but he glowered instead. "I don't have a hotel. Is this how Americans treat others? He was compensated to take us to Newark, and he abandons us in the middle of Connecticut? If it were worth my while, I'd file a complaint with his firm."

"I understand," I offered. "Under other circumstances, it would be a dick move on his part."

"A *dick* what?" he asked. "I'm not familiar. Is that a crass American way of saying inappropriate?"

Well, okay then. I regretted my offer, but refused to provide him additional reasons to sully my fellow countrymen by losing my cool. "Um, sorry for being *crass*. Perhaps you should retrieve your order so the rest of us can place ours? Good luck with your travels."

His face softened with a hint of embarrassment. He nodded, grabbed his sandwiches and exited the line. I approached the deli case and ordered a plethora of meat, knowing there would be enough to last me several days, even if my friend Mateo came to weather the storm with me. After loading the cart, I made my way to what appeared to be the shortest cashier line, which was about fifteen customers deep. Mr. Howard was a couple of people in front of me, being dramatic with sighs and eye-rolls every few minutes. An older woman next to him, whom I assumed was his mother, patted his arm. At one point, he turned to survey the length of the line, and he spotted me behind him. I saw him whisper to his companion, and she looked over to me as well. I wondered if he had told her I was a *crass* American and she wanted a better view of what one looked like. Instead, she smiled at me, touched his arm once more then walked around the couple behind her to speak with me.

"Hello. I'm Mrs. Howard. My son told me about your gracious offer," she informed me. Unlike her son, she was warm, if a bit formal. She had an air of elegance, like her son, with her refined accent, tailored clothes and a fashionable hairstyle that I doubted she managed on her own. "I just wanted to thank you. He told me he neglected to do so, and I wouldn't want you to think we're ungrateful."

"Oh, it's fine. I hope he didn't think I was rude," I said, wondering why I was feeling apologetic. I had always been too eager to please. "I think I may have used language to describe your driver that was…salty."

I internally chastised myself for speaking like a pirate, and wondered if she would think I was an idiot—another positive impression of Americans for this family from wherever.

She laughed. "Oh please, I'm sure my son was thinking the same salty thing." Then she whispered, "He becomes quite testy when he's stressed."

I smiled, liking her. "Yes, I saw that," I acknowledged. "But I understand. So, did you guys find a hotel to stay at?"

She furrowed her brow. "No. My son has been checking whilst waiting in line and, so far, everything seems to be booked. I'm afraid we'll have to find a place of lodging and plead for a chair or sofa to sleep on, even if it's in the lobby. Although on the way here, we heard a radio announcer speak of places of education sheltering people during the emergency. By chance, is there one of those within walking distance?"

I was horrified to think of this older woman walking miles to a school in the pouring rain and wind, then sleeping on a gym mat. While it was a terrible situation for anyone, from the looks of her, I was certain she had never experienced something that primitive. I suspected her son hadn't either, though I might have enjoyed watching him try. "I don't think any are within walking distance," I stated.

Mrs. Howard frowned. "Oh. We'll have to get a cab then. Perhaps you know the address of a school that we can provide to the driver?"

An internal voice was urging me to give her the name and address of the local elementary school, but another voice was guilting me to refrain. It wasn't as if taxis would venture out in this storm to transport them anyway. "You shouldn't stay at a school. I don't think you realize how much you'll be roughing it," I explained. "When I was a kid, my family had to stay at one during an ice storm. You had to wash in group showers, eat food provided by local charities and sleep on the floor with dozens of people lying around you. It was tough for me when I was young. I can't even imagine..."

"How an old dame like me would survive it?" she finished, but smiling to show she wasn't offended.

"No. Not *old*," I clarified.

"It's quite all right," she soothed, as she and I inched closer to the cash register to keep pace with the moving line. "I'm sure you're correct. It does sound unpleasant. I don't like the sound of a group shower. However, young man, I've lived through worse. Desperate times call for desperate measures, and all that."

"Look, it might seem audacious of me, but you guys can stay at my house until the storm passes," I blurted. I didn't know if it was a wise statement, but I felt relieved I had said it. Now, if they refused, I could go home without guilt. If they said yes, at least the mother seemed nice. I'd ignore the son. I still had no idea who the assistant was.

"Oh, that is very kind of you," she replied. "But you must have your own family to care for, and we wouldn't want to intrude."

I had one more chance to latch onto her words and bow out. I didn't. "No. No family. Just me. I have a three-bedroom, two-bathroom house and there's a couch that can be slept on, too. It would be more comfortable than a school."

She looked appreciative, but also skeptical. "Why would you make such a generous offer to strangers?"

I shrugged. "Desperate times, and all that," I answered, mirroring her earlier comment. "I promise I'm not a psychopath. I've never invited people I don't know into my home. However, I can't in good conscience let you stay at a school. It will be just a night or two anyway. I have a whole-house generator, and now I should have enough food. I guess it will help me sleep better knowing I didn't turn you away."

Mrs. Howard smiled. "Americans are so giving. I, like you, wouldn't choose to cohabit with strangers, but my instincts tell me you're a nice man. And we were ready to share space with strangers in a school, and I would think that's far riskier. Are you sure you don't mind?"

I nodded. "Sure."

She surprised me once again, pulling me into a hug. "You are a dear boy. We'll compensate you, of course."

I waved a hand through the air. "It's not necessary. Consider it Connecticut hospitality."

Mrs. Howard grinned and rubbed my arm, thanking me once again. I glanced toward her son, who looked dumbfounded by the sight of us. His expression turned grim. It made me wonder if I should have listened to the first voice in my head that told me to leave them to their own devices.

* * * *

Carrington

My assistant and friend, Stefan, trying to stay dry whilst huddling under the narrow overhang of the front entrance, shot me a questioning glance when my mother and I emerged from the store. The forward young man had charmed my mother and convinced her that staying at his house was a solution for our lack of shelter. Although I couldn't find a feasible alternative, this plan felt reckless and impulsive.

"Sir, who is this?" Stefan asked, pointing to the American who had rolled out his cart behind us.

Before I could answer, the chap extended his hand to my assistant. "Eric. Eric Turner."

The introduction didn't erase Stefan's look of confusion or compel him to extend his hand in return. The man who called himself Eric Turner lowered his hand as if it had been slapped.

"Okay," Stefan stated, shooting me a look that implored clarification. "Where's our cab? You texted me from the market you'd be ringing for one. If we don't depart soon, we'll miss the flight."

"Whilst stuck in that line, I was searching the internet and saw our flight was canceled," I replied. "And to worsen matters, my search for suitable quarters was fruitless. There is nothing available."

"I'm guessing people were anticipating power outages and booked rooms days ago while they still could," Eric Turner interjected. I must have looked perturbed at his intrusion, as he gulped and glanced at his tennis shoes.

"I'm sorry, *but who are you?*" Stefan prodded with more of an edge.

"Stefan! Mr. Turner offered to help us with our dilemma," my mother chastised. "He's allowing us to stay at his home."

"Stay at his house?" Stefan exclaimed before looking back to me. "Is that wise? Does he know about us?"

"Know what about you?" Eric Turner inquired, apprehension on his face.

"Oh, nothing dear," my mother responded. "He just means that we're not American and may have different customs, but I'm sure you already knew that from our accents."

I could tell from Eric Turner's expression that he was doubting my mother's explanation, and from Stefan's face that his question was answered that Mr. Turner was unaware of our identities. Because I hadn't a notion what we'd do if Mr. Turner were to leave us in a lurch as had our driver, I felt compelled to provide a more believable response. "Mr. Turner, what Stefan was alluding to is that he and I are a couple. Will that be a problem?"

Eric Turner seemed to focus on me, which prevented him from seeing the looks of surprise from both Stefan and my mother. "Oh," he answered, swallowing hard once again. "Um...no. I'm gay too. I guess that makes it easier. I was worrying I might have left something hanging around my house that would out me." He appeared uncomfortable before adding, "I mean, not porn or anything. I don't even have porn. Not that I want porn. I just..." His face was now bright red and he stammered the rest. "I just wasn't sure what little thing could be...anyway, I just didn't want anyone to be uncomfortable. You never know who is open-minded and who is not."

My lie had elicited that surprise confession, but none of it mattered, considering we'd be gone in a couple of days. "Ah. Well, very good then. Perhaps we should be on our way before we get wetter?"

Eric Turner was still looking at me, his natural color returning. "Yes, of course. I'll get my car from the parking lot and pull it up to the curb so you can stay dry under the overhang. Just watch the cart for me."

When he was about ten feet away, he turned back to shout to us, "This worked out well. Now nobody needs to sleep on a couch. Mrs. Howard, you can take one room, and the gentlemen can share the bed in the other."

I tried to smile in return, but I thought it displayed more like a grimace. I turned to my mother, who looked amused, then Stefan, who appeared to be mortified. "Oh, don't you two give me grief. I had to come up with something to cover your mistakes. Maybe try a little harder to keep me alive, if you please."

Chapter Two

Eric

Mrs. Howard must have realized how awkward it was that I didn't know their first names as we began loading the groceries and their luggage into the cargo section of my car. "Please call me Olivia," she invited, handing me a fancy bag with her right hand while balancing an umbrella in her left. "Our assistant is Stefan, who should have told you that himself when you introduced yourself earlier," she noted, shooting a reprimanding look his way. "The other one failing to exhibit good manners today is my son, Carrington."

Of course, his name was Carrington. It was suitable for a self-pretentious prick. Carrington seemed more annoyed than embarrassed by his mother's chastising, ignoring her and making his way to the back passenger door. "You may want to sit up front," I warned him. "You being the tallest and all," I explained when he shot me a questioning glare. "It's just that the back seats are kind of tight. At least that's what I've been told."

Carrington huffed, but heeded my advice and piled into the front passenger seat. I walked Olivia to the door behind him, opening it for her and helping her inside. Once Stefan loaded the last of the luggage and took his place behind the driver's seat, I hopped in to take us on the ten-minute journey home.

"What a charming little town this is," Olivia observed, glancing at the main street we were traveling. The quaintness was evident even in the middle of a storm.

"Thanks," I answered, making eye contact with her via the rear-view mirror. "We have more houses from the seventeenth and eighteenth centuries than any other town in the United States — well, except Marblehead, Massachusetts."

"Does secondary placement merit mentioning?" Carrington asked.

I pretended it was a comment made in jest, and tried to make a joke in return. "That's why some friends and I are going to Marblehead this summer on an arson mission."

Carrington glanced at me with horror, then he must have realized I wasn't serious. He rolled his eyes and directed them back to the windshield. "It's interesting what Americans consider historic. Those houses would be considered new construction in our country."

"Carrington, be polite," Olivia admonished. We sat in uncomfortable silence for a few minutes.

"So, what country *are* you from?" I ventured, noticing the three passengers exchanging furtive glances in response.

After a pause, Olivia acknowledged my question. "It's a small country that most Americans have never heard of. It's near Finland."

Okay. Whatever. If I found out later it was Sweden, I was going to be insulted by their assumptions regarding my intelligence. It felt like they were avoiding mentioning the name of the country, but I wasn't going to push it. I was more concerned about why they were so secretive about *everything*, and wondering anew if I was inviting danger into my home.

"We're almost there," I informed them, turning off the main street into my development. As I slowed to pull into my driveway, all three passengers studied my house with varying degrees of curiosity. "Home, sweet home," I mumbled, worrying their silence conveyed disappointment. I gathered from their clothes and manner that they were wealthy, and my house was upper-middle class, at most. I was proud of it, though. Upon seeing it, I had fallen in love with the saltbox colonial reproduction, its wooden post fence, the expansive yard with mature trees and plantings and the barn-style detached garage. The neighborhood comprised other homes with an Early American architectural style, creating a cohesive feel to the area.

"Well, it's lovely," Olivia exclaimed with a look of delight that appeared genuine.

I looked to Carrington, whose scowl remained. As if catching himself, he nodded in agreement with her. "Yes. Indeed."

I handed Carrington a key and pointed to the side door. He looked perplexed. "Let yourself and your mother in so you don't get too wet. I'll unload the car with Stefan." I caught a glimpse of Stefan in the rear-view mirror, and he didn't seem to mind me including him on the task.

"Will I set off a security alarm?" Carrington asked.

"It's not turned on," I assured him.

"But you do have one? One that is operational and can be activated this evening, correct?" Stefan piped up.

"Uh, yes," I responded, wondering if the worry was related to their secretiveness, or if it was Stefan's assessment of the neighborhood's probable crime rates. "But I can assure you, the area is very safe. The worst you ever hear about is an infrequent car break-in by an under-privileged kid from Hartford. Even then, it's because somebody left valuables in an unlocked vehicle. I always garage the Audi."

Stefan looked out of the windows in every direction, almost as if preparing to ward off a would-be thief. "Yes, it looks peaceful, as you said. Still, best to secure the alarm."

They were giving me serious creep vibes. It was too late to back out of my commitment, though. While the security system would protect me from those outside my home, it wouldn't protect me from my house guests. I made a mental note to place a kitchen knife under my pillow before sleeping.

Chapter Three

Carrington

Once Eric Turner showed us the rooms where we'd be lodging, he descended the stairs with the bed linens and towels to put them through the wash. That left me alone with Stefan, who was in security mode, peering out through the bedroom windows to ensure the perimeter was secured.

Mr. Turner was young, and I was wondering what his occupation could be that he could afford this home. Although it was modest compared to anything I had ever lived in, I had traveled the world enough to know it was many steps above what the average citizen could afford—even in America. Perhaps it was his age that grated on me. It was embarrassing to be beholden to a man who looked no older than a recent college graduate. He seemed sweet and, by any objective person's assessment, cute to the point of adorable. Those traits emphasized his youth, making me feel even more inadequate about needing his help for mere survival.

My mother came out of her guest room and into ours, a scowl on her face. I imagined she was unhappy with the quarters she was assigned. At least she wouldn't have to share a bed with someone.

"Mother, it may not be on par with our most recent accommodations, but it's quite nice for a middle-class home. Keep in mind, you were the one who made this arrangement, and it's safer than staying at a school or a hotel lobby where any number of people could recognize us."

"That's why you think I'm upset? Carrington, I am so disappointed with you right now," she declared. Then, looking at Stefan, she added, "Both of you."

"Disappointed? Why?" I asked, though I imagined it related to her earlier comments about my manners, or lack thereof.

My mother crossed her arms and frowned. "Don't be daft. It's unbecoming, as your behavior has been all day. I know you're concerned about what's happening, but it's unlike you to treat someone this way. This young man has been gracious, and I meant it when I told him his home is charming. It reminds me of where I grew up, unlike the grandeur you've always been surrounded by. Instead of showing him gratitude, you've acted like his purpose is to serve you — and that he's failing. If I were him, I would have asked us to leave. Instead, he's on the main level freshening linens for us. What he must be thinking!"

Stefan, who had been quiet throughout the excursion, defended us before I could. "With all due respect, madam, we have no idea whether Mr. Turner can be trusted."

My mother waved a dismissive hand through the air. "Rubbish. How would he have known we would stop at that food mart for lunch? How did he just happen to be standing nearby when the driver decided he wouldn't proceed with our travels?"

Stefan wasn't swayed. "The driver could have been an operative from the start. He was the one who suggested where we stop for lunch, if you recall. He could have signaled Mr. Turner when and where to be so he could secure us in his custody."

"Stefan, Mr. Turner offered us a ride, which my son shot down. Carrington said that Mr. Turner was ready to let us venture on our own at that point. It wasn't until I approached Mr. Turner that he made the offer to stay at his house. How would he know I would go to him? If Carrington hadn't told me what happened, we would have left that store and been on our way. To where, I have no clue. Not to mention, if the limousine driver had been part of a plot to harm Carrington, why didn't he do it during the ninety minutes he had us confined from Boston to this town? Why would he orchestrate an elaborate scheme to pass us to someone else? On top of that, Mr. Turner doesn't look the part of some undercover hooligan."

"Looks can be deceiving," Stefan countered.

"And your speculations are far-fetched. Nothing has transpired that would support your scenario."

Stefan pondered for a moment, but nodded. "Okay, I agree. Mr. Turner might just be a clueless chump, but we should remain guarded."

"Stefan! What has possessed the two of you? A clueless chump? The man is a saint, and you'd do well to remember that when you dine on his food this evening and sleep in his guest quarters afterward. After the way we've treated him, I'd be embarrassed for our country to tell him where we're from."

Remembering my position and my duty to represent our country, I felt a wave of shame. Of course, she was correct. I had been letting my frustration, safety concerns and feelings of inadequacy drive my actions, which had been insufferable at best. Before Stefan could antagonize my mother further, I interceded. "Yes, you're quite right. Our behavior was inexcusable. I'll apologize to him."

My mother's posture relaxed a bit. "Well, that's a start. And stop being so critical. Whatever this man has, I'm sure he worked hard for, and wounding his pride is not who you are."

I looked around the room once more, beginning to appraise it with an unbiased eye. I had to admit it was tasteful, albeit sparse. Everything about the house had simple lines and décor, typical of middle-class homes in eighteenth-century America. Mr. Turner seemed intent on embracing the fact that his home was an architectural reproduction, and it shamed me once more that I had mocked his heritage.

"How are two grown men going to sleep on that bed?" Stefan pondered. "It's too narrow."

"Well, that shouldn't be difficult for two people in a romantic relationship," my mother snapped. I assumed her sarcasm meant she didn't believe we'd shown appropriate contrition.

"Of all the things to come up with, you came up with us being…homosexual lovers?" Stefan complained to me.

"One of you can sleep on the floor," my mother scolded. "But when you're outside this room, you two had better behave like you're in love now that you've put that notion in Mr. Turner's head. You've already said and done enough to raise his suspicions without adding to them."

"I guess on the bright side, if he thinks we're a couple, he won't proposition one of us," Stefan conceded.

"You can't be serious, Stefan. After the way you two have been behaving, I'm sure he has no interest in either of you," she chided. My mother then focused a critical glare on me. "Now, I'll be going downstairs in a few minutes to keep our host company. I expect you will precede me to extend your apologies?" She turned to exit, making it clear it wasn't a question.

Chapter Four

Eric

I had a load of laundry in the dryer and food laid out on the counter, ready to prepare the evening's meal. The wind had picked up, and I wondered how long it would be before my generator would have to kick on. It had an automatic switch, ready to take over if my house lost power. It had never been needed, however, so I hoped it would work. The one thing worse than a house full of strangers would be hosting them without utilities.

I was beginning to chop celery for the pot roast when I heard footsteps descending the stairs. I turned — Carrington was approaching the kitchen.

"Everything squared away?" I asked, turning back to my chore while awaiting his response.

"Yes, thank you," he replied. He stood silent for a moment, so I turned back to him with a quizzical glance. He looked down at his shoes, some embarrassment reflected on his face. "I'd like to apologize for how I've behaved toward you. You've been most kind, and I've been rude and ungrateful." He raised his cobalt blue eyes up, laser-focused on how I'd react.

At first, I nodded. His intense stare didn't alter. "Okay. Thank you for saying that. Do you want to help me make dinner?"

From his reaction, it was as if I'd asked him if he wanted to help me scalp a neighbor. "Um..."

I jumped in to spare him. "It's okay. Go watch the television or read. Whatever."

"No," he protested. "I want to help. I just don't know how."

All the swagger and sourness from earlier was gone. He seemed relaxed now, and it highlighted his attractiveness. I knew he was taken, but I couldn't help but admire him like the time I had first seen him. His hair was a rich light brown with darker highlights, brushed back and falling into waves in all the right places. His eyes were emotive, and his angular face was highlighted by high cheekbones and a strong, squared, dimpled jaw. His lips were a soft pink and shaped for kissing. And I thought to myself, all of that belonged to Stefan, so I willed my eyes to look away. "Uh, that's okay. I'll teach you. Nobody knows how to cook — until they do. The secret is, if you can read and follow directions, you can cook. Do you want to finish chopping the celery? Just cut them to the size I've been making them." I handed him the knife. Pointing to the chuck roast, I added, "I'll start the rub for the pot roast."

"Pot roast?" he asked with concern.

I assumed it was a dish his country didn't make, or he was intimidated by the prospect. "Yes, I'll make it with potatoes, carrots, celery, some onion and garlic and a red wine-beef broth mix. There are other seasonings too, but nothing too complicated."

"I don't eat meat," he stated, as if his diet should have been common knowledge.

"Oh," I sputtered. "Gosh. That's...okay. You can have the vegetables, right?"

"Not if they've been cooked in beef broth," he responded. "I'm quite all right and can do without dinner. I don't wish to be a burden."

"You can't just have a sandwich for the day. Hey — you had a sandwich at lunch," I remembered.

"A roasted vegetable sandwich," he clarified.

I prayed I had lots of pasta in the pantry. The vegetables wouldn't last more than a couple of days, and it was anyone's guess how long we'd be stuck together. "Is there anyone else who is a vegetarian?" I asked, hoping the answer was no. Otherwise, they were going to be scrounging for berries from my bushes.

"Only me," he assured me. "And everyone else can have dairy."

"You can't have dairy either?" I exclaimed. "You've just eliminated ninety percent of the food in my house."

"I have a dairy allergy," he explained. "I'll make do. I don't wish to create difficulties."

"This will be interesting." I sighed. "Um, well — on the bright side, it seems to work for you. You have awesome skin and a rocking body." As soon as the words escaped my mouth, I realized they could be perceived as flirtatious. I felt compelled to add, "I do photography as a side job, so I can appreciate when a subject makes my work look even better. Not that you'd be posing for me, of course." I had to shut up before he thought me insane.

Carrington looked bashful, but gave me a slight grin and side eye while he started cutting the celery. "What sort of photography do you do? Models?"

"Amateurs wanting to be models," I explained, starting the rub for the pot roast. "I haven't even done that since moving to Connecticut last year. I did a lot of photography when I lived in the city — New York City, that is. Way more aspiring models there. When my firm for my real job wanted to relocate me for a bigger assignment, I was sad to give up the photography, but more money and a lower cost of living are hard to turn down."

"What's your real job?" he asked, seeming to be interested as opposed to making small talk.

"I lead a project management office for one of the large insurers. Hartford is the insurance capital of the world. Our headquarters are downtown. I miss city living, but I also like the peacefulness of this town and its history." The blood rose to my cheeks when I recalled Carrington slapping me down for suggesting the United States had any meaningful landmarks. "Brief as it may be," I added.

Carrington must have remembered his earlier jab, for now it was his cheeks that blushed. "Your country has a proud heritage. I was being disagreeable when you spoke of your town. I, once again, must apologize. The area is charming. Maybe, once the storm passes, if there is time, you can show me more of it."

I nodded and smiled, but I thought it was odd that Carrington wouldn't have included Stefan — at a minimum — in that suggestion. As if suspecting shenanigans, Stefan entered the kitchen with Carrington's mother in tow. He shot a look of shock in Carrington's direction, and I hoped he hadn't heard his boyfriend's last comment. "What are you doing? You should put down that knife before you cut yourself," he exclaimed to his partner. "You don't know how to do that."

Carrington appeared flustered, then annoyed. "I can assure you I am capable of cutting a celery stalk."

"Yes, of course you are," Olivia intervened. "Stefan, why don't you let the boys finish what they're doing? Carrington is in good hands. You and I can read in this sitting area."

"Dinner will be ready in an hour," I told them as they walked into the family room. "I have an Instant Pot." Of course, they had no idea what that was, but it made sense to me to explain the quickness of cooking a large slab of beef.

"That sounds marvelous, dear," Olivia remarked. "My son won't eat the meat, though, I'm afraid."

"Yes, what are we going to do about that?" I asked Carrington. Before he could answer, I offered to roast the carrots and potatoes for him, and make a side salad.

"I've been enough bother," he protested.

"I want to," I assured him, because the person before me was nothing like the cranky man I had met earlier. Carrington gave me his first big smile, revealing large, straight white teeth. I was afraid my knees would go weak. "So, um...I'll just start those now." I feared my face was giving away how I was feeling, and was thankful Stefan wasn't in the room to see it. I spent the rest of dinner preparations looking at Carrington as little as possible.

Chapter Five

Carrington

"What was that?" Stefan asked as soon as we had retired behind the guest room door.

"What was what?" I volleyed back, not caring for his tone.

"Your behavior has been odd since we went downstairs," he replied, appearing as annoyed as he was confused.

"I'm sure I don't know what you mean."

Stefan put his hands on his hips, eyeing me up and down as if the answer could be found on my body if he looked hard enough. "You're showing so much interest in that man. If I hadn't known better, I would think he was an old mate of yours. All evening, you were asking questions about his job, his family and his friends. You helped him cook, you helped him clean up when we were done and now you've offered to help him if something should go bump in the night."

It was true that as Stefan and I had bid goodnight to my mother and to Eric, I had invited our host to wake me if something happened during the evening which necessitated assistance. "A hurricane is coming, and the edge of the storm will be upon us overnight," I reminded him, pointing at the window as if Stefan wouldn't hear the howling wind otherwise. "It seemed like the hospitable thing to do, as did helping him with dinner and clean-up. Mother was right. He's being generous. He isn't here to serve us. As for me asking him questions, it's called conversation. It also kept him from asking *us* questions, did it not?"

Stefan sighed and nodded. "Yes, I suppose. I feared you were beginning to like this chap, and it wouldn't be a good idea to let down your guard."

I couldn't help but roll my eyes. "Well, I do like him. After spending the day with him, do you still suspect Mr. Turner is someone other than whom he claims to be? If he was any more innocent, he'd be a choir boy."

"I suspect many choir boys are anything but innocent," Stefan retorted. "And it's funny you should use the analogy of a boy. He seems barely into adulthood, and all those American 'golly gee' puppy-dog expressions don't help. How does someone like that become a vice president at a large firm? It defies logic."

I laughed at Stefan's description since it wasn't off the mark. Although Eric's youthful qualities had irked me when I had met him, as the evening had worn on, I found them more and more charming. "Eric seems intelligent enough to hold a position of authority. He also shared too many details for it to be untrue."

"I know it wasn't fabricated," Stefan conceded. "I looked him up on LinkedIn whilst you were in the kitchen perfecting your culinary skills."

I crossed my arms to show my dissatisfaction with Stefan's sarcasm. "Perhaps you should use the internet to find a course that teaches the appropriate way to address someone in my position."

Stefan frowned, nodded then looked down at the floor. "Yes, of course. My apologies, sir. I fear our longstanding friendship sometimes makes me forget myself."

Now I felt like a bastard. "Oh crap, Stefan. Don't do that. I told you not to call me 'sir' when we're alone. I just don't fancy being spoken to like I'm a daft adolescent. I appreciate your caution and desire to protect me. You are a wonderful assistant, security guard and a best friend. Just trust my instincts more. I didn't get to where I am by being clueless."

Stefan nodded once again, still uncomfortable, but appearing to relax a bit. "I know that, sir — Carrington. I never meant any disrespect."

I thought changing the subject would be advisable to end his embarrassment. "I know. So, I am sure you will not disrespect me by criticizing my decision to sleep in the nude this evening."

I thought Stefan's eyes would pop from his head, but to his credit, he tried very hard to retain his composure. "Um, as you wish. I was planning to sleep on the floor anyway."

Unable to hide my amusement any longer, I began to chuckle. "It was a joke. I do not sleep naked. I hope you do not either."

If I hadn't known better, I would have thought that Stefan looked hurt for a moment before donning a shy smile. "I do not."

"Then there will be no need to sleep on the floor. I'm sure we can endure a night or two of bumping into each other. I apologize in advance for any knee jerks to your legs."

The camaraderie that Stefan and I shared in private returned. "I sleep in a fetal position. My knees might end up hitting you in a more vulnerable spot."

"Ha. You'd wish me to believe it was accidental, wouldn't you?" I asked.

Stefan chuckled. "Imagine explaining that soreness in the morning? You could tell Mr. Turner that I need to scale back exercising my buttock muscles—that it was like slamming your crotch into a couple of boulders when we made love."

The blood rushed to my cheeks. Stefan and I had shared many off-color remarks in our history, but this was the first one that suggested a sexual relationship between us. The fact that it had described me impaling him created the visual, and I found I couldn't look him in the eye. "Um, that might be too descriptive for polite breakfast discussion." I started to retrieve toiletries from my baggage so I could bring them to the lavatory to prepare for bed.

Stefan seemed oblivious to my uneasiness. "I was joking, of course. Although you know, we should act a little more like a couple tomorrow. You paid a lot more attention to him than you did me. As your mother said, we should try to be convincing."

I gave him a quick nod of agreement, then bolted from the room with a foreboding sense that conditions were going to be hard to control—and it had nothing to do with a hurricane.

Chapter Six

Eric

I emerged from my room just as the door to the guest room opened. Though it was dark in the hallway, I could make out that the shadowy figure approaching me was Carrington. He had taken the time to throw a robe over his pajamas. If I hadn't been concerned about the source of a loud noise, I might have been more focused on the fact that I was walking around in a T-shirt and sleep shorts. I was always shy, and being half-dressed when someone else was over-dressed wasn't a comfortable situation for me.

"Did you hear that bang?" I asked him.

"I did. Do you think your house is secure?" he whispered.

I shrugged and started down the stairs, Carrington on my heels. Once I was on the first floor and wouldn't disturb the other guests, I turned on some lights. "I think it came from the backyard," I said, looking to Carrington, who appeared more uneasy than I did. I walked to the French doors that overlooked my enclosed patio and flipped on the exterior lights. "Shit."

"What is it?"

I wiped a hand over my face, not happy with what I saw. "A tree fell on my patio fence. It brought down a panel and it looks like the whole structure could be compromised. I wonder if it cracked any of the patio pavers. That tree may have to be cut up by professionals. It's huge."

"At least it missed the house," he consoled. "It could have been worse."

He was right. If the tree had fallen in a different direction, it would have hit the room where Olivia was sleeping. I couldn't imagine how horrible that would have been. Still, my sinking heart saw the inconvenience and the repair costs. "Well, the night's still young," I mumbled.

"Hey," he whispered. I was still staring at the mess that was my patio. Carrington touched my shoulder, and I turned to his compassionate stare. "It will be okay."

"I have a $2,500 deductible," I complained. I could tell he didn't know what I meant. This wasn't a rich person's problem.

"Perhaps Stefan and I could help remove the tree," he offered.

I laughed. "Dude, I don't think you realize how much work cutting up that tree will be."

He looked perplexed. "Dude?"

"Don't focus on my American phrasing right now. I'm too upset."

He gave me a slight nod. "Of course. My apologies."

The windows were doing their best to protect us from the driving rain and vicious winds, but their rattling was making me nervous. "Maybe we should move away from the glass," I suggested. We walked to the kitchen, which had one small window over the sink.

"I'm amazed that the others can sleep through this," he observed, looking back toward the bellowing French doors that lined the rear wall of the family room.

"Has Stefan always been a sound sleeper?"

Carrington looked surprised by my question. Did it cross a line to ask? It had been an attempt at small talk. "Um, yes. I guess." Even though I had the overhead lights at the lowest dimming position, I could see Carrington blush. Perhaps people of proper society didn't share details regarding a partner's sleep habits. Before I could contemplate further, Carrington's stomach rumbled, which elicited a deeper blush from him.

"Are you hungry?"

Carrington shook his head 'no.' "It's the middle of the night. I don't require replenishment."

"You didn't have much at dinner. I felt terrible watching you settle for a few vegetables."

He shook his head 'no' again, but a slight smile confirmed that he was just being polite. "Carrington, please. Let me get you something."

"You have much bigger worries," he interjected.

"None that can be addressed now. Your hunger, however, can be. I'm sure I can find something that you can tolerate." He was about to protest, but I held up a hand to silence him. I opened the refrigerator — most everything inside had some type of meat or dairy, other than eggs.

"Want fried eggs? I'm trying to think how I can prepare them without butter," I mused. If I had known of Carrington's limitations when I was still in the grocery store...

"Don't cook anything," he implored. "It's too late to go through that effort."

I started to rummage through the cupboards and spotted a large bag of ready-made, butter-free popcorn. "Do you like popcorn?"

Carrington looked at me with uneasiness. "You don't have to give me your popcorn."

"Stop," I commanded. I retrieved a large bowl and dumped the bag's contents in it, handing it to Carrington. He paused, then nodded with a smile, taking it with appreciation.

"I love popcorn," he admitted, grabbing and shoving in a handful. I had noticed at dinner that he put large quantities of food in his mouth, causing his whole lower face to contort and move while he chewed. It didn't seem to align to his 'hoity-toity' life, but I was glad. There was something about the way he ate that I found masculine and sexy.

I looked away when I realized I was staring. "I have more bags in the pantry. Please just help yourself whenever you'd like."

He was about to put another handful of popcorn in his mouth, but paused and looked at me with bewilderment. "Why are you being so nice to us?"

I shrugged. "I'm a nice guy...I hope."

His mouth formed that little grin that I was beginning to love, and he continued to eye me with a mix of surprise and admiration. His piercing blue eyes giving me that much attention was starting to affect me. I felt heated and exposed, standing before him in my boxers and too tight T-shirt. Thinking about that also caused my dick to stiffen a bit. I leaned into the island that separated us so he wouldn't notice.

"Why are you single?" he asked.

That question didn't help me relax. "Um, I don't know. Hard for a guy to find eligible men in this one-horse town."

"One-horse town? I'm guessing that isn't a literal thing?"

I laughed. "No. I mean, it's a rural town—it's not a gay mecca."

"But you recently moved from New York City," he remembered. "I'm sure there were lots of men to choose from there."

I swallowed hard. It was a reflex that I had since I was a child, something that signaled to anyone watching that I was nervous. I hated that about myself, but try as I might, I could never shake it. "None of them wanted to *choose me*, I guess."

Carrington looked at me as if I were a con man who had just offered a suspicious deal. "I'm quite certain that's untrue."

"Why?" I asked, somewhat surprised.

He glanced down with a bit of bashfulness. "You're kind. You're successful." He bit his lower lip and raised his eyes back to my face. "You're very good-looking."

"Don't."

Carrington looked panicked. "I'm sorry. I wasn't soliciting sexual favors from you."

Of course, he wasn't. That was the thing. Every man I had ever found attractive didn't reciprocate. For some reason, I was always drawn to the wrong men—often straight ones. Maybe it was the aggressiveness of the gay men who approached me that repelled me. Too many men liked to grab. Having grown up in a home where physical affection wasn't displayed, I found the forwardness of many gay guys jarring. On the rare occasion I would find a gay man like Carrington that was my type, they were already taken or they weren't interested — or in this case, both.

"No, I wasn't thinking that. I know you love Stefan." Carrington didn't respond, which I thought was strange. "I just meant you didn't need to flatter me. I'm a realist. You and Stefan are like models. Believe me, I know. I took enough photos of aspiring ones during my side work to know the real deal. You two are better looking than anyone I ever photographed, in fact. So, I know gorgeous, and I know average. Nobody's going to take photos of me. And you know as well as I, in the gay world, good looks are king."

He shook his head. "I'm not trying to flatter you. I don't know why you think you're average looking. You're beautiful. I would want to take pictures of you if I were a photographer."

I didn't know whether he was being genuine, but I wanted to discuss something other than my physical appearance. "Can I get you something to drink? You must be thirsty now that you've been eating popcorn."

Carrington sighed. "I'm not changing the subject. Why are you critical of yourself? Who did that to you?"

I did the hard swallow thing again. "What? I told you, I'm a realist. Even my own mother once said to me, 'you may not be an attractive person, but you're one of the smartest'."

He grimaced. "Yes, you're bright, but with all due respect to your mother — who I'm sure is a lovely person — I wonder if her eyesight is failing. This must not have been a recent observation on her part."

"It wasn't," I acknowledged. "She and I don't talk much. Let's just say I was an unattractive teenager — braces, long hair, skinny."

"And you've metamorphosed into the man you are now. I'll bet if you asked her today what she thinks, she would tell you that she's amazed at how you look."

I barked a laugh. He didn't comprehend from my comment that my mother and I had no interactions whatsoever. "Yeah, I doubt it. So, what do you want to drink? Water? Juice?"

Carrington looked resigned. "Water would be nice. Thank you." I reached into the refrigerator for a bottled water and handed it to him. As he opened the cap, he shot his eyes back to my face. "Can I just tell you why I think you're beautiful, then I'll drop it?"

I sighed. I did want to hear, but I assumed it would be about my personality. While friends and acquaintances often told me I was a good person, those compliments felt like encouragement that it didn't take attractiveness to be loved. "If you promise to drop it…"

He nodded. "Your inner beauty shines through."

As I had expected. "Got it. I'm going back to bed. Do me a favor and turn the lights off before you head upstairs."

Carrington held up a hand to stop me. "Wait. I'm not finished. What I wished to say is, you are a stunning gentleman, and the niceness you have makes you shine more."

I crossed my arms, pulling away from the island. I didn't have to worry about an erection, as I was now tired and becoming sad that whatever patronizing thing Carrington would say next would leave me depressed. "Okay, what's so stunning?"

He smiled. "Well, your face is as cute as a cherub's. You have those big brown eyes that are full of expression and emotion. You have that patrician nose that I envy, and that pout of a mouth makes adorable shapes when you're irritated or anxious. And speaking of when you're nervous, your eyes become wider and you swallow in such a vulnerable way. It's quite endearing. Your cheeks also take on the prettiest color. You have rich dark-colored hair, and from what I've seen, you have smooth skin over toned muscle. I'd have to wax to get that look, and I'm just not interested. Do I need to say more?"

I gulped. I hoped he didn't think I did so because he thought it was *endearing*. I was beginning to believe he was serious, and I felt a little heady. "Um, thank you. Those were very nice things to say, though I don't know why you'd want to wax. You don't have hair on your back, do you?"

Carrington laughed. "No. I have hair on my pecs, my arms and my legs. Not ape-like, but I don't like body hair. Maybe that's why I prefer women."

"Huh?"

Carrington opened his mouth to speak, then snapped it shut. He had a guilty look on his face like the boy who got caught putting a frog on the teacher's chair. "Uh, yes…about that."

"You're bisexual?"

He sat quiet for a moment, staring down at the bowl of popcorn before lifting his eyes back to mine. "I don't wish to lie to you anymore. You've been very kind to us, and we've been dishonest with you from the start. It's just that we didn't know if we could trust you. I know now that we can."

I was confused and becoming annoyed. They were all lying? About what? Carrington being bisexual instead of gay? Why would that matter? "I'm tired. Just tell me what's going on. Are you putting me in some kind of danger?"

Carrington shook his head no, but his expression seemed to convey uncertainty. "I don't think so."

"That's comforting," I said, unable to avoid sounding sarcastic. "Are you a criminal?"

He huffed a laugh. "Not at all. Have you heard of Yastarus?"

"The country? Of course."

He looked surprised. "I told you you're intelligent. I'm quite amazed at how few Americans have heard of it."

"Well, school system quality varies across the country. What does this have to do with anything?" I asked, becoming impatient.

He paused for a moment, then answered in a matter-of-fact tone. "I'm the president of Yastarus."

I waited for the punchline, but Carrington continued to sit in silence. "I'm sorry. What?"

"We were here—in Boston specifically—for a follow-up visit my mother had at a hospital that treated her for a rare illness. They provide the best care in the world for the disease." I was about to express my concern when he held up a hand. "Not to worry. It was to check that she is, in fact, cured now that she's finished treatment. We received very good news, indeed. We were booked on a flight out of Newark because it was a direct flight home—something we couldn't find out of Logan Airport in Boston. That's why we had a driver taking us through Connecticut when we encountered this storm you're experiencing. We thought we could outpace it."

"You're the president of a country?" I asked, unable to hide my skepticism. If it was the truth, he must have thought my inability to keep up disproved that I was as smart as he thought.

"Is your cell phone nearby? Do you still have service despite the storm?"

I shrugged, but pulled the phone from the charger that was plugged into a kitchen outlet. "Yes, it seems to be working."

"Look up the president of Yastarus," he commanded.

I typed and the result popped up on the screen. "It's showing Carrington Von Dorran is the president. You said your last name is Howard."

"It's an alias," he explained. "Google images."

I did as he instructed. There were pictures of two different men that were identified as Carrington Von Dorran—one of them was the man sitting before me. 'President of Yastarus' was printed under each photograph. As I kept scrolling, it became evident that one was a senior and one was a junior, with both having served as president. "Carrington Von Dorran the Second—that's you?"

He smiled. "Yes. There won't be a third. If I have a child, that wretched name stops with me. My father was president before I was. When he passed three years ago, his vice president—Antony Vishkov—became president. After a few months of serving, reports of rampant corruption and fiscal mismanagement contributed to his downfall. He had also been signaling to Russia that the country was eager for an alliance—perhaps even open to becoming a Russian territory as we once were at the time of the Soviet Union. It was a serious miscalculation of what the people of Yastarus wanted. They identify as Scandinavian, and the majority want NATO membership. Vishkov was forced to resign and my father's political allies pushed hard for me to run for the vacant seat, certain my name would be enough to resume power, despite my political inexperience. They were correct. My father was one of the country's most popular leaders, and support for me was high. So were expectations."

"But you're so young," I murmured, still absorbing the news.

"I'm thirty-six," he stated. "Any Yastarus natural-born citizen aged thirty-five or older is eligible for the presidency."

"So, your mother was the first lady at one time," I concluded.

"Yes," he affirmed. "She didn't love it. Mother didn't want me to run for the office, but I was sure it was what my father would have wished. Also, I couldn't bear to think about the country continuing to move in the direction it had under Vishkov."

"Where are your Secret Service agents?" I wondered.

Carrington laughed. "We don't call them that. My protection, on this trip, is Stefan."

Stefan's name reminded me that his alleged relationship was now in question, based on Carrington's earlier confession to liking women. "So, you two aren't lovers, are you?"

Carrington blushed. "No. That's one of the lies I didn't feel comfortable perpetuating. You overheard Stefan ask me if you knew about us. I wasn't prepared to tell you who I was. I'll explain why in a moment. But at that point, I tried to think of something that would be innocuous to an American that would divert you from the truth. Knowing that your country is far more accepting of homosexuality, especially in the Northeast, I formulated that excuse. It turned out to be coincidence that you were, in fact, gay yourself."

"How could you be traveling with just one guard?"

"Yastarus isn't the United States. We're a very small country with a fraction of your national budget. The trip was deemed inconsequential, and we made the decision to leave the rest of our security behind to protect the Yastarus government officials who remained. It wasn't until we were departing Boston that we received intelligence reports that there is a Russian threat to my safety."

"Wait. What?" My stomach flipped.

"I don't believe we're in danger," he rushed. "Of course, upon receiving the news, I was eager to return home to safety. That was why I was so frustrated earlier today when we were stranded. However, I would think we're off the radar. Who would ever suspect I'm staying at your home?" He smiled. "I'm sorry. I know there is a small element of risk. If you wish us to leave, we will do so, post haste."

Send them into a hurricane and a possible Russian threat? That wasn't an option. "No, I wouldn't do that."

Carrington sighed with relief. "Thank you. I promise that if I have any inclination that my whereabouts are compromised, your safety will be my priority. I will leave before you can even say goodbye."

I was surprised that his promise made me sad. The revelation also made me suspect that his earlier praise of me had been an attempt to convince me that he was gay. "Okay."

He quirked his head and tried to read my mind. "What's going through that pretty head?"

I swallowed hard again—he must have thought I had a medical issue. "You don't have to keep up the guise. You're straight. I get it. I'm not going to ask you to leave. You don't need to pretend that you think I'm attractive anymore."

Carrington blanched and appeared alarmed. "I wasn't pretending. It's true that I've never been attracted to a man before you…" He reacted to his own words with surprise. "Oh. I think I just said I was attracted to you." He ran a hand over his face, then looked back to me with shock. "I think you were right. Maybe it's best we retire for the evening."

Carrington pushed the bowl of popcorn a few inches away, avoiding my gaze once he had seen my surprise. "Um, maybe you can cover this," he suggested, pulling away from the counter stool. "I'll bid you good-night then." With that, he nodded and scurried out of the kitchen and up the stairs before I could say anything further.

Chapter Seven

Carrington

Between thinking about what I had uttered to Eric, the continuous wind and rain pounding the house and a snoring Stefan within millimeters of my ear, I hadn't slept the rest of the night. I heard Eric exiting his room and going down the stairs. I glanced at the clock he had left on the guest room nightstand, and it indicated that it was a little after seven in the morning.

I thought about rising as well, but I wasn't sure I wanted to be alone with Eric again. My feelings about him were confusing and troubling. I had told Eric I had never been attracted to a man before, but that was untrue. I had been enamored with a male friend when he and I had been teenagers. The boy was a fellow football player, but at the time, I had dismissed my yearnings to being young and hormonal. Once I had discovered women, that boyhood attraction seemed an aberration and unimportant. Now, here I was twenty years later, feeling like an awkward teenager once more — experiencing desire mixed with embarrassment and fear. There was no way I could act upon these feelings. I was the president of Yastarus, and its people didn't elect me thinking I fancied men. We just needed to leave Connecticut as soon as the storm broke, and Eric would be forgotten as I resumed my busy schedule.

Stefan let out a combination of a snort and a choke, which must have jolted him awake. He was surveying his surroundings, and it seemed he had forgotten where he was. Once he had his bearings, he looked at me and grimaced. "Sorry, did I wake you?" he mumbled.

I rolled my eyes. "Impossible. I never slept with all the noise."

He wiped a hand over his dampened face and turned toward the battered window. "Hmm. Yes, the storm is quite loud."

"Yes, I suppose *it* is loud too," I complained. "I was hoping it would become white noise and drown out the incessant death rattle emitting from your orifices."

It was difficult to embarrass Stefan, but this time he did appear shamed. "I apologize. Was it that bad?"

"I was about to ask Eric if there was a nearby exorcist we could summon," I deadpanned.

He paused before smiling and rasping, "Your mother sucks cocks in hell."

"I beg your pardon?" I demanded.

Stefan appeared confused then alarmed. "Oh! No, I don't mean *your* mother. It's a line from the movie — *The Exorcist*. Your mother isn't even dead. And if she was, she wouldn't be in hell doing that!"

"God, stop!" I snapped.

He laid his head back on the pillow, looking up at the ceiling, as did I. It reminded me of when we had been mates in college and would sometimes go to the riverbank on a nice day, and lay in the sun to talk about school, politics and girls. The memory made me think of how Stefan might recoil if I shared with him my thoughts about Eric.

"Are you going to be in a crabby mood because I kept you awake?" he asked. "Not to take advantage of it, but I could explain to our host that it is why you aren't affectionate toward me today. It will eliminate the need for a ruse."

"We don't need a ruse," I sighed. "He and I spoke last night. I told him everything."

Stefan couldn't hide the panic in his voice. "I see. Are you sure that was wise, Carrington?"

I nodded, unsure if he was looking over at me to see. "He's a good man. I am *sure* of that."

"Okay," he whispered. "But you should impress upon him not to tell anyone. Your safety is assured because we stumbled into this place. If our whereabouts are compromised..."

"I know," I acknowledged. "I'll say something to him. Our conversation ended a bit...abruptly...before I could ask for secrecy."

From the way I stated the last sentence, Stefan sensed my discomfort. "And why is that?" He paused, then got a knowing look on his face. "Oh. He made advances toward you, didn't he? I knew he was interested in you. The way he was fawning over you during the meal preparation and afterward. You know, I find that quite offensive considering he thought we were a couple."

I cast him a glance of annoyance. "He wasn't fawning."

Stefan crossed his arms over his chest. "He looked at you like you hung the moon."

I returned my gaze to the ceiling. "Well, that's because I did. Right after I created the earth and sun."

My bed mate snickered. "Okay. Just another ruler who fancies himself a god."

I smirked. "You know I don't. But you think *he* fancies me a god, huh?"

Stefan rolled his eyes. "Check your ego. I didn't go that far. Hanging the moon is just an expression. But yes, I think he fancies you."

I turned to stare at my companion — he was serious. "Well, he didn't do or say anything inappropriate. He was quite respectful of our alleged relationship. On the contrary, it was I who crossed a line."

He turned to me, curious. "How so?"

My friendship with Stefan was solid, of that I was certain. I knew I could share, but I was hesitant. Saying it out loud again was like confirming a change in my sexual orientation. But I wasn't sure that was true, as sex itself was not something I had considered with Eric. I couldn't deny, though, that I enjoyed looking at him and being with him, and had a desire to hold him. At one point, watching his mouth, I had even wondered what it would be like to kiss him. There was no way I could rationalize those thoughts as heterosexual. "Have you ever wondered what it would be like to experiment with another male?"

Stefan's eyes grew large. "Experiment? As in have sex?"

I huffed. "No, experiment as in do chemistry tests with him. Yes, to have sex."

He grimaced. "You don't have to be mean. You're grouchy this morning. What did you say to him anyway? Something about sex thoughts with a boy when you were younger? It's not a big deal. Who hasn't?"

I looked at him, and he became uncomfortable under my scrutiny. "*You* have?"

Stefan shrugged. "Every guy has. People know about gay sex, so you can't discuss it without picturing it. It doesn't mean you want to act on it."

"Did you ever want to act on it?" I pressed.

"How did this become about me?" he bristled. "What did you say to him?"

Now I shrugged. "I may have said something about being attracted to him."

"What? Are you insane? Even if you were attracted to him, you can't tell him that! Do I need to remind you how that will play back home?"

"I know!" I barked back. "I'm well aware of my lapse in judgment."

"What did he say in response?"

"Nothing," I replied. "I told you before about the abrupt end to our discussion. I left the room as soon as I blurted my confession."

We remained silent for a few moments, each unsure what to say next. Stefan sighed. "Why him? I mean, if you were going to contemplate such an act after all these years, what made him so special? There were more attractive men who would have been willing."

My gut reaction was to defend Eric. I remembered how he had been critical of his own looks, and I couldn't understand what he and Stefan were missing. "I don't agree. For the sake of argument, however, who do you think was more attractive that would have indulged this curiosity?"

"Me!" he spat.

I was stunned. My jaw dropped and I stared at my companion as if seeing a stranger in the bed next to me. "Stefan...I don't even know what to say. You've never said anything to indicate you had feelings."

He turned away from me, facing the wall. "I didn't think there was any chance of you reciprocating. I didn't want to ruin our friendship. I didn't want you to hate me."

I reached over and stroked his bare arm. I had never done that before, but I didn't find it unnatural or unpleasant. He was my dear friend, and I had hurt him. "Stefan. I'm sorry. I didn't know."

He still didn't face me, but he was willing to converse. "For many years, I waited for a possible opening. Maybe a hint that you were interested, or even just horny enough to settle for me relieving you. It would have been enough. I was in love with you."

"You're in love with me?" I gasped.

Stefan turned to me once again, a bitter look on his face. "I said I *was* in love with you — when we were boys and all through college. After hearing you talk about girls, seeing you date them for years, I got the point. I moved on. Still, it hurts to hear that you met this chap Eric, and in one day, you're thinking about shagging him."

"I'm thinking no such thing. I just find him...alluring. I'm sorry. If I had known you have these feelings..."

"Had," he corrected.

"I wouldn't have told you about last night." I paused. "Are you gay? You've dated as many women as I have."

He laughed, but the tone was bitter. "Used them would be more like it. I didn't want you to know the truth. I've been afraid what you — my family and friends — would think of me. I've been with men, but it's always been clandestine affairs."

"I see." But I didn't. The past few hours had been confusing as I realized things about myself and Stefan that I had never thought possible just a few days earlier. "Is there someone in your life?"

"No," he whispered. "I think you set the bar too high for me. I never connected with anyone the way I did you."

We remained silent again for a bit before I commented, "Well, it wouldn't have worked between us, anyway. A few nights of those boar-like noises coming out of your mouth and nose, and I would have had to suffocate you with a pillow."

My humor had its desired effect, as he laughed. "Funny. Nobody else ever complained. I guess they were too grateful to be in the presence of such handsomeness."

I laughed. "And humility."

"Said the man who fancies himself a god," he countered. "But may I ask you? If you can have an attraction to a man, why wasn't it with me? We already had the emotional connection, and I have been told I'm quite fetching."

"Mothers don't count," I joked. He didn't laugh. "Okay. It's a fair question. You are very handsome. I'm not blind. I've been quite envious over the years. Even Eric said you could be a model."

"Did he?" he asked with some surprise. "I didn't think he could see anyone else in the room when you were in it."

I smiled. I didn't want that to make me feel warm inside, but it did. "He said we both could be models."

"Hmm. So, he fancies himself a three-way, huh?"

I could feel my cheeks flush at the notion. "He strikes me as way too shy and innocent to think such things."

Stefan laughed. "He's a man. There's no such thing as a guy who doesn't think about sex. My guess is, he wanked himself to sleep last night picturing himself in a Carrington-Stefan sandwich."

"I'm sure I don't know what that is," I lied. "Your nasty cravings would have sunk us if your snoring didn't."

Stefan just laughed louder. "Please. You forget what you've told me regarding your thoughts about some of the women you've dated. I dare say relating the desires you had would make most members of proper society squirm."

"Because they'd be trying to hide their arousal," I shot back.

"Okay, forget what you think Eric wants. Tell me, how did he find the valve that opened the flood of these feelings?"

I knew the underlying question remained why I wasn't attracted to Stefan. "I meant what I said. You are a handsome man. You are more attractive than I. I'm not sure why Eric isn't more drawn to you than me, especially if what they say about gaydar is true."

"It isn't," he answered.

"Be that as it may," I continued, "I can appreciate your physical attributes, but they don't affect me the way Eric's do. Please don't take offense. From a technical perspective, I would say that you are more attractive than him."

"But?"

"But I guess I'm not drawn to other men that look like me. I haven't been drawn to other men, period. Eric—I can't figure it out. It is confusing and quite scary," I admitted.

"Is it his personality?"

I contemplated the question. "There is something quite endearing about his kindness, his vulnerability, and his demeanor. And when I look at him, I find him to be adorable. I just can't picture myself being amorous with a big, hairy, alpha male."

"Is that your way of explaining why you weren't attracted to me?" he deduced.

I grinned. "I guess. You and I are of like builds and temperaments. It just isn't what I picture for a romantic partner. I'm sorry. Am I offending you?"

"I guess not," he conceded. "I understand. You like twinks."

"I do not. I may not be a homosexual, but I know what a twink is. I don't want an androgynous, wispy, fragile male that resembles a child. Eric isn't a twink. Yes, he's a good deal younger, but he's well-built and masculine, albeit in a gentler quieter way. But along with compact muscle, he has a sweet, emotive face, smooth skin and a dignified beauty." Stefan was silent, so I looked over to him, and he appeared to be in shock. "What?"

"You've got it bad for him," he murmured.

"I do not," I protested. "This is a momentary fascination, and it will be gone as quickly as it came. The sooner we leave the United States, the better."

Stefan didn't look convinced. "I agree with you about one thing. We need to leave. In the meantime, you need to avoid Eric. We can't have him telling reporters that you had a thing for him."

"He wouldn't do that," I argued.

"You don't even know him well! The fact that you keep projecting sainthood on him tells me that you are in denial about the extent of your attraction to him. Just heed my advice and stay clear of him until we're out of here."

I felt compelled to defend Eric further, but that would validate Stefan's conclusions. Instead, I nodded in agreement.

Chapter Eight

Eric

After making breakfast for everyone and laying it out on my dining room table, I passed Carrington in the hallway on my way to my bathroom. His morning greeting was a quick nod followed by a rapid glance down at his feet. It reinforced that I had made the right call to have eaten alone before he and his companions descended, knowing Carrington might still be struggling with his late-night confession. Though it had been thrilling for me to hear the gorgeous man profess an attraction, it was obvious it had troubled him.

I jumped into the shower, thankful to still have hot water running in the wake of the storm. The all-house generator had come in handy. It was still windy, but the rain had ceased and I would be able to venture outside to survey the damage. I imagined that roads and airports had sustained enough to limit travel, but I hoped my guests would be able to depart the next day. I would be a bit sad to see Carrington leave, but since nothing would come of our mutual attraction other than awkwardness, it was for the best.

Once I was washed and dressed, I called my friend Mateo. Mateo had been a bar-hopping, party-going companion when we had both lived in New York City, and he had followed me to Connecticut soon after I relocated. It was easy enough for him to establish a hair-styling salon here, and it was already rivaling the success he had enjoyed in the city. When he had made the move, he told me he would enjoy being the prettiest fish in the pond—with 'the pond' being the Hartford gay scene—as opposed to being one of many in the large city. After having bagged the handful of desirable men available, he started complaining that the pond was more like a swamp with nothing worth fishing for. As a result, he had begun spending more time with me to fill his social calendar, settling for sports and movie viewing, or helping me with projects around the house. Each visit entailed me listening to his woes about the dearth of men and his chronic horny state, followed by a lament that I wasn't his type, which would have allowed him to use my body for relief. Seeing as he was drawn to hunky men, his comments didn't bother me. He wasn't what I go for either. Mateo was handsome enough with his dark, chiseled features, perfect black hair and muscular build. But his personality was more compatible with what I sought for a fun outing, not a romantic relationship. I did appreciate, though, that he had befriended me, and he had been loyal and kind to me since.

After I checked to see how he and his apartment had endured the storm, he informed me that he was without power and close to losing the battery charge on his phone and the food in his refrigerator. I suggested he come stay with me, warning him that he'd have to settle for a sofa as I had other guests. That piqued his interest—even more so when, under pressure, I confessed to him that there were attractive men present. I explained as much as I could without revealing their identities. As luck would have it, Mateo also preferred almond milk and dairy-free butter to regular, so him bringing over some of his salvaged food would allow me to cook for Carrington.

"A friend of mine is coming to stay with us. He's without power, and it's too hot and humid for him to stay in his apartment without fans or air conditioning," I informed the trio of guests.

Olivia registered mild concern, but Carrington and Stefan exchanged glances of panic. Carrington explained why he and Stefan were alarmed. "I told Eric the truth last night, Mother. He's been kind to us. I didn't feel comfortable lying to him any longer."

His mother's reaction was surprise, but she shifted to a composed, unreadable expression. "Yes, of course."

"Now that you know our identities, you know why bringing your friend here could be problematic," Stefan replied.

I nodded. "I understand, but you'll see once you meet Mateo that it will be fine. He's so not interested in politics. It's a fifty-fifty chance he even knows who *our* president is, let alone who the president of your country is." I felt guilty once the words left my mouth. I was portraying Mateo as an idiot, which he wasn't. Of course, he would know the name of the president of the United States. He just wouldn't care who it was as long as they were a supporter of gay rights and immigration reform. Mateo found the news to be too depressing to watch or read, figuring there was little he could do to change things anyway.

"So, you didn't share with him anything I told you last night?" Carrington asked, unable to hide the fuller meaning of his question.

I swallowed, thinking about the moment Carrington had told me that he was attracted to me. If it weren't for Olivia sitting there watching me, I would have become aroused with the memory. "Of course not. I wouldn't betray your confidence."

Carrington nodded with relief and clear appreciation. "Yes, I know you wouldn't. Forgive me."

"Good news is, he's bringing his food, which includes many vegan and non-dairy items. You'll be able to eat real food."

Carrington looked solemn. "Doesn't matter. We'll be on our way as soon as we can find suitable travel arrangements."

"Dude, I've already checked. There are no flights leaving the Northeast any time today. That's if the roads are even clear enough for you to make it to an airport. You're here for at least another night," I informed him.

Olivia smiled. "That is kind of you to let us stay a bit longer. I'm sorry we are a bother."

Stefan retained the look of panic he had when he first learned of Mateo's pending arrival. "But where will everyone sleep?"

"Mateo can sleep on the couch." I shrugged.

"But..." Stefan paused, looked over to Carrington, then back at me. "Um, now that you know the president and I are not a romantic couple, I was hoping I could sleep on the sofa this evening. It was tight in the bed, and it was also brought to my attention that I'm a bit of a snorer."

I couldn't help but chuckle at Stefan's discomfort. It was easy to picture an irate Carrington griping to him about the noise. "Oh. Well, yes, I can see why the bed is small for two people who are not inclined to cuddle."

Olivia blanched, and Stefan and Carrington each blushed.

"Perhaps Stefan can sleep in the bathtub. I'm sure you have an extra pillow and blanket you could loan him," Carrington stated. I was unclear if he was teasing. Stefan was mortified.

I rushed to his rescue. "Um, that doesn't sound very pleasant."

"Well, neither is the sound of a buzz saw in your ear for eight hours," Carrington uttered with disdain.

"I understand. I would offer to let Mateo share my bed, but he snores too. I needed to stay at his apartment one night when my roof was leaking. I made the mistake of accepting his offer to share his bed. It wasn't very restful," I conceded. After that excruciating night, I had suggested to Mateo that his snoring problem stemmed from swallowing incorrectly, but he wasn't interested in listening. I turned to Stefan. "Where is your tongue right now?"

The three guests looked at me with a mix of bewilderment and curiosity. "Beg your pardon? Is that an American way of asking why I'm not defending myself?" Stefan asked.

I shook my head. "No, I meant literally—where is the tip of your tongue when you have your mouth closed?" I clarified. Now the three stared at me as if seeing a lunatic.

"Answer him. I'm curious to see where this is going," Olivia commanded, still looking like she was searching for a large net to drop over me if my explanation proved me insane.

Stefan glanced at all of us with astonishment, but when he saw nobody was shutting down my question, he swallowed and forced an expression and stance of dignity. "Where else would it be? It's in my mouth."

Carrington and Olivia were trying not to snicker at his response. "But the tip of your tongue," I pressed. "Where in your mouth is it landing when you swallow, when you have your mouth closed?"

"For the love of God, what madness is this? It's in back of my teeth," he shot, shaking his head to display how obvious the answer should be.

"As I suspected," I stated. "It shouldn't be there."

Stefan curled his lip. "And where else would one's tongue be? And please remember there is a lady present before you provide us with an inappropriate joke."

Olivia's tittering signaled she was more amused than offended.

I flushed, however, at the idea that they thought I was suggesting something sexual. "Oh no. I was going to say that the tip of your tongue should always be at the roof of your mouth when you aren't speaking or eating."

While they all had looks of confusion, I could see they were double-checking where the tips of their tongues were in that moment. "Nonsense," Stefan huffed.

"No, it's true," I insisted. "I used to swallow incorrectly too, and I used to have my tongue resting against my teeth. But when I was thirteen with a mouthful of crooked teeth and an overbite, my parents brought me to an orthodontist. The doctor told me that before he would put on braces, I had to learn to swallow properly. Otherwise, the pressure of my tongue against my teeth would just undo the orthodontist's work once the braces were removed. You learned how to swallow that way because, as a baby, it was the way you could stop the flow of milk coming from a nipple when you couldn't intake more to your mouth."

"My God, man, what are you going on about? What has this to do with my snoring? Stefan snapped.

I felt I was staring down three inquisitors, now all awaiting an explanation for my craziness. I always did something nerdy to alienate people.

"I'm sorry," I blurted. "I'm making a mess of my point. I learned to swallow with the tip of my tongue on the roof of my mouth and learned how to keep it there when my face is in repose. It's where it's supposed to be naturally." I paused to take a sharp inhale. "You can't snore if your mouth is closed, and you can't open your mouth if the tip of your tongue is on the roof of your mouth. So, if you learn to rest your tongue in the right place, you will sleep through the night with your mouth closed."

I could see that Carrington and Olivia were once again checking where the tips of their tongues were placed, but Stefan was staring me down with wild eyes. "You're quite odd."

I swallowed and regretted having said anything. "Um, yes. I'm sorry. I was trying to be helpful. I talk too much."

Olivia tried diplomacy. "Well, I didn't find it odd. It was quite enlightening. I'll have to be more aware of how I swallow."

Stefan glared. "Well, seeing as I shan't relearn how to swallow within the next twenty-four hours, perhaps we could resume our discussion about sleeping accommodations."

"Olivia and I are in the two larger beds. I don't suppose the two of you would want to share a bed?" I asked, looking to Carrington and Olivia.

"No, we would not," Carrington protested. "I am well past the age of sleeping with my mum."

Olivia shrugged. "Suit yourself, but it isn't I who will sleep on a floor, thank you very much."

I sighed. I was about to suggest Carrington take my bed and I would put a blanket on the floor in the living room, as far from a snoring Mateo as possible. Before I could, Carrington responded to Olivia. "Of course not, Mother. It seems the feasible solution would be for me to share a bed with Eric." He turned to me with an unreadable expression. Stefan's, however, was very clear. It was a mix of horror and anger, and I presumed it was because he didn't trust the gay guy with his buddy. "I mean, if it is all right with you, Eric."

The three looked to me, awaiting my response. My face flushed and there was a lump in my throat. "Um, sure. That would be okay."

Chapter Nine

Carrington

Eric's friend, Mateo, had just arrived with food in what he called a 'cooler.' He and Eric were unloading and trying to find space in Eric's already overfilled refrigerator. Unlike Eric, Mateo was a man I would have guessed to be gay. He was flirty and made big gestures as he spoke. I was certain Stefan would take an immediate dislike to him. Instead, Mateo had made Stefan chuckle a few times whilst they bantered in the kitchen. Sometimes Mateo would put his hand on Stefan's arm whilst emphasizing a point, and Stefan didn't appear inclined to rebuff him. I found it odd that he seemed to trust Mateo more than Eric, as the former struck me as someone who'd be inclined to gossip. I hoped Eric and Stefan remained vigilant about what they shared.

Once the kitchen was in order, I was shocked to hear Stefan offer to help Eric and Mateo with the clean-up outdoors. It made me feel guilty enough to volunteer as well, but Stefan insisted I stay inside to keep my mother company. Of course, his real motive was to ensure I was safe behind the walls of Eric's home...and I would be away from my newfound crush.

When they opened the patio doors to venture outside, a whoosh of heavy, damp air sucked in. I couldn't imagine that it was healthy for the three of them, fit as they might be, to be working in those conditions. I sat on a chair that faced the French doors to the patio, watching them picking up branches, cutting larger limbs and trying to buttress the now sagging fence. Before long, a sweating Stefan and Mateo removed their shirts and tucked them in their waistbands. I had been feeling a heightened awareness of male sensuality since meeting Eric, and observed the naked torsos in a way I would never have imagined just a few days earlier—wondering if they would arouse me. Though I could appreciate that both men were in amazing shape, their pumped-up chests and bulging arms weren't enticing. I just couldn't imagine wanting to be held by them, and their faces—though striking— were too hard and masculine for kissing.

Eric continued working at a punishing pace, sopping wet in his white Henley shirt. His shyness allowed him to undo no more than a couple of buttons which bared a small part of his smooth, tanned chest. His rolled-up sleeves revealed hairless, toned and bronzed forearms. The cotton fabric clung to him and had become translucent, making him seem sexier than if the shirt had been removed. His carved pecs and nipples were thwarting the shirt's attempts at modesty. Eric had on a pair of tight work jeans that hugged his ass and thighs, and I couldn't help but marvel at his form. He had some meat in the seat, as they say — two perfect globes defying the laws of gravity. Watching his lithe body move was making me excited. I forgot my mother was nearby until she made her presence known.

"Stefan seems to be getting on better with them," she commented, approaching the back of my chair.

I pushed forward into a more upright position, hoping it would position my misbehaving member into a less obvious state. I was glad she was behind the chair as opposed to facing me. "Hmm? Oh, yes. Well, it seems he's less concerned now about Eric's friend than he was before meeting him."

"Maybe it's all the attention Eric's friend is giving him. I think he's smitten."

I turned to her in surprise. "Who? Eric's friend or Stefan?"

My mother smiled. "Indeed."

I didn't want to betray Stefan's secret. "I don't know what you mean. I'm sure Stefan is just being polite."

"Is he? I haven't noticed him go out of his way to be polite to others in the past. In fact, I would say he's been somewhat rude to Eric, wouldn't you?"

I was becoming anxious. If my mother suspected Stefan was gay, was she going to wonder what that meant for me — his longtime friend? "I think he just didn't know if he could trust Eric."

My mother sat in the chair next to mine, still looking out at the three working men. "But he can already trust Mateo?"

Now I was becoming agitated by her line of questioning that felt like she was saying something without saying it. "What are you suggesting, Mother?"

She pursed her lips and sat silent for a moment. "Do you not know? I find it hard to believe you've been mates since childhood, but you weren't aware that Stefan likes men?"

I was shocked. "Pardon? How do you know this? I just found out last night!"

Now it was her turn to look surprised. "Oh. I'm glad I never said anything. It was his truth to tell you."

"But, how did you know? He's dated girls for as long as I've known him."

My mother looked at me now with sad eyes. "My dear boy, you really have been oblivious, haven't you? I used to wonder if there was a mean streak in you, that you let him pine for you and you played daft. Or maybe it was just you loving the attention. But I saw the hurt in his eyes when you would talk about a girl you were dating or when you'd mock him in jest. I used to wish, for his sake, he'd meet someone and fall in love so he could forget about you."

"Forget about me?" I whispered. "No. Close friends don't forget about each other. But he did tell me last night that he fell out of love with me. I suppose anyone gives up after years of disappointment." I sighed. "So, you're okay with Stefan being homosexual?"

"Why wouldn't I be? It's not my life to live nor mine to judge."

"That sounds more like tolerating someone rather than embracing them," I mumbled.

"I have mixed feelings when it comes to Stefan. I have affection for him because he loves you and keeps you safe. I also worried because he was *in love* with you. Unrequited romantic love can lead to unhappy outcomes — for both parties. I didn't want to see him pained, but I was more afraid that he could hurt you.

In general, though, I've never cared about whether someone is gay. You know your uncle, my brother Charles, is gay. We were always close and I couldn't understand why people felt it was their prerogative to tell him whom he could love. People claim it's about the Bible, but I think it's just an excuse to hate others who aren't like you. Most of those people disobey many other passages of the Bible and think nothing of it. I guess that's why I never go to church—even if our country's people want to condemn me for that. Their hypocrisy angers me, but more than that, it bores me. Maybe it's my Scandinavian blood."

"But Father went to church. He opposed gay marriage," I reminded her.

"In public, yes. When he was president, there wasn't majority support for same-sex marriage. In private, he thought the opposition was absurd and primitive. I refused to compromise my principles that way. As I said, hypocrisy bores me."

We paused and I thought about her comments regarding my uncle. "Mother, I remember when you were close to Uncle Charles. Why haven't you been these last few years?"

Her eyes welled a bit. "We had a falling out. He was angry that I didn't speak out for gay rights as First Lady, and he resented your father for coddling the far-right. I tried to explain that Yastarus is always one step away from realigning to Russia, that we had to choose our battles and try to unify the conservatives and the progressives. Charles believed that blood should have trumped my nationalist sentiments—that fundamental human rights should have been my priority. I never spoke out against gays, as you may recall. But he's right—I didn't advocate for them either. Now that a small majority of our people support same-sex marriage, it may seem to you like our inaction was cowardice. But back then, it could have been a cultural wedge the far-right used to tip us back to a federal semi-presidential republic, which is just a political label for a dictatorship. I didn't see how that was a long-term win for anyone's rights—including Charles'."

"But I'm on record as supporting same-sex marriage, and you were quoted as supporting my advocacy. Why hasn't that mended fences between you and Uncle Charles?"

My mother frowned and looked at her clasped hands. "I hurt him. The same way I thought you, and your role in the government and in our family, might wound Stefan one day. I thought he could turn his back on you. When your father was president, Charles used his position with a prominent paper to write harsh editorials about him and me—letting everyone know that we supported gays but didn't have the courage to do so in public. Of course, he was correct, but your father denied it, which just made the gulf between Charles and us wider. Both sides forgot that we once cared for each other, and I don't know if there's any coming back from that."

I nodded because I wasn't sure she was wrong. "I didn't know that was happening. I shied away from Father's presidency and the associated media. I never thought I'd one day take up the baton, and I never thought I'd discover my best friend is gay. At least with Stefan, we sustained our bond. Now, I can support him in whatever he chooses."

She nodded and smiled a bit. "That shouldn't be difficult in today's more open-minded society. He's not a public figure, and people will understand your loyalty to a longtime friend. Eric, though, might be a harder pill for people to swallow."

"I beg your pardon, Mother? What about Eric?"

She turned to face me. "You are doing a marvelous job of fooling yourself about the men around you. Maybe it's being your mother, but I've never had a problem reading you. I knew before you did which girls you liked, and I've never seen you quite as undone as you seem to be around this young man."

"Mother…"

She cut me off. "Carrington, if you want to lie to me, then you can tell me as the president of our country that you deny my allegations and order me never to speak of them again. But as my son, don't lie to me. And for heaven's sake, don't lie to yourself."

I looked down at my lap, as if some magic words might be written there. I didn't know what to say. "I'm confused. I've never felt this way about a man before. I don't know what's happening to me."

She let out a loud exhale. "Darling, as I said, I haven't seen you act this way around *anyone* before — man or woman. The way you were with him last night whilst preparing the meal, and all through dinner — it was like you had a warm light around you. I've never seen you so enthralled and eager to impress. If he was just another in a line of interests, I would tell you to put the country first and forget about him, you'll meet a nice girl one day and all that rubbish. After all, you're already facing a credible death threat from far-right extremists, and falling for a man would make things more precarious."

I studied her pained expression. "I feel there's a but in there…"

She looked as though she might cry, something I hadn't seen her do since my father had died. "But you're my child. You may be the most powerful man in our country, but you'll always be my boy. And a mother's greatest wish is to see her child happy. I can't tell you what will bring you contentment. But I'll support you, whatever it is."

I shook my head. "I don't know if it's this. We don't know each other that well, do we? I can't stop thinking about him, though. It's like this man is becoming all-consuming and I hate him for it."

She laughed. "My dear, I know you don't hate him. And from what I've seen from him, he likes you, too. Have you noticed the adorable way he looks at you? Those blushing cheeks and that cute way he gulps when he's in your presence. I just want to squeeze him!"

I looked at her in shock, causing her to chuckle. I then snickered in return. "Well, join the club. At least the people of Yastarus won't turn on *you* for doing it."

She paused for a moment. "Carrington, I think you're too confused to leave things unresolved. You'll always wonder. I'm not saying he's your true love. You may find you don't even like being physical with a man. You never have been, have you?"

This wasn't the conversation I wanted with my mother. "Good Lord! Mother, please. No, I haven't, but I don't wish to speak with you about sexual relations."

She nodded, sparing me additional misery. "I understand, but you need to talk to him or seek advice from Stefan. Figure out what you want. I'm sure Stefan will be discreet about you and Eric if you want to see where this takes you. Eric could come to Yastarus to visit. What you do or don't do with him in private will be your business. But you could see if your heart wants him."

"And if it does? What then? I'm the president," I mumbled.

"For another two years," she reminded me. "You didn't want to be president. You did it for your father's memory. Don't run for re-election, regardless of what happens with Eric. Follow your bliss, Carrington."

We sat silent for a while, and I felt appreciation for having a mother who was willing to risk our family reputation for my happiness. "I know I said I didn't want to discuss sexual relations, but if I ended up with him, then it would be sexual. Would you be able to look at me and him and still love me, knowing…that?"

She put a hand to the side of my face. "I would love you no matter what. And mothers don't think about their kids having sexual relations, regardless of their orientation. It's one of those things our brains are programmed to block, just as yours no doubt blocked you from thinking about me and your father."

"Yuck," I whispered, which elicited a laugh from her.

"You see. Programmed. That's why tonight, I will be sound asleep when you're in bed with him. Fancy little maneuver on your part to make that happen, I might add."

"Excuse me? I didn't do that to have sex with that man. I'm not ready for that," I exclaimed, though the thought had crossed my mind once Eric had agreed to the arrangement.

"Very well," she conceded. "But if and when you are, be careful. I hope you'll be safe."

"Mother, I'm thirty-six years old," I complained, knowing I was blushing.

She rose from the chair and put a hand on my shoulder. "I meant protect your heart...and his. I'm guessing he's a bit of a novice in this department as well. He strikes me as too shy to be a Romeo. Be kind to each other, whatever happens, and you'll end in a good place."

Just when I thought she had ended the conversation with sweet words, she had to ruin it. Walking away, she added, "Maybe take some water out to the boys. I know you've been straining to get a better look at your soaking wet man."

I put my head in my hands and moaned, which was followed by her laughing as she exited the room.

* * * *

After realizing how creepy I was being watching the three men sweating, even to the point of being mocked by my mother, I decided to make myself useful and move my personal belongings to Eric's bedroom. It occurred to me that, unlike the guest room, his room wouldn't have a bureau of empty drawers awaiting the belongings of visitors. Leaving a pile of clothes on his bed seemed rude and intrusive, so I opened a few drawers to see if any had capacity. After opening one that was filled to the brim with socks, I tried the one below. It was full of undershirts and underwear. Now I felt like a pervert because I found myself checking out the type of undergarments he wore. It seemed he had a penchant for black trunks, though there were a couple of briefs and some traditional boxers as well. Picturing him wearing them was beginning to turn me on, so I slammed the drawer shut to turn off my mental movie projector and respect his privacy. Perhaps checking one more drawer would reap results and, if not, I would give up and ask him later where I could store my belongings.

Upon opening the third drawer, I gasped to see sex toys—a plug, a vibrator and a large flesh-colored dildo. By its side was a half-full bottle of lubricant. I closed the drawer as if it had burned my hand. I turned to make sure nobody had seen me invading his space, feeling more guilty than embarrassed. I chastised myself for not having thought about how there might have been personal items that were not my right to see.

I dropped my clothes on the end of his bed and sat on a nearby chair. The toys made it clear there was one thing he liked, and it forced me to think about whether it was something I could consider. As I thought about his bottom, I was becoming aroused once more, this time imagining what it would be like to enter him. I knew I was well endowed, and my first reaction was that I would hurt this smaller man, but the dildo wasn't petite. I had never dared to ask a female companion for anal sex, and it had never been offered to me. It was easy to understand why. One thing felt too big for the other to be pleasurable. Still, the mental projector re-started of its own volition, and I could see Eric, naked on his back, knees pulled up and waiting for me to penetrate him.

I bolted from the chair and took deep breaths to calm myself. Staying in his room would just invite the images to return, so I headed down to the kitchen to retrieve the water bottles as my mother had suggested earlier. If I wasn't helping with the outdoor efforts, the least I could do was replenish the men who were.

Once outside, bottles in hand, I marveled at how they had continued their tasks in the blazing heat. The dew point had to be comparable to what I had experienced when visiting southern American states, something I found oppressive.

Stefan saw me approaching first. "You read my mind. I was just about to ask Eric if we could take a break and get ourselves something to drink."

Eric looked up with surprise, then embarrassment. "Oh. Guys, I'm sorry. I just got caught up with what I was doing. You don't even have to be helping me. Stop whenever you like, and help yourself to whatever I have when you want it."

Then he stopped talking and was staring at me with an unexpressed question. That might have been because I was gawking at him, his face wet and every muscle of his torso visible through the pointless garment he once called a shirt. "Um, I brought you water."

Stefan chuckled. "I just noted that. I didn't think you brought them out here for yourself. That would be cruel."

Mateo laughed as well. "Sure would. Would you hand one over? It's hotter and moister than the devil's bunghole out here."

Eric rolled his eyes. "Mateo, stop it."

Mateo pretended to be taken aback. "What? Did we time-warp back to nineteenth-century England? Maybe we did since you think it's too scandalous to take off your shirt. My God, Eric, it's over one hundred degrees with one hundred percent humidity. What are you hiding anyway? A giant Mickey Mouse tattoo on your back?"

Even through the sweat and bronzing skin, I could see Eric blush. "No. I don't have tattoos."

Mateo took a swig of the water, then exhaled. "Right now, that's better than sex." He then poured some down his chest, catching Stefan's attention. It was comical how I now seemed so aware of Stefan's attraction to men when I had been dense about it before. "It's nice and cool. Stefan, try it."

Stefan hesitated, then smiled, unscrewing another bottle top and pouring it down his chest. Mateo didn't even attempt to hide his appreciation, watching every drop on Stefan's chest and stomach like a dog waiting for its master's okay to lick up a treat. I glanced to Eric, who was observing the soft porn exhibit with desire and unease, eyes wide and biting his lower lip. He looked over to me and blushed before looking down at the patio as if hoping an angel would rise from the pavers to stop the decadence.

I was torn from the reverie by Mateo laughing. "Sorry, straight guy. I guess this is too homoerotic for you."

It took me a second to conclude Mateo was speaking to me. I was of the mindset that I wasn't heterosexual anymore, I realized. "Um, it's okay," I managed. "Besides, Stefan is straight, too."

Stefan shook his head. "Carrington, I told them earlier that I'm gay."

"You did? Why?" I didn't know why I was asking. It was none of my business. I was just surprised that he had tried to keep it a secret for years, and now he was outing himself to everyone and their dog and cat.

The furtive glance Stefan shot Mateo gave me my answer, but he shrugged to signal it wasn't a big deal.

Mateo grinned. "That just leaves you, big guy. Are you sure you don't want to join the party? Gay guys have more fun." He shot a sarcastic look Eric's way.

"Well, most gay guys do. This one's decided he wants to be Amish."

Eric sighed and rebuked him with little energy. "Shut up."

Mateo was undeterred. "It's true. When we both lived in the city, I'd drag him to the clubs and you wouldn't believe the number of guys who wanted his ass. He was almost as popular as I was." Mateo turned and winked at Stefan.

Eric was becoming more agitated. "Mateo, stop talking."

"It's a compliment. Guys saw me hanging with him, so they were always asking if I had his number. They started wondering why he was even going out because he'd never go home with anyone. He wouldn't dance with anyone but me." Mateo was explaining this to me and Stefan, as if we had been asking for the backstory. He returned his gaze to Eric. "Dude, people began to think you were my straight buddy." Mateo returned his glance to me and Stefan. "Nobody ever appealed to him, or he didn't believe they were attracted to him."

Even Stefan seemed to pity Eric's discomfort. "Some men are bashful. People can project the wrong intentions on introverts."

"He's wasting his youth," Mateo reasoned. "In the gay world, you've got an expiration date at forty — earlier if you aren't hot enough to begin with."

"I'm forty," Stefan whispered with embarrassment.

Mateo looked stricken. "Shit. I'm sorry. I would never have guessed. You are scorching hot. I take back what I said. Nobody would say no to you."

Stefan shot me a glare, the meaning clear that I was the exception and, therefore, the foolish man who had lost his chance. "Thanks. There have been a couple who didn't find me hard to resist. I guess I should count my blessings it wasn't a majority view."

Mateo nodded in agreement. "You've been blessed all right, and that's just based on what I see from the waist up."

Eric was becoming more fidgety, looking everywhere but at one of us.

"Maybe that's a conversation better left between the two of you in private," I suggested.

"You're right," Mateo said, but gave me a mischievous wink, implying he thought I was encouraging the two to hook up. "As for Eric, he's cute, but he won't age as well as a muscular hunky dude. I was worried about him when he moved up to this Stepford Wife state. I can count on one hand the number of gay men you'd sleep with, and I can count on one amputated foot the number of them you'd want for a partner. I felt obligated to follow him to make sure he didn't join a monastery."

Eric let out a huff, his eyes pained. "I think we've done enough for the day. I'll go shower and get dinner started." Before I could think of anything to say that would make him feel better, he was already halfway across the patio.

I started to follow but felt Mateo's hand on my arm holding me back. He explained, "I give him tough love sometimes. He needs it, and you give friends what they need."

I tried to hold back the anger I was feeling toward Mateo. He would wonder why I was so invested. Nevertheless, I couldn't withhold the sarcasm. "And I see your tough love has been working so well. He's filled with confidence now."

Mateo reacted like I had slapped him. "I...I just try to point out that he shouldn't worry so much and he should have a good time."

"Maybe what he wants isn't what you want. Maybe he's waiting for the right guy."

Mateo nodded. "I know. But he's had lots of bites at the apple. He could get to the core and realize there's nothing left even though he's still hungry."

Stefan piped in. "Carrington may be right, though. You were kind of harsh." He looked over at me. "Maybe people should back off and stop speculating on what he wants." He narrowed his eyes, wanting to send me a message. "Eric is a grown man. He may not want *anyone* in his life, and he doesn't need prodding from us."

Mateo nodded again. "Shit. Now I feel bad. I was just trying to help. I'll go talk to him." I put a hand up to stop him this time, but he brushed it away. "Don't worry. No tough love. I'm going to apologize and tell him to trust his instincts. What do I know? It's not like I'm with someone either." With that, he grabbed his shirt off a nearby fence pole and retreated to the house.

"What the hell was that?" I barked at Stefan.

He squirmed a bit. "You mean Mateo flirting with me?"

"Surprising as it was that you were encouraging it, I was referring to the way he was treating Eric."

Stefan's mouth tightened and he jutted his chin like he was ready to do battle. "First off, you of all people have no right to deny me a little fun with another guy. You're a big reason I lost so many years as it is, and you sure aren't hiding your little crush on our host. Christ, I can't believe Mateo couldn't see it. You were eye-fucking Eric the entire time he was standing there."

"What? I wasn't," I stammered.

Stefan smirked. "I haven't seen you even look at a pretty girl the way you were feasting on him." He rolled his eyes. "I'm your mate, don't lie to me about it."

His words reminded me of what my mother had said. Everyone close to me was beginning to think me dishonest. "I...wasn't thinking about sex. I don't deny I find him...breathtaking, though."

My friend's face softened a bit. "Well, I'm beginning to see it. He's not what I go for, but he is very cute. That body is more jacked than I would have thought. Even I was waiting for him to take the shirt off."

I felt a surge of jealousy. "Mateo wasn't enough to be salivating over? And what do you think will come of that, anyway? You live halfway across the world from Mateo."

Stefan had a victorious smile. "Indeed. Maybe you should apply that logic to yourself. I'm willing to settle for a quick shag with a hot man. I'm not so sure that's going to be enough for you. I'm looking at Mateo with lust. You're looking at Eric with little heart emojis."

"I'm not in love with him. I don't even know him," I protested.

"You'd do well to remember that," Stefan warned. "You want to attack Mateo, but he told me some things. Eric has baggage. Mateo's been there to help him every step of the way."

"What are you talking about?" I demanded, though I wasn't sure I wanted to hear anything negative about Eric. Maybe I *was* projecting heart emojis.

"Eric is almost a virgin at the age of twenty-six. You might think that's quaint, but I think it's indicative of issues. Mateo said that he came out to his parents whilst attending New York University, and they cut him off. He finished school on scholarships and part-time jobs. When he graduated, he had no money and no place to go. Mateo befriended him and took him in."

I couldn't understand how any mother could disown someone as kind as Eric. "My God," I whispered.

Stefan continued. "Mateo even moved to Connecticut, leading Eric to believe that he wanted a change of pace. But the truth is that he cares for Eric like a brother, and he was afraid for him to be alone. So, before you criticize Mateo for being tough on Eric, you should consider how much he's done for him. He said Eric has very low self-esteem, and he sabotages opportunities with men. That's something else you might want to think about before you go down this path to disappointment."

"Perhaps Eric hasn't found the guy who will treat him the way he should," I countered.

"Maybe," Stefan concurred. "I'm just saying, you're already confused, and you're falling for someone else who's confused." Waving his arm toward the destruction from the hurricane, he added, "It's a storm brewing, and this could be the outcome."

I pondered all that Stefan had shared. "Or maybe it's two people who found someone else to cling to in the storm." I bit my lip and raised my eyes to gauge Stefan's reaction.

He had a tired look. "It's obvious you want it to be."

"So, what do I do with the limited time I have left with him? Will telling him how I feel scare him away if he's so skittish?"

He clapped a hand on my shoulder. "Carrington, I don't know. I'm not comfortable with any of this. He may not even be interested in you. Maybe we're misreading him. You realize that, don't you? Plus, he's suffering from emotional trauma that you're not going to be able to cure. Everything about your interest in him is risky — to your ego at a minimum if he rejects you, to your political career at worst if he doesn't."

"Yes. He hasn't shared if he feels the same attraction. Maybe I'm not someone a man would fancy."

Stefan laughed. "What am I? I hope you're not suggesting I'm less than a man."

"Of course not!" I defended. "I'm sorry. I meant a man who isn't biased because he's my friend."

Stefan rolled his eyes. "Our country's best-selling magazine named you its most eligible bachelor and one of the country's ten best-looking people. I'm certain a survey of gay Yastarusian men would support that."

I felt more heat and it had nothing to do with the blazing sun. I had never contemplated that I could be a pin-up to gay men. "Thank you, and I don't take for granted what a compliment it is that you felt that way. You know how much you mean to me." He nodded. "It's just that man. He's done something to me."

My friend sighed. "Then I hope he isn't Russia's secret weapon."

I knew Stefan was being flip, but it was the prodding I needed that I'd exceeded the thirty minutes I was waiting between check-ins regarding affairs back home. The vice president had been informing me that there was nothing of consequence happening, and that it might even be good that I was out of sight, as it had quieted intelligence reports about a possible attempt on my life. Still, the Russian threat wasn't gone, and I knew Eric could become a high-risk complication for me. Still, I couldn't bring myself to leave without unburdening myself. Like my mother said, I couldn't depart the United States feeling so confused. Doing so would also put me at risk because I would be distracted, wondering 'what if.' With help and discretion from her and Stefan, I believed Eric and I could find a way to explore whatever we were feeling, providing he was feeling anything at all. I was relieved that we had changed the sleeping arrangements, and I would now have Eric's undivided attention for the night.

Chapter Ten

Eric

A couple hours after dinner, I made up the couch for Mateo. He had apologized to me for embarrassing me in front of Stefan and Carrington, and he had even shared that they both had defended me once I had left them. He thought Carrington had seemed irate, which gave me a warped sense of pleasure. Of course, I had forgiven Mateo. He was just being himself. When all was said and done, Mateo would always have my back. I wanted to share with him how I was attracted to Carrington, but I knew he would caution me to avoid disappointment. After all, he didn't know about Carrington's confession.

Once Mateo was curled up on the couch, content to doze off while watching television, Stefan and Olivia bid me good-night and went upstairs to their rooms. From the way Stefan had parted with Mateo, I suspected they had concocted a middle-of-the night rendezvous. There had been a wink and a couple of knowing glances. I didn't mind as long as they didn't soil my upholstery if they chose the couch as their setting. The sofa was a Queen Anne reproduction that had cost me a week's pay.

"Um, maybe I should go change first?" I suggested to Carrington. "I can leave the lights on for you in the bedroom and master bath for when you're ready to come up."

He nodded in agreement. "I'll turn off all the lights down here and be up in about five minutes."

I could tell he was as nervous as I was. No doubt, he was concerned I was going to make a move on him in bed. Awkward as it would be, I would have to assure him once he was beside me that he didn't need to worry. He had a bigger risk of Mateo sneaking in on him than me mortifying myself by trying to be with someone who didn't want me.

Once upstairs, I rushed through brushing my teeth and washing. Although my night-time routine was limited to cleansing my face, I scrubbed everywhere — just in case lightning were to strike. As Mateo always said, "*Prepare for the unexpected to avoid regrets later.*"

I was lying back on the bed, head propped up on a couple of pillows, when Carrington entered the doorway and peered my way. "Okay to enter now?"

"Yes, of course," I responded. "Um, help yourself to whatever you need in the bathroom."

He smiled, grabbing some garments before going into the ensuite and closing the door behind him. I was glad I had put on antiperspirant, because my nerves were shot. I took long breaths, reminding myself that nothing might happen other than exchanged pleasantries and wishing each other a good-night.

After a few torturous minutes passed, Carrington emerged, wearing a white T-shirt and a pair of clingy light-blue boxer briefs. The tight cotton on top teased me by hugging the buds of his nipples, and the fabric on the bottom clung to his long, thick cock. I tried to look down, but that just drew my eyes to his exposed, muscular legs. The calves were dusted with light brown hair and his thighs were smooth and beefy. I looked to the window, as if something very interesting were happening outside.

He walked to the bed, pulling back the covers enough to slide in. The heat from his body was instantaneous.

"You're wearing pajamas," he commented.

I made eye contact with him. "Huh?"

He looked apologetic. "I pulled back the covers enough to see you're wearing pajamas. You're not doing that because of me, are you?"

"Um, you were wearing pajamas last night. I didn't want to make you uncomfortable."

Carrington grinned. "To be quite honest, the pajamas were uncomfortable. I wish no offense, but even with air conditioning, your upstairs quarters are a bit stuffy. I figured you'd be okay with me dressing this way, since it's how you dressed last evening."

I was about to point out that my boxers had been longer and looser than what he had donned, but I didn't want him to know I had been scrutinizing. "Oh, well, I'm sorry you weren't comfortable."

"It's okay," he said. "I just feel bad that you're going to get hot. Why don't you take your top off?"

I looked back to his face, wondering if he was being polite or suggestive. "Um, won't that make you feel weird?"

He grinned. "If by weird you mean horny — maybe. I guess that would make you more uncomfortable, wouldn't it? I'm sorry. You're just so beautiful. Truth be known, I was hoping you would take off your shirt when Mateo was goading you earlier."

I gulped. "You were?"

"Eric, I told you last night — I'm attracted to you. I spent all day trying to convince myself that it was a fluke. Maybe I was in some emotional state last night. But being around you today hasn't changed anything. I'm willing to admit it to myself now." His blue eyes were like lasers on me, and I wasn't sure I could withstand the onslaught. "If you don't feel that way about me, I understand. I'll close my eyes, be a perfect gentleman — a disappointed gentleman — who will not bring it up again. I know you have a specific type in mind when it comes to potential suitors."

I groaned. "Mateo… Is that what he said? Listen, I just don't want a guy who comes up to me and starts grabbing, wanting to get off on me. I want to like them first. I never thought it would take so long to find a man that I liked enough to want more from them." He nodded, but I could tell he missed the meaning of my words. "And now I found one."

He beamed. "Do you mean me?"

Carrington seemed hopeful, so I felt emboldened to be honest and a bit playful. "Yes, despite your ridiculous little tantrum in the grocery store. I thought, 'too bad that cute guy is such a diva'."

He didn't stop smiling. "I *was* a prima donna. I turned around and you were there, discombobulating me with your kindness and warmth. I thought, 'how dare he try to assuage my outrage!'"

I laughed. "Sorry about that. I'll know next time to let you have your hissy fit."

He chuckled in return. "Please do. I'm rather fond of my tantrums. People jump to attention when I have them."

"Hmm. You like people bowing to you, huh?"

He shrugged. "I am a president, after all."

"Yes sir," I joked. "At your command, sir."

Carrington's eyes clouded. "I hate to tell you how much that just turned me on."

"Uh oh. You're not an S and M master type, are you?" I asked, though suspecting he wasn't.

He shook his head. "Nothing like that. But having you do as I tell you does have its appeal."

"Oh?"

"Mm-hmm." He nodded. "Now, take off your shirt."

It was just a shirt, and I knew I was in good shape. But I wasn't built like Carrington. I was nervous, but under his watchful gaze, I found myself unbuttoning my pajama top. "Um, you're straight. What if you don't like what you see? I mean, I even have a farmer's tan."

He looked sympathetic. "Eric, I promise there is nothing about you that I can imagine not liking. But if you don't want to, then don't. I would never try to force someone to do something that makes them uncomfortable. But now I must know, what is a farmer's tan?"

I was about to answer, but instead I mustered the courage to finish removing the shirt. I let out a sigh when I got to the last button, and pulled the fabric away from me before I could second-guess myself. "That's a farmer's tan," I answered, letting my body speak for itself. My face, neck, throat and forearms were dark from my day's activities, but the rest of me was my usual pallor. "I guess I should have listened to Mateo about working shirtless."

I dared to peek at his face for his reaction. He looked amused. "You thought that would make you unattractive?"

"I'm no Stefan. Or Mateo, for that matter," I whispered.

Carrington surprised me by taking my face into both of his hands. "No, you're not. I'm glad. I'm not attracted to them. They're handsome. *You're beautiful.* Look at you."

"I'd rather look at you," I admitted, staring into his eyes.

"Okay, that's fair. Look all you want, because I can't take my eyes off you," he said in a raspy tone. My dick twitched.

"So, you can be attracted to a guy's body?" I wondered.

"Apparently," he confirmed. "There's a part of me that's saying I'm very much interested, if you know what I mean. You look better than I hoped. Your chest...it's exquisite."

My eyes widened in surprise. "It is?"

His tone had a sleepy, sexy quality to it. "Mm-hmm. So smooth, and yet so toned. You have nice pectoral muscles, and your nipples are...perfect. One of the things I like best about women is their breasts. I'm a breast man. Love their big nipples too. Makes me want to lick and suck them every time I see a nice pair. I think one of the reasons I don't like guys is their chests just don't interest me that way."

I frowned. "Are you saying my chest reminds you of a woman's?"

He chuckled. "No, Eric. But some of the things I like about a woman's breasts are why I like your chest. I told you, I'm not a fan of body hair. I don't like bulging muscles either. And a lot of guys have small nipples — just kind of unnoticeable. You, on the other hand, while strong, have that silky skin and those quarter-sized nipples that are lying there so nice and erect, I want to lick them."

"Oh," was all I managed to whisper.

"And that beautiful, flat hairless stomach — heaving with nervousness and anticipation — is driving me crazy," he added.

"Um, you hate body hair a lot, huh?"

He chuckled at that. "I guess it sounds like I have a body hair phobia. I don't. I just know what I'm attracted to."

"I have pubic hair, and a little in my arm pits," I confessed, now silently cursing every follicle. At least I had trimmed the hair in both areas a couple of days earlier.

"Good." He smiled.

"Good? But..."

"I don't want someone who looks like a prepubescent child, for heaven's sake. Like I said, I love your muscles. You're very much a man, just a very angelic-looking one. And it's intoxicating when it's the packaging for a very sweet soul."

"I think you're the best-looking man I've ever seen," I blurted. I shut myself up, realizing I sounded like an eager, starstruck teenager.

Carrington didn't seem to mind. He had a big smile. "Yes? Tell me what you like. I enjoy being flattered."

I grinned. "All hail the president, huh?"

He gave me an appraising look. "You're an angel, but you have a little devil in you, too. Your mouth can be fresh." Then he smiled. "You're perfect."

"Fresh? I'm always sweet. I'm practically Amish, remember?" I mock-protested.

His expression became solemn, and I wondered how my playful banter offended him. "About that," he started. "I have a confession to make. Not as earth-shattering as admitting I'm attracted to a man, but one that may make you angry with me."

I had no idea what he was talking about. How would me joking that I was always sweet elicit a confession from him? I knew things had been going too well. I imagined this would be the point in the conversation where he'd tell me that he had ordered political foes executed, or some equivalent that would be too horrible to ignore. "Okay," I managed.

"Earlier, I came up here to move my belongings into your room. I wasn't thinking. I just started opening drawers to put away my clothes, and, well," he explained, darting his eyes over to my dresser.

For a moment, I had no idea what he was referencing. Then it hit me. I put my hands over my face and moaned. "Oh God."

"Please don't be embarrassed. I'm the one who should be. I had no right to go into your things. In my defense, I wasn't trying to be invasive. I just wasn't thinking. I'm so sorry I disrespected you."

I looked up at the ceiling to avoid his scrutiny. "I forgot they were there. I don't ever use them."

He had the audacity to chuckle. "Um, okay, but the bottle of lubricant was half-empty."

I returned his glance with a grimace. "You're trying to torture me, aren't you?" He began to laugh. "I thought you weren't snooping. You sure seemed to have checked every detail." He just laughed a little louder. "Okay, I've used them, but it's been a long time."

"Eric," he prodded when I went back to looking at the ceiling.

"I'm telling you the truth," I mumbled.

"Look at me," he ordered. I didn't. "Please." Then, I did. His face was remorseful. "I'm sorry I embarrassed you. It just didn't feel right not to tell you. Don't be angry. The thing is, I think it's hot."

"You do?" I asked in surprise.

He returned a hand to the side of my face. "Mm. I've been thinking about you and that larger sex toy all day. I would love to watch you with it."

I gulped. "Oh."

He smiled. "I'm hard as your bedpost right now, picturing it."

In reflex, I shot my eyes in the direction of his crotch, but it was covered by the blanket. "I don't think I can do that," I managed. "I'd feel too self-conscious."

"In time," he said. "Once you realize I'm not judging you. It's you having the power to make me weak."

"I thought you like to be the one barking orders and being in charge," I reminded him.

He smiled. "Oh, I'd be barking orders, all right. It doesn't mean you wouldn't still be the death of me."

I tried to remember what had triggered the topic of my sex toys. "How did me joking that I'm always sweet make you think about the dildo?" He darted his eyes away. "Oh. It was you calling me out as a liar for my Amish comment."

He pulled my face back into his hands. "I'm glad you aren't a part of some celibate sect. That would be such a waste. I love that you can be naughty. You're full of surprises."

"Did you like to watch girlfriends play with sex toys?" I asked, unable to hide my inexplicable jealousy.

"Never happened," he stated.

"Why not?"

Carrington shrugged. "I guess because I always hooked up with society types, or at least women who tried to be what they thought a man in my position wanted them to be. I enjoyed sex with them, but they always held back. I think they thought if they appeared to be having a good time, I'd think less of them. I was never even sure if the orgasms they had were intense. Maybe they weren't even real. It's hard to be in relationship after relationship like that. You begin to wonder if you're just a bore in bed."

"I doubt it," I assured him. "We haven't even done anything, and you've already had my...dick stiffer than I think it's ever been." I flushed, then silently chastised myself for doing so, feeling it would remind him of the prissy society girls.

He gave me a quizzical look. "Dick? I assume it's your word of choice for your manhood? I'll remember to use it henceforth."

"Huh? What do you like to call it?

He smiled. "Well, now I like to call it a dick. Yes, it has a blunt, masculine sound to it."

I chuckled. "You're kind of weird. Maybe the girls didn't know if they were supposed to moan or laugh."

"Why not both?" he asked. "Why can't sex be fun?"

"Hmm, to quote you — indeed. Perhaps I shall strive for that, henceforth."

He gave me his big-toothed smile and tapped me on the shoulder. "Don't mock my way of speaking, Mr.

Turner. I learned English at Oxford University and blend well when in London, thank you very much."

I pretended to become serious. "High-society London, maybe."

He rolled his eyes. "Back to your dick predicament. Are you still suffering from said stiffness? Do you think we should do something to remedy it?"

I gulped. "Um, I didn't think you'd want to see a guy's dick, let alone do something with it."

"As opposed to doing something with a woman's dick?" He snickered. I looked at him with confusion. "You said a guy's dick..."

"Oh," I whispered. He did go back and forth between hot and silly.

"I'm sure you have a beautiful dick." He grinned. "Everything about you so far has been a work of art." He paused and became serious. "But I appreciate you thinking about it. I am nervous, truth be told. I don't know what I'm doing. I just know I like being with you. This conversation is one of the most fun I've had in a long time."

"Me too," I confessed.

"I'd like to kiss you," he whispered. "Would that be permissible?"

I swallowed hard and nodded. I couldn't think of anything I wanted more. He moved his face to mine, taking one last look at my lips before pressing his own against them. His mouth was warm and strong, and a lock of his long, brushed-back hair fell forward, tickling my nose as he moved his face to get a better angle. He seemed frustrated that he still wasn't close enough, moving his body onto mine.

"Are you okay? Am I too heavy?" he whispered. I shook my head no without answering, pulling his mouth back to mine. I wanted him so much. I mortified myself by making little sounds when he started tasting me with his tongue, inserting it between my now parted lips. "Yes, Eric, I love the way you moan," he whispered, before taking my mouth once more.

"Will you take your shirt off too?" I begged. "I want to feel your chest against mine."

He raised his torso so he could remove the T-shirt, revealing his lightly haired chest. It was a thing of beauty. His pecs were mounds of muscle, and his nipples were about the same size as mine and just as hard. With him leaning over me, they were pointing down at my mouth, like an invitation to be sucked. I took the chance and bent up toward him, taking his right tit into my mouth, licking, and sucking. He moaned and grabbed my face with urgent hands, pressing my mouth against his wet nub. "Oh God, Eric. I love watching that little mouth," he gasped.

"I want you so much," I admitted. "I wasn't kidding when I said you're the best-looking guy I've ever seen."

Carrington pushed me back down on the pillow and latched his mouth on my left nipple while tweaking and rubbing the other one. I put my right hand over my face, covering my excitement and hoping to stifle my noises. "Don't," he panted. "Let me see you." He moved my hand away from my face and surprised me by grabbing my dick through the pajama pants. He started moving his hand up and down, creating glorious friction. I couldn't stop my cries. Carrington began kissing my neck and throat, lifting his face from mine to watch me squirming in pleasure. "You are so beautiful," he rasped.

"I'm going to come," I warned.

He donned a mischievous, lustful grin. "Yes, do it, baby. I want to see that sweet face of yours when you come."

I couldn't hold back any longer. I knew I was going to mess up my pajama pants, but the ecstasy overtook me. I came as his hand ground into me, almost lifting my legs from the mattress. I did my best to keep my voice low, muttering a few F-bombs while tugging at my own hair. When my emissions stopped, Carrington pushed his mouth back to mine. When he pulled away, he smiled. "Sweet Eric."

"Carrington," was all I could whisper, then I grabbed his hair to tilt his mouth back to mine. He kissed me much more softly.

After a couple of moments, he smiled. "You good?"

I nodded. He looked down at my messed-up pajama bottoms. "Sorry about that," I said.

"For what?" he asked. "Don't start feeling guilty."

"Are *you* okay?" I wondered. After all, he was the straight guy who had just had sex with a man.

"Will be if I can ejaculate. Would you mind?" I shook my head, though unsure what he wanted to do. He shocked me by reaching into my pants and rubbing his hand all around my cum. "Enough to feed an army," he joked.

"The Yastarus military has an unusual cuisine selection," I commented.

"We try not to waste," he deadpanned. He then took his cum-filled hand and slipped it into the front of his shorts. "Eric lubricant," he explained.

He started jacking while resuming our kissing, and I found it thrilling he would be okay with using my emissions as a means for slicking himself. Within seconds, he pulled his face away and began panting. A vein in his forehead became prominent when he was starting to orgasm, and he dropped his face onto the pillow while grunting and gasping. I held him tight through his release, stroking his back then rubbing soothing circles on it when I knew he was finished.

"Are you okay still?" I asked, fearful that now the regret would set in.

He raised his head from the pillow to look at me. "I am. Don't worry. I'm not going to have a straight man freak-out. In fact, I dare say, I've never felt anything that intense."

I felt a surge of pride, even though I know I didn't do much of anything. "Me too."

He brushed back the hair from my forehead, gazing at me affectionately. "What are you doing to me, Eric Turner?"

"Whatever you want," I whispered back.

He smiled. Then he reached over to the box of tissues I had on my nightstand, grabbed some and threw a wad at me. "You clean yourself, and I'll clean myself. Then, let's cuddle. Or do you not do that?"

"I do that," I replied with eagerness. He chuckled. After we both wiped ourselves down, I told him to just throw the tissues on the floor and that I'd pick them up in the morning. I didn't want him to leave the bed. Once we had discarded the cum rags, he rolled to his side and pulled me up to him. "Mm, this is nice," I admitted.

He put his strong arms around me, kissed me on the forehead and rubbed my lower back. "Sleep well, sweet Eric."

* * * *

Five years earlier

My newest college friend, Troy, had just left my parents' Caldwell, New Jersey, home to head back to NYU. He had come to stay as a guest for the Thanksgiving break since the dorms were going to be closed, and Troy's parents didn't want to pay for him to travel home to California for such a short school vacation. Troy had taken the train so he could get back when the dorms reopened on Saturday, but I had stayed behind and would be driven by my parents the following day.

My parents had been quiet the entire time Troy had been with us, bordering on rudeness. They hadn't said much to me either, so I knew they were upset about something. I was embarrassed and angry with my mother and father for making my friend so uncomfortable. We were now sitting down to dinner, and the tension was palpable.

Once the three of us were seated, my mother addressed me without eye contact. "You're at an age where we would have thought you'd be bringing a girl home some time. Are you still not seeing anyone?"

There was a tone that signaled where the conversation was heading, and bile rose in my throat. "Um, no, I haven't met anyone."

She stabbed at a piece of meat, but didn't eat it. "You're not going to meet a girl when you hang out with people like Troy."

I looked to my father, but he was eating with a scowl on his face, avoiding eye contact with either of us. I knew what my mother meant by her comment, but I thought it would be smarter to play dumb. "I don't know what you mean." I forced a piece of meatloaf into my mouth, but felt like my throat would close if I tried to swallow it.

"He's not the first friend you've had that's one of them," she snarled, pushing her fork into mashed potatoes then dropping it to the plate.

I knew she meant gay people, but I hoped staying silent might encourage her to change the subject. I shoved another piece of meatloaf in my mouth, wanting to finish as soon as possible so I could leave the table.

"I don't hear you denying your friend is a queer," my father snapped, also dropping his fork on the plate, then wiping his forehead. I was wishing he would at least look at me, but he didn't. It was becoming clear that both he and my mother were certain I was gay, and they couldn't bear to be around me.

Since both were just staring at their uneaten food, I knew they were waiting for me to speak. "Yes, he is," I confessed.

My mother looked like she was about to cry, but I found it elicited from me irritation as opposed to empathy. I hated that their bigotry made me the bad guy in the scenario. "I've been sick since that...boy...got here, wondering if you're like him," she muttered with disgust.

"I haven't slept with Troy, if that's what you're suggesting," I protested, thinking it might be enough to slow down the inquisition.

She looked like she was about to vomit. "I don't want to think about that. Are you attracted to any girls?"

I tried to be evasive once again. "I'm not attracted to anyone. I'm just trying to focus on school."

"So, you don't like boys?" she pressed.

"I don't like anyone," I reiterated.

My father pushed his plate away and bellowed, "Goddammit, are you a homo?"

I gulped. He hadn't beaten me since I had started college, but he seemed close to doing so now. The look of disgust on my mother's face made me realize she would welcome it. I was scared, but I was also tired of being so. It was obvious that any answer other than 'I'm straight' would lead to the same nasty outcome, so maybe it was better to tell the truth and be done with it. "Yes," I whispered.

My father picked up his glass of water and hurled it at me. It hit my shoulder before bouncing and smashing against the wall. He stared me down with unadulterated hatred, then stormed from the room. I looked over to my mother, and she was crying. I knew it wasn't with sympathy for me. After a few minutes, she spoke. "I didn't want to believe it. I don't know what's wrong with you. We never did anything to cause you to be this way."

"I know," I managed.

"Your father told me that if he found out you're like Troy, he wants you out and you can find a way to pay for college yourself," she informed me.

Although I knew the answer, I didn't want her to absolve herself from being a co-conspirator, so I asked, "And what do you want?"

"I want you to be normal!"

"Do you want me to leave?" I asked, trying to keep from sobbing.

She glared at me. "If you're not going to change."

I swallowed, a tear escaping. "I can't change."

My mother shook her head in disgust. "You should pack your things. I'll drive you to the train station, and

I'll give you money to get you back to school. The semester, including room and board, is paid for. You'd better think about how you're going to support yourself once the semester is done."

Within an hour, I found myself sitting in the passenger seat of my mother's SUV, willing myself to keep my dignity and stay calm. My mother didn't speak during the ride, nor as I was exiting and retrieving my bag. I thought she might at least say goodbye or suggest that she'd call some time, but she said nothing. I shut the door and watched her drive away — knowing I was dead to my parents.

* * * *

Present day

"Eric! Eric, wake up," the voice was saying. It was unfamiliar. No, wait. It was Carrington, and I couldn't understand why he was standing with me watching my mother drive away. "Eric," he called again.

I opened my eyes, feeling disoriented. "What?" My mind was fuzzy.

"You were having a bad dream," Carrington was saying.

I looked around. I was in my own bed, and Carrington was sleeping with me. "Oh," I managed, rubbing my eyes. Carrington was staring at me with concern. "I'm sorry."

"Don't be sorry," he said. "Eric, you were tossing and making this pained sound. I was frightened."

"Sorry," I repeated, even though he had told me not to be. "It was stupid. Just reliving something that happened a long time ago."

"Do you want to talk about it?" he asked.

"No," I whispered. "I'll try to be quiet."

Carrington pulled me into his arms. "Eric, I'm not concerned about that. It's all right. I'll hold you until you fall back to sleep."

"You don't have to," I said. "I can't fall back to sleep once I wake up from a nightmare. No reason for both of us to be up until dawn. You already didn't sleep last night."

His pretty eyes never left mine. "I'll be going home soon. I'm content to spend more time with you. We can talk."

I grinned a little. "I never would have thought when I first met you that you were going to be so nice." He grimaced. I would have to stop reminding him of his unfortunate first encounter with me. "Maybe that's why I'm drawn to straight guys. My mother used to talk about how gay men were disgusting with their filthy sex acts."

"Well, you're gay. Do you think about filthy sex?" He smiled, no doubt waiting for a snarky answer.

I touched his glossy hair. "Seems I do when I'm with you."

Bingo! He laughed. "We can have sex if you'd rather. Would that help you sleep?"

"Mm. I don't know about that. But it would be kind of nice to have sex with someone more than once."

He looked surprised. "You've never had a repeat performance with someone?"

I shook my head no. "I've never been with anyone I wanted. I was always glad to get away. That's why I never did much with them to begin with."

"Do you want to talk about why?"

I kissed him. "I don't want to spend my limited time with you crying on your shoulder. I'd rather be licking it."

Gareth Chris

He laughed. "You'd rather lick *my shoulder?*"

I fluttered my eyelashes to be funny. "Well, what else are you offering me?"

He laughed again. "Oh baby, don't tempt me."

I rolled us so that I was on top of him. "Do I tempt you?"

"You know you do," he responded. "But you know what? This blatant flirtatiousness isn't you. It's not that I'm not enjoying it, but I feel like you're manipulating me to avoid talking about things that trouble you."

"Ugh." I rolled to my back. Reaching over to the nightstand, I retrieved a pack of breath strips and gave him one before popping another in my mouth.

"That bad, huh? I guess morning breath starts right after midnight." He sighed, popping in the strip.

I laughed. "I wanted it for myself. I'm sharing to be polite."

He leaned toward me and started brushing my hair with his hand. "You always try to please. Why is that?"

"Because I'm a nice guy?"

He smiled. "Yes, you are. But it seems very important to you to please others, even when it isn't something you want. Why did you go home with men you didn't wish to be with?"

I looked at the ceiling fan instead of his penetrating gaze. "I don't know. I started off by saying no to them. I tried to come up with excuses that wouldn't hurt their feelings. Most guys would let it go after a while. A few others didn't. They wore me down."

Carrington continued stroking my hair and it was soothing, making it easier to share. "You had the right to say no. You *should have* said no."

I shrugged. "I know. After being with me, they were disappointed, I'm sure. I could never bring myself to get into it. I don't like sex with strangers. It was always the same. They'd blow me, then I would feel obligated to do the same. I'd never swallow, though. I just couldn't. It felt like something too intimate to offer someone that I didn't know — that I didn't even like. It would make me think about what my mother had said about gay sex. These were men I didn't have any connection to, yet we were doing stuff that you'd think a caring couple would do. I'd always feel guilty afterward. I'd head home, brush my teeth, jump in the shower and scrub myself clean, swearing I wouldn't go to a club again. But the hormones would act up and I'd venture out, thinking maybe it would be different the next time. Perhaps I'd meet some Prince Charming who'd want to date before getting in the sack. It just never worked out that way. I decided it wasn't worth it. Much to Mateo's chagrin, I became a stay-at-home, work-focused boy."

We remained silent for a few minutes. I thought I had bored poor Carrington to sleep. I turned to look at him, and he still had the same intense gaze fixed on my face. "I'm so sorry, Eric. I hate that people abused your kindness, and that includes your parents."

I raised my eyebrows in surprise. "Other than what I told you about my mom's views on gay sex, what makes you think they abused me?"

Carrington pursed his lips, seeming to question whether he should reply. "Mateo may have shared some things."

I let out a sarcastic laugh. "Ah. Yes, I'm sure he did. He can't help himself. What did he tell you?"

"Well, he told Stefan, who told me," Carrington clarified. "That they disowned you when you were at university. He said you earned more scholarships and secured work to finish college, then landed yourself a job upon graduation. In just a few years, you've done well for yourself, Eric. I'm impressed. Stefan told me Mateo is, too, and that he speaks of you with affection."

"He helped me a lot," I affirmed. "I owe him. That's why I tried to be more like what he wanted in a friend. A guy who'd go to clubs with him, pick up guys and share sex stories after. I did try."

Carrington tilted my chin toward him so we could lock eyes. "Another example of you sacrificing a part of yourself to please another. You do see how that's going beyond being a nice guy, don't you?"

I sighed. "Our company healthcare plan offered five therapy visits at no cost. I figured it wouldn't hurt to go to one. I was having trouble with an abusive boss. She made me work way more hours than anyone else, rationalizing that all my co-workers had families and I didn't. The therapist asked me if I ever told her that I wouldn't do it, and I said I didn't. I didn't want to upset my boss."

"There's a pattern here," Carrington said.

"Hmm. Once the therapist delved into my family history, he said the same. It was funny. Without me even telling him, he deduced that one of my parents was an alcoholic. In this case, it was my father. He asked me if my dad was abusive and if he had a lot of fights with my mom. I told him yes. The therapist then summed up my issues as stemming back to that."

"How so?" Carrington asked.

"The therapist said that as the only child, it was a very unstable and precarious world for me. To cope and survive in it, I began to be the peacemaker. I became good at helping the other side understand the other's perspective. I tried to do everything to please them so they didn't have something else to fight about. Relatives used to say I was the perfect child." I sighed. "Except I wasn't. I wasn't the attractive son they could boast about. I wasn't good in sports, which was a disappointment to my father and I wasn't as tough as they thought I should be. I did get good grades in school, though. That, at least, made them somewhat happy. Until I blew it to shit by turning out gay, that is."

There was a deep frown on Carrington's face. "I don't ever want to meet them. I could never forgive them for what they did to you."

I brushed my thumb over his lips. "You won't ever have to. I haven't talked to them in years. I tried once. When I landed my first job in the city, I called my mother. I had a new cell phone, so she didn't know it was me calling. I asked how she was, and she said she and my father were fine, and asked what I wanted. I told her that I didn't want anything, and before I could say another word, she replied 'good' because they had given me years of love and financial support — and me choosing a disgusting lifestyle was the thanks they got for it. She told me not to bother her again, so I haven't."

"You can't still love them!"

I shrugged. "A small part of me did for a while. I'd remember the few good times and some things they did. They were kind to me at Christmas and on my birthday. They bought me a lot of presents, which is weird. It did feel like they loved me sometimes, but all the hitting, expressed disappointment and criticism made it confusing. I've gotten to a place where I know I can't live for them. Long way of saying, I guess they're as dead to me now as I am to them, and I don't cry about that anymore."

Carrington's face looked pained, and I felt bad that I was making him unhappy. I had said enough. "My mother always says, be kind to others because everyone carries a burden, and it's often one we don't see," he shared.

"Your mother is nice," I said. "Would she be upset if she knew about us?"

He upturned his lip a bit. "She already does."

"What?"

He chuckled. "She figured it out. She knows me so well."

"Does she hate me now?" I worried.

He laughed again. "Not at all. She told me she wants to squeeze you because you're so adorable. I told her to back off. You're mine."

"I'm yours?" I asked.

Although it was dark, I could see Carrington was blushing. "I'm sorry. I didn't mean that the way it sounded. Of course, you're not mine. I just meant, I wanted to be the one to win your favor."

I smiled. "You talk funny."

He play-punched me on the shoulder. "*You* talk funny."

Once we stopped laughing, I whispered, "I know I don't know you well, but I know whoever gets to be yours one day is a very lucky person."

Carrington's pupils enlarged and he pulled me into a kiss. I tasted the mint from the mouthwash strip, felt the wetness of his lips and tongue and basked in the heat of his breath. I wondered if he could feel my dick hardening against his thigh. "Eric, would you do me a favor?"

"Hmm," I responded, somewhat dazed — resuming the kissing I was enjoying so much.

He pulled away, catching his breath. "Eric, don't do anything just to please me. Okay? It's all right if pleasing me is giving you pleasure, too. But I don't want to be another man you remember as someone who took advantage of your nature."

"Carrington, you are not doing that. I have loved every minute of this. I promise, you can tell me what to do that will please you, and it will be my pleasure, too."

"Why? What's different about me? You don't know me well. You said you wanted to wait for Prince Charming."

I pondered. "Well, you're not a prince, but you're a president. Kind of close." He chuckled. "You're way better looking than any other guy I've been with, and my dick gives you its seal of approval." He laughed some more. I became serious. "And I may not have known you very long, but it seems to me that there are people you can be around for years and not truly know. Then there are people you meet, and you feel like you've known them for years. I already trust you." I swallowed hard. "And I like you a lot."

He kissed me. "I like you a lot, too. I'm glad we're sharing these firsts together. It could never have been any other man for me."

I tried not to focus on the word 'firsts, as it implied there would be other men to follow. In my head, I was already fantasizing about something everlasting. "But you'll be leaving."

He began to stroke my hair again. "Come visit. My mother already suggested it. I'll show you Yastarus."

"I work." I pouted.

"You don't get holiday?"

"You mean vacation, funny talker?" I joked.

He ignored my barb. "Take vacation. Right away. We can be discreet. Of course, I'll pay for everything. You just need to show up. What do you think?"

"Maybe," I replied. It would require checking with my supervisor, finding someone to watch the house and many other things I hadn't yet considered.

"It's a yes or no question," Carrington pressed.

I laughed. "You always get what you want?"

"No," he responded. "So please say yes, but only if it would please you too."

I paused, looking into his eager eyes. "Yes."

* * * *

Carrington

"I'm glad you'll be coming." I smiled. I knew I would be taking a risk bringing a male lover to my bed in Yastarus, but with Stefan's and my mother's help, I was sure we could make it work.

"Do you mean to Yastarus, or in my pants?" Eric snickered.

I chuckled in return. "So cheeky. I should put your bare bottom over my knee and give you a well-deserved spanking."

Instead of the laugh I expected in response, his eyes popped and his dick prodded my waist. "Um…"

I looked at him with surprise. "Oh my, you'd like that wouldn't you?"

"What? No," he protested.

I ran a hand through his hair as I had already learned it soothed him. "I would be okay if you did. I would never hurt you. But administering a few playful slaps on the bum, just enough to make your cheeks pink, might be fun for both of us. I must confess, I fancied playing with your bum when we were outside yesterday."

His dick had become engorged, and his face was a mix of astonishment, apprehension and lust. "Oh."

I kissed him. *If you* desire a little spanking. There are so many things I wish to try with you. I'm sure we could agree on a few."

He was silent for a moment, and I could tell he was busy thinking again. "Can I ask you a question?" he ventured.

"Of course," I answered.

"I'm not just a list of gay sex things to check off, am I? I mean, when we get to the end of the list, will you...dismiss me?"

I pulled him close to me and spoke with a softer tone. "Eric, no. My words were unartful. You are not a checklist for me. I love sex, but like you, with people I care about. If I didn't already feel affection for you, I wouldn't be talking about more adventures. The expedition would be over already."

He grinned, satisfied. "Sorry. I'm kind of insecure, I guess."

I nodded. "You think?" I ruffled his hair. "I understand, though. Thank you for telling me about your childhood. It's going to be my mission to make you see what an amazing man you are. After all, it takes a special person to awaken someone else's buried sexual orientation. I don't know if I would have ever realized this had I not met you. The funny thing is, I'm feeling at ease with it. That's because of you. You just seem right for me."

He beamed a little. "Yeah?"

"Hmm," I hummed.

"Carrington?"

"Yes?"

Eric blushed. "I think I'd like to be spanked the way you described it."

I grinned. "I know, baby. Your dick finds ways of communicating what your mouth holds back. Are you relaxed enough to sleep now?"

He nodded and sighed in contentment, laying his head on my chest. After a few moments, he was breathing heavily, and I knew he had fallen asleep. I was glad he would have a night where he would be able to find peace after waking from a nightmare.

Chapter Eleven

Eric

I woke, my face pressed hard against Carrington's strong chest. I turned a bit, and some drool slipped from the corner of my closed lips, dribbling down his breastbone. I internally chastised myself for being disgusting. I pulled my head up, praying he was sleeping and wouldn't notice, but of course, those darned blue eyes were open and looking right at me.

"I'm sorry...about the drool," I muttered.

He smiled. "At least it's warm. I'd ask how you slept, but I'm pretty sure you were dead to the world after we spoke."

I ran a hand through my now unruly hair. "Did I sleep on your chest the entire time? You must not have gotten *any* sleep."

Carrington rolled me to my side, and he lay facing me. "See how easy it was to turn you. If it had been bothering me, I could have fixed it."

"But did you sleep?"

He shrugged. "A few hours. I will admit, there was one point when I woke up and my arms were numb from being wrapped around you. I had to lower them to my sides. It made me sad. I enjoyed cradling you."

I reached over and rubbed the arm that he wasn't lying on. "I'm sorry. You should have pushed me off."

I was still moving my hand up and down his arm, marveling at the strong, hairy forearm and the smooth, hard biceps and triceps. I leaned in and started kissing his throat. He began to moan.

"You're a devil. A devil with an angel's face, doing a devil's work," he whispered.

I grinned. "Well, we all have to have a hobby."

He laughed. "As I said last night, I like you a lot."

My smile faded. I know he had said those same words the prior evening, but they still pulled at my heartstrings when repeated. "Me too."

His face sobered. "Speaking of hobbies, I'd love for you to show me your photography studio. It's in the basement, right?"

I was sure I looked puzzled. "How did you know that?"

"I overheard you talking to Mateo."

I gave him a side eye. "Eavesdropping, eh?"

He shrugged. "I may have been wanting to learn more about you. Come on. Show me some of your work. I'd like to see it."

That made me happy. "Okay. But, did you want me to do anything else for you first?"

Before he could answer, we heard the shower faucet turn on in the guest bathroom. "Hmm, seems the others have awakened," he said with disappointment.

"Ugh," I muttered, flipping onto my back. "Bastards. I can't do anything when I know they're out there walking around."

"I quite understand. It is a bit of a mood killer. Perhaps you should get breakfast started whilst I'm in the shower. I'll be down after I check in back home. I'll also have to see if there are any flights out tonight."

I frowned. I knew the time would come for them to leave, but it felt too soon. "Okay."

He was still staring at me. "Okay? So, why are you still in bed?"

I looked at his amused expression, rather liking his teasing. I pretended to be grumpier than I was, flipping off the blankets in a huff, uncovering the half-naked man whose boxers were tenting. "Oh my." I grinned.

Carrington didn't hide himself. He looked at me with hooded eyes. "Did you do that on purpose?"

"What? No, I swear!" Since he still made no move to cover himself, I took it as an invitation to look. "You are so fucking beautiful," I whispered. "I wish I could photograph you, just like you are now."

For once, he appeared as nervous and shy as I was. He even swallowed. "Yeah? I think I'd like that." He then regained his composure. "Of course, we can't. I couldn't take the chance of a photo like that leaking." I might have appeared offended. "Not that I don't trust you," he added. "It's just, risky…"

I paused to think about it. The prospect was too exciting to dismiss. "I could delete the photo after I take it."

He looked bewildered. "Then what's the point of taking it?"

I grinned. "Taking sexy photos of you would be the point. Enjoying the process."

He smiled. "Would you teach me to take photos so I can take some of you too?"

That wasn't as thrilling. "Um, I'm not sure I could do that…"

He fake-pouted. "So, you get to have all the fun?"

I sighed. "Okay, I guess we can take turns taking photos."

He gave a victorious, all-teeth exposed smile. "You with the dildo."

"What? Hell no," I protested.

"Hmm, we'll see," he replied.

"Maybe you with the dildo," I countered.

He was taken aback for a minute. "If I do something with the smaller toy, will you do something with the dildo?"

"What? You're kidding right?" His expression didn't change. "Why do I need to have the dildo instead of the smaller toy?"

He laughed. "You're more experienced at handling something that size. I have a virgin ass."

"I do, too. Silicon objects don't take your virginity," I muttered. When I looked back at him, he had a resolute expression, and I realized he was serious about the bargain. I was about to protest again, but my dick wasn't objecting. The thought of seeing Carrington naked and pleasuring himself with a toy was making me crazy. "Okay, fine."

He looked shocked, then a bit scared. "Really?"

"Yes," I spat, pretending I was doing this just for him.

He seemed to pick up my habit of gulping when nervous. "Okay."

"Okay," I agreed, rising from the bed. "By the way, you have nice legs."

He blushed. "They're legs. Not that interesting."

I gave his exposed legs another look-over. "I disagree." I reached over to glide my hand up his strong, hairy calf, then over his beautiful knee and up his thick thigh. "Amazing."

His eyes were full of lust. "Nobody's ever been turned on by my legs before," he admitted.

"Then the girls you dated were stupid," I joked. "I could look at your legs all day. You'll have to make a habit of wearing short-shorts."

He chuckled. "I don't think the president can walk around wearing shorts of any type."

It was a reminder that he was a president of a country halfway around the world, and he would be heading home to it later in the evening. It brought the moment to a depressing close. "I should go make breakfast. I'll just go into the bathroom to brush my teeth. Then the shower is all yours."

I stepped out of bed, and I could tell he was pondering the mood change, but I didn't want to tell him my thoughts. I would try to enjoy the time I had with him. There would be time for crying tomorrow.

He must have wanted to reignite my playful spirit, as he called from the bed. "In your drawer of underwear, did you happen to have a jock strap?"

I turned to look back at him, but his slight grin belied that it wasn't a serious question. "You went through my underwear drawer too?"

"I didn't sniff any." He answered, as if that forgave him for rummaging through people's bureaus.

I was flustered. "I don't know. Yes, I have a couple. Why?"

"Mm." He licked his upper lip. "I think I'd like for you to wear one today under your jeans. I want to know that sexy butt is bare under your pants."

My eyes grew wide as I became paralyzed in place. He laughed, which caused my face to flush. "Okay, fine. You wear the other one!"

That wiped away his smile. "What if I get stopped by TSA? Strip-searched?"

Now it was my turn to grin. "Hmm, that would be a sexy scene."

"You're into role-play, huh?" he asked, but I could tell he was intrigued and turned on by the idea.

"Guess you'll have to put on the jock strap to find out," I dared.

"What size is it?"

"Small. I have a thirty-inch waist," I explained.

His lips raised in victory. "Too bad. I wear a medium. I have a thirty-two-inch waist."

"Ha! It will fit. In fact, that's even better. I like the thought of you being crammed into my strap. Maybe that will teach you not to spy on me."

He looked a little uncomfortable, but gave me a reluctant nod.

* * * *

Once I was downstairs in my kitchen cracking eggs, Mateo approached me from behind donning a big smile.

"Good morning," I grunted.

"It is, isn't it?" he beamed.

I chuckled. "Someone get lucky last night with a certain house guest?"

He had a boastful smile. "Sure did, and Olivia has the tits of a teenager and one sweet pussy."

My jaw fell and I dropped an egg I had been meaning to crack in the bowl. "What?"

Mateo bellowed. "You're always gullible. So sweet."

I rolled my eyes and gave him a chastising look. "Olivia is a classy lady. Don't be talking about her that way."

"So, what do you think of Stefan?" he asked.

"I like him better since he helped me with the outside chores. Up until then, I thought he was a douche."

"Stop it," Mateo ordered, slapping my arm. "He's a good guy."

"I take it you two hooked up while I was in bed," I figured.

"Hooked together like a strand of Christmas lights," he confirmed. "Eric, he's a god. You should see his body."

"I did, remember? You two were putting on your little show on my patio," I reminded him.

"Okay, well the rest of him is just as hot. It's no wonder he's a model. I'll need to google him later," he added.

I remembered that when Mateo had asked what Stefan and Carrington were in the States for, Stefan replied that they were models and here for a commercial gig. "Um, I don't think he's that famous, though, is he? Maybe he's not on the net? I'm pretty sure they said they're struggling to get noticed."

Mateo dismissed that notion with an eye roll. "That's crazy. They're gorgeous. I'm sure Stefan has some kind of presence on social media. Even you'd come up if I google you. I just need his last name. I can't believe I forgot to ask for that. Hey, what is Carrington's last name? I can look him up."

I started to panic. "Um, funny thing. I never asked him his either. So, what do you want to eat?"

Mateo was looking at me like something was off, then came closer and began to sniff me. "Hmm."

I pulled away in annoyance. "What are you doing?"

"You smell funky," he answered.

"Shut up," I demanded, turning to the stove to put the eggs in a pan. "I didn't shower yet. I need to wait for Carrington to finish."

Mateo moved behind me and I could feel his nose brush my neck. "That's not it."

I was getting nervous and moved away from him like he was threatening me with a dagger. "Get away from me!"

My command didn't hinder Mateo. He stayed by the stove with an expression of contemplation. Then, his eyes widened as he noticed the front of my pajama bottoms "Oh my God, you had sex!"

"What? Shut up. You don't know what you're talking about," I protested.

"Dude, there's evidence. And I have a nose for this stuff. You smell like sex." After a brief pause, he added, "And like *him*!"

I began to stammer. "I. I don't know…"

"I thought he said he was straight," Mateo wondered.

"He is…for the most part," I replied.

"You little slut." He laughed. "You turned a straight guy."

"Mateo, stop. Jeez. You can't turn someone gay. You want that to become a right-wing talking point?" I shot.

"So, what, he's bi?"

I went back to the eggs. "I guess. I don't know. He told me he's never been with a man before."

"You believe him?" Mateo asked, unable to hide his skepticism.

"I do," I affirmed. "I'm sure of it. God Mateo, don't say anything please. He's just getting used to the idea that he's attracted to me."

"Just to you, huh? Not me or Stefan?" he asked.

I almost felt guilty that I had to tell Mateo that he wasn't on someone's 'must screw' list. "Sorry. He said he doesn't like hairy, muscular guys."

"Hmm," Mateo murmured. "Did you do something this time, or did you just nibble at his dick and spit out his juice like you always do?"

I felt my face flush. "Mateo…God! I'm sorry I ever told you stuff."

He shrugged. "Yeah, yeah. So?"

"We just jerked off together, okay? Please stop asking me questions about this," I pleaded.

"I see," he replied, tapping his index finger against his lips. "Makes sense. Straight boy figures mutual masturbation isn't too gay. College experiment kind of thing. Does he seem to want to take it further?"

"Maybe," I shared, not wanting to say too much, but also interested in Mateo's perspective.

"Don't get too attached. He lives halfway across the world," he pointed out.

"Thanks, Captain Obvious," I said. "I have just one word for you. Stefan."

"I don't have illusions about that being more than a great fuck," he explained. "I mean, I like him. But come on, how would it ever work?"

I nodded, thinking the same about me and Carrington. "Don't say anything to anyone."

"Do you think I'm going to out him to his mother? I'm not an ass."

I glanced at him, biting my lip. "His mother knows."

"His mother knows what? Did she walk in on you two?" he wondered.

"What? No! She doesn't know we had sex…"

"I'm not even sure I would say you had sex," he deadpanned.

"Fine, but she doesn't know anything about that. He told her he's attracted to me. I think he told Stefan too."

Mateo looked astonished. "No shit. Wow. That's big. This doesn't sound like a guy who just wants to rub one out on the sly."

I shrugged. "But they don't know that he acted on it, and they won't know if you keep your mouth shut."

"You sure?" he challenged. "You reek of sex, dude."

I sniffed my arm. I didn't smell anything. "Well, it's a good thing the others don't have your coyote sense of smell when it comes to post-coital activities."

"Hmm," he muttered. "I wouldn't be so sure. You smell pretty spunky. I heard your shower go off a few minutes ago. Go upstairs to bathe and put on some clothes. Those pajamas need to be bleached or something. I'll finish making the breakfast."

"Okay," I surrendered. "Don't forget Carrington doesn't eat dairy. I laid out his stuff over there."

Mateo grinned. "You have a love note for him you want me to put on his plate?"

"Shut up," I demanded, starting to leave the kitchen, almost bumping into Carrington as he was entering. "Oh. Sorry. I was just heading up to shower."

"Okay," he replied, a solemn expression on his face.

"What's wrong?" I asked.

"I, um, talked to Stefan and it looks like we can get a flight out of Newark a little sooner than expected. We'll need to leave after breakfast."

I felt my stomach drop. I should have known things would end this way. I was at least pleased that Carrington appeared to be disappointed. I nodded to him, then left the room.

Chapter Twelve

Carrington

Mateo and Stefan joked and yapped through breakfast like two sated lovers. I could imagine what they had been up to whilst Eric and I had been intimate and sleeping the night before. I wondered if my mother, who was also at the table, was aware of the shenanigans that occurred a few hours earlier. She was quiet, observing the other men with casual interest, sometimes looking to me with an expression of concern. I thought she might have sensed I was feeling glum.

I had been saved by my phone ringing. I decided to take the call in Eric's parlor, since the caller was the head of Yastarus Intelligence. He had good news — they had located the terrorist cell that was planning an attempt on my life. They had captured three of the four men who had been plotting a threat, but one of them had escaped and his identity was unknown. Although our country didn't advocate or practice torture, the authorities were going to implement every legal means of pulling information from the captives regarding the fourth individual. In the meantime, the head of National Security, Nils Lagerfeld, was recommending that Stefan and I remain in our current location a bit longer. Their thinking was that the fugitive was in Yastarus and, therefore, not as much of a risk to me if I stayed put whilst they hunted him down. They were much more concerned about me landing back on Yastarus soil.

I was thrilled at the thought of spending more time with Eric, but I didn't want my countrymen to view me as a coward. Lagerfeld conceded that if within a few days they had not apprehended the fugitive, I could return. We called the vice president to let him know of our plans, asking that he continue to oversee the day-to-day business of Yastarus. The citizens would be told I was still in the United States handling diplomatic matters, but continuing to manage my presidential duties from afar. To further dispel suspicion, it was decided my mother would travel home within hours, and she would be greeted by heavy security at her destination.

I informed my mother of the plan, and she felt relief that some of the terrorists were captured, but concerned the danger wasn't yet over. "Intelligence will get the information they need," I assured her. "In the meantime, you'll be flying into Poland under your latest alias. Lagerfeld will have a security team to greet you and take you by the presidential limo to Yastarus. Once you're back at the residence, keep a low profile and allow security to do their job. Make an appearance so people think everything is fine, and reinforce that I stayed behind to handle diplomatic matters with the

United States. Lagerfeld told me that he has America's cooperation to corroborate the story. In the meantime, I told Mateo that you need to head back early for a personal matter, and he was kind enough to offer to drive you to Newark. I think he was happy to do so once I suggested Stefan accompany the two of you. He doesn't need to know that Stefan is there for your security."

"And what about *your* security whilst Mateo and Stefan are driving me to New Jersey?" she worried.

I smiled. "Mother, the fugitive is in Yastarus, and nobody knows where I am. I will be fine. Stefan will be back later this evening."

She nodded, though there was still concern etched on her face. "Very well, but don't go sightseeing."

I laughed. "I promise. I will stay here with Eric."

My mother couldn't help but grin a bit. "It doesn't sound like that will be too much of a hardship for you."

I became serious. "I know you must go pack, but I did want to thank you for your support yesterday. It means a lot to me, Mother."

"So, you spent the night with him and you still have feelings for him?" she asked.

"More so," I responded. "I don't think I'll awaken tomorrow and realize I'm not attracted to him. I like him, Mother."

She sighed. "It's unexpected, of course. But as I said, if he makes you happy, then that is what matters. Convince him to come to Yastarus soon. We'll tell people it's gratitude for him having sheltered us from the storm—that is, once we can tell people about everything that happened with the threats against you. I don't see why anyone would question his presence. You and he will just need to be discreet."

"Of course," I agreed. "Thank you, Mother."

She patted my cheek and exited the room to head upstairs and pack her bags. Within seconds of her leaving, Eric entered the parlor. "Hi," he whispered.

Seeing his fresh-scrubbed face and styled hair made me feel gushy, and I had to remind myself that this must be my new normal. "Hi yourself."

"I waited for her to leave the room. I didn't want to interrupt," he said. "Is it true? Are you staying? Mateo told me that he and Stefan are taking your mother to the airport, but you will be remaining behind."

"Yes, if that is okay with you," I confirmed. It occurred to me that I never asked permission, assuming Eric would welcome the extended stay.

He answered my question by rushing to me and embracing me. I pulled him tighter and gave the top of his head a quick peck. His hair smelled like coconut, and I felt like I could stand there and inhale it forever. "What changed?" he asked when he pulled away.

After I explained to him the events of the morning, he donned a worried expression similar to my mother's. "Don't fret," I said, brushing my thumb over his cheek. "This is good news. They've caught all but one of them, and he's halfway across the world. They'll apprehend him."

"Don't go back until they have," he implored.

I moved my thumb over to his lips, grazing them. His eyes were pleading with me. "Eric, I can't do that. If it isn't within a couple of days, I must return. I have an obligation to my country's people."

He paused, then nodded. "Then I'll go with you."

I raised an eyebrow in surprise. "You're sure you can take a holiday that soon?"

"I'll make it work." He nodded. "And it's a vacation. You talk funny."

"*You* talk funny," I answered, picking up on what was becoming a routine for us.

"I can't wait for them to leave. No offense to your mother," he said, blushing.

"Imagine, the house to ourselves for the day," I grinned. "Whatever will we do?"

Eric smiled. "I believe you wanted to see my studio. Do you still want to?"

I nodded. "Indeed. I'm looking forward to seeing your...talent."

He laughed and hugged me once more. He wasn't the only one eager to see the trio head to Newark.

Chapter Thirteen

Carrington

My mother had given me and Eric each a kiss on the cheek goodbye. Stefan gave me a quick hug and Mateo saluted me, then whispered something in Eric's ear that made him blush before hugging him farewell. I suspected he knew what was happening between his friend and me.

Once they had pulled out of Eric's driveway, I turned to my host. "So, just you and me."

He swallowed, but looked as eager as he did nervous. "Should we go back inside?"

I followed his slender frame back through his side entrance, and took him in my arms as soon as the door was closed. "It's been but a couple of hours, and I've already missed this," I admitted.

He hummed. "Me too."

I ran my hands down his back, then lower onto his buttocks. The thick fabric of his jeans couldn't conceal the hem lines of his boxers. I sensed an opportunity. "I thought you and I had an agreement that you'd put on a jock strap?"

He looked at me with surprise, not expecting that would be the direction of the discussion. "Um, I was going to, but I thought you would be leaving this morning."

"So?"

He seemed nervous that I might be annoyed. "I...I was thinking it didn't matter."

I gave him a stern look. "It mattered to me. I would have wanted to grab your bum when nobody was looking. Imagine the disappointment I would have had on top of needing to leave you. I thought you were good for your word to me."

He looked panicked. "I am. I mean, I would have been." He saw my expression didn't change, and his voice faltered. "I'm sorry, Carrington."

I smiled a little to let him know I was playing. "Well, I think you should get a spanking for disappointing me, don't you?"

His eyes lit up, then he grinned a bit, understanding that I wasn't upset but was enacting his fantasy scenario. "A spanking?"

"It's up to you," I offered, just in case he was apprehensive. I wanted to make sure he enjoyed everything we did together. "If you don't think it merits a spanking, then I will respect that. I will defer to your judgment."

He acted as though he was considering the situation. "Um, maybe a small spanking? It was a misunderstanding, after all. I guess I deserve it, but not too hard."

I nodded, trying to maintain an authoritative posture. "Very well. A mild spanking is what you shall get. Now, go upstairs and put on the jock strap like I told you to. You can put your jeans over them if you're uncomfortable presenting yourself half-dressed." He looked at me with uncertainty. "Go put it on."

He nodded, his body a bit shaky. As he began to walk away, he stopped when he realized I was following him. "Why are you coming?"

"I'm going to wait in your quarters whilst you change in the ensuite. I'll be sitting on the bench in front of your bed," I informed him.

"Oh. Okay," he whispered.

Once we were in his room, he opened the drawer and pulled out a black jock strap and held it up for me to see. "Is this all right?"

I nodded and motioned for him to go to his lavatory. He did as he was told, closing the door behind him. I was curious as to whether he'd emerge without the jeans. I had left it up to him, and I was wondering if he was becoming comfortable enough with me to take a bold stand. When he emerged from the bathroom, he had on his jeans, though they weren't zipped. His black short-sleeve polo shirt skimmed his waist, so a strip of his stomach and the waistband of the jock were exposed when he reached up a hand to scratch his head. "Good man," I complimented, motioning for him to approach me.

"Um, what are you going to do?" he asked.

"I'm going to put you over my knee, and I'm going to give you a few slaps for being naughty. Come here."

Once Eric was before me, it was clear that he was unsure whether he should bend over. I took his hand and pulled, causing him to crouch over me. I helped position him such that his bottom was raised up over my lap, his head hanging down past the left side of the bench. I didn't remove his jeans—not yet. Instead, I brought down my hand and smacked the seat of his pants. I made it firm, but painless. He made no sound, and I wasn't sure if he was enjoying it or hating it. I brought down my hand again, but Eric remained silent. I ceased with the slaps, pondering whether this was having the desired effect on him.

"Are you done spanking me?" Eric asked, peering up at me, looking puzzled.

"I think the padding of your jeans is making this ineffective, don't you? I would like you to push them off, please."

He raised his head up, a moment of shyness and uncertainty on his face. "All the way off?"

"Yes, please," I confirmed, trying not to show any expression. "The sooner you do it, the sooner we can take care of this matter."

He bit his lower lip, but hooked his hands on his waistband and pulled the jeans down to reveal his beautiful ass. It was even better than I imagined. He had creamy skin and a hairless crack. I helped draw the pants down his legs and over his feet.

I was afraid I'd lost my voice and would be unable to speak. "Eric, you are the most beautiful creature I've ever seen. Your bottom could inspire the greatest painters."

He snorted a laugh at that. "Um, I thought you were going to spank me, not wax poetic."

I chuckled. "Such insolence." With that, I brought down my hand on his bare skin, and he let out a mild yelp. There was a light shade of pink where I had slapped him. I brought down my hand again to the same spot, causing him to flinch, but also to moan with pleasure. I massaged his ass cheeks to assuage any sting, then smacked his right buttock, then his left. Just as he was feeling the tingle of those slaps, I spread him open. He squirmed a bit in surprise, a reflex to pull away. "Shh, shh," I soothed. "Trust me."

"I just don't want you to be grossed out," he shared.

"Baby, I am so not grossed out right now," I promised. I massaged his cheeks again, then spread them to see his little pink hole. I never thought I'd think an asshole was cute, but his was like the rest of him—adorable. I had a desire to lick him. "Your hole is hot. So pretty, just like the rest of you."

He snickered. "Bet you say that to every asshole."

I smacked his bottom again, this time a bit harder. "That's for being one," I joked. I then massaged his rosy buttocks, and bent over to blow cooling breath on them. I pulled him open and brushed my thumb around the edge of his anus, and he let out a little cry. "Get on the bed, face down," I commanded.

He bounded off me, his length pushing at the tight fabric of the jock, looking like it was desperate to be freed. He jumped on the bed, burying his face in the pillow. He turned back to look at me, still a bit unsure. "Like this?"

"Not quite," I remarked. "Spread your legs." He swallowed hard, but did as he was instructed. "Wider," I ordered. He stretched his legs open to expose his hole to me. He had hidden his face in the pillow. I got up on the bed and crouched over him. "Eric, turn your face to the side so I can look at you."

He did so, but didn't make eye contact with me. "It's kind of embarrassing."

I rubbed his back and leaned over to kiss his cheek. "You have nothing to be ashamed of. You are fantastic. I am so fucking hard right now looking at you. Eric, I love burying my face in pussy. Looking at your ass, it makes me think of that. Knowing you might take my dick there someday is such a turn-on. I fancy rimming you. Would you be okay with that?"

His eyes were like saucers, his lips parted with shock. "Um, are you sure?"

"Kiss me," I demanded. He did, opening his mouth to let me in. I licked his tongue and his lips, and he gasped for breath. "Eric, I've never had the opportunity to do this to anyone. I wish to do this for you."

He gulped. "Uh, yes? Okay."

I moved back away from his face, then pushed his shirt up to reveal most of his back so that he was exposed and vulnerable—just the way I wanted him. I alternated spreading his ass cheeks, followed by thumbing his anus. He started whimpering and grinding his crotch against the mattress. Once I knew he was excited beyond care, I pressed my tongue into his ass crack. I loved the feel of the two hills of flesh on each side of my mouth. I pushed my tongue up against his warm hole, circling it. He was moaning and panting. "Oh fuck!" he cried.

"That's it, baby," I soothed. "Let go. Just let me make you feel good." I went back to plundering his most private place with my tongue until he was weeping for release. I slapped his buttocks a bit harder than before, and pulled the elasticized straps of his jock to let them snap against his tender flesh, never lessening the pressure of my tongue. Within minutes, he climaxed, screaming my name, mixed with garbled gibberish and a few F-bombs. When he collapsed from his release, I kissed his ass cheeks. He was gasping and heaving, and his bottom was wet from my saliva and from his sweat.

"Oh my God," he kept mumbling into the pillow.

I moved my body higher on the bed so I could give him my full weight. I kissed his neck, his cheek, and his hair. "Relax, baby."

After a moment, he tried to turn over, so I lifted enough to let him do so. "Carrington," he whispered.

"Yes, Eric?"

"Are you…still liking this?" He gave me a look that made me realize every new act would have him worrying it would be the one that would turn me off to him.

"Yes," I replied with conviction. "I love everything with you, Eric."

"I want to see your…hole sometime. I'd like that," he admitted.

I realized the courage it took for him to show me his, considering I felt shy about showing mine in return. I knew I'd need to at some point if I didn't want to be a hypocrite. I avoided his request by rolling him to his side and pulling him to my body. "I might make a mess on your jeans," he said with concern, looking down where our crotches met.

I pulled away from him a bit to see how wet he was, and saw some of his cum leaking out the front of his jock and down his thigh. "Eric, you are a cum machine. Those balls of yours must work in overdrive." His face turned red, and I kissed his cheek to let him know I wasn't mocking. "It is so fucking hot."

He smirked a bit. "It's funny to hear you, Mr. Oxford University, use the F-bomb."

I grinned. "Don't ever tell my mother I swear. It's a pet peeve of hers. I try to limit my cuss words to dirty sex-talk interactions."

He moaned. "Mm, I like it when you talk dirty."

"Yeah?" I asked. "Is that one of your kinks? You like dirty talk?"

He nodded. "I guess. Although, I have to say, I've been with a couple of guys who talked dirty to me, and it didn't turn me on. But it's hot when you do."

I cuddled him, not caring that his semen was getting on my trousers. "I suppose when you like someone, it makes all the difference."

He grunted in agreement. "Like the fact that you don't mind me getting you messy? I can't imagine you'd be okay with other guys getting cum on you."

I laughed. "I'm not sure how they would. Are they just shooting it at me from across the room? Since I wouldn't be having sex with them, it's an inconceivable notion."

"So, you've never been attracted to any other men?" he asked with skepticism.

I reflected. "When I was a teenager, there was a mate of mine who I thought was cute. I didn't understand those feelings. I liked girls, so it was easy to dismiss it as heightened affection for a friend. When I'd think about something sexual with him, I inserted females into the fantasy. You know, like a three-way. Maybe it was my brain trying to shield me from something that would have been too scary to contemplate. Then, as I got older, my conditioning was to focus on women, so I guess that's what I did."

"I still don't understand why me..."

I kissed his forehead. "You're like what I imagine the Greek sculptors used as a muse. You remind me of the statue of David, masculine yet so much more beautiful than other men. Your personality is sweet and youthful.

I find it enchanting. But I've seen you take charge and that's hot, too. You're a perfect combination."

I leaned in to kiss him, but he pulled his head back.

"I know where that tongue has been," he protested with a smirk. "Use your mouth for talking instead. Tell me what it's like to be a big politician."

I shrugged. "I don't think of myself as a politician." He looked confused. "I know. I know. I'm the president, so yes, of course I'm a politician. It's just that I feel like it's all been a charade. I didn't want the role. I've had government jobs, thanks to my father, since I graduated from university. It's been somewhat interesting, at best. To keep my party from fracturing between two rivals with very different views, I agreed to run for the presidency because I was a popular choice, thanks to my father's legacy. To keep the other party, which I find dangerous, from seizing power, I just let them sweep me into office. The rest, as they say, is history."

He frowned in thought. "Are you good at it?"

I sighed. "I don't know. I suppose. Things seem to be going well. It's not that I can't do it. I just don't love doing it."

"So, you won't seek re-election?"

"No," I replied. "I can't communicate that, of course. I'd be a lame-duck president and would be unable to move forward any necessary legislation. But no, I won't run again. I'll support the vice president, who would be a worthy choice. He's a good man."

"What will you do?" he asked.

"Don't laugh," I pleaded. "I want to go into sports medicine and therapy. It's what I studied."

"Do you play sports?" he wondered.

"I used to. I was quite good at football—what you Americans call soccer."

He got a knowing look. "That explains the legs."

I flushed. "And I'm pretty good at tennis and golf. Of course, since becoming president, I haven't done any of those things."

"Hmm," he muttered. "Our presidents always seem to be on the golf course. Anyway, why do you think I'd laugh at your career ambition? I think it would be a noble profession. Although, I don't love the idea of you ministering to young, athletic bodies all the time," Eric admitted.

I ran my thumb over his lips. "I'm a one-woman guy. Or, in this case, a one-person guy. If I'm seeing someone, I don't dally with other people."

He paused. "Wait. Are you saying you're with me…like that?"

I realized what I had admitted and exhaled a deep breath. "Uh, I guess I am starting to think we're together. Of course, it takes two to make that kind of commitment. I know we've just met, so I understand if you don't feel the same." I was hoping he did.

His face lit up. "I would like that. I know it seems fast, but I can't picture wanting to date someone else right now. And to be honest, I'd be jealous if you wanted to. I'd like to see where this goes."

I hugged him in. "Me too. Dating, huh? I like the sound of that."

"Speaking of beautiful bodies, when are we going down to my studio so I can photograph yours?" Eric probed, a flirtatious gleam in his eye.

"Such an eager young man," I remarked. "Don't forget, you said I could photograph yours, too."

He grimaced. "Hmm. Guess I'll have to take the bad with the good."

I snickered. "And don't forget the stash of sex toys in your bureau."

"It's not a stash!" he exclaimed. "There's only four toys."

"Four? There's a fourth? I saw three."

His face reddened. "Um, maybe."

"What?"

He began to stammer. "I don't know what you call it. It's some, purple thing you insert. It's long, but not as thick as a...dildo. It's the narrowest of the ones I have, and it doesn't vibrate or anything. I think it's for beginners or to prep you for something bigger. Or maybe some people just like it smaller. I don't know." He paused, looking frustrated. "God, stop talking about it!"

"I'm not. You're the one talking about it," I reminded him.

He rolled his eyes. "Well, you made me."

"So, you were going to have me use a bigger object on myself when you've had this smaller toy that I could have used instead?" I pointed out, though somewhat amused.

He looked guilty. "I thought you'd like the vibrator better." I gave him a side-eye that showed I wasn't believing him, but he continued. "It pulses and vibrates, and it has multiple speed options."

"So, you thought I'd be intrigued by the gadgetry's technology," I quipped.

He blushed and shrugged before mumbling, "It's kind of cool."

I pretended to be disappointed in him. "Eric, Eric, Eric. I thought one spanking today would be enough, but I'm thinking you might need another. Maybe I was too gentle with you."

"Maybe. Can we go downstairs now?" he begged.

"You're up for this already? You just came a short while ago, and it was your second time in the last several hours," I observed.

"So ready," he murmured, pressing his erection into my hip to prove his point.

"Very well." I smiled. "I need to satisfy my young beau."

"Hmm. How do you make outdated phrases sound sexy?" he asked.

"They sound sexy to you because you're besotted." I chuckled.

"I am," he admitted. "Okay, let's go downstairs. It's like when I was a kid on Christmas morning. I'm excited to unwrap my present!"

I was elated by his exuberance. "Get your toys and we'll go." He hopped off the bed and reached to the floor for his jeans. "Why are you putting those back on? I'll be taking them off of you again. Please don't tell me you're too shy to walk bare-bottomed in front of me after what we just did."

He glanced over to me, swallowing hard. "Um, I suppose not. But I thought we were going to take turns shooting photos? Don't you want us to start at the same place—clothing-wise?"

I was pleased that he wasn't retreating back to his insecurity, and there was a different reason for the jeans. "Ah, fair enough. But if you're going to cover up again, then I'd like to choose what you'll be wearing. Lead me to your dressing room."

He gave me a questioning glance, but turned and opened the door to his walk-in closet. "Um, not a dressing room, but…"

I started to peruse the hanging shirts and pants, feeling the textures and picturing each item on Eric. I settled on a black button-down shirt. "Put this on," I commanded. "Roll up the sleeves and leave half the buttons undone." He had a shy expression, but he nodded. I continued checking out the trousers and found a pair of dressy black shorts. "And put these on as well. Put on a pair of your black boxer briefs underneath them."

He was flushed, but nodded his assent. "Should I put on socks and shoes?"

"Put on a pair of whatever shoes you'd like," I instructed. "No socks. Then meet me downstairs."

I didn't wait for a response. I exited his room, eager to start the next adventure to show Eric just how beautiful he was.

Chapter Fourteen

Eric

My nerves were jangling as I descended the stairs to my basement, wondering how I could be so horny yet so timid. I felt silly carrying the sex toys, so I stuck them in a shopping bag to bring with me. I entered my studio where Carrington was studying the many photos I had up on the walls. He turned with appraising eyes when he heard me enter the room.

"You're breathtaking," he said. "You blew out your hair for me too, didn't you? It's thick and full, so soft around those chiseled features."

I wished I didn't flush, but I knew I had. I never would understand what he found attractive, but I was so appreciative that he felt as he did. "I wanted to look nice for you," I admitted.

"You succeeded," he affirmed. "And you wore the shirt just as I requested. Thank you. It's very sexy. And your legs…just beautiful."

I smirked. "I thought legs are just legs?"

He remembered his own comment and pursed his lips, trying to suppress a smile. "Such insolence. I'm going to spank you for withholding the information about your fourth sex toy and for this latest naughty comment. Do you know when?"

"When?" I breathed.

"When that dildo is all the way inside you. I want you to feel my slaps on the inside as well as the outside," he informed me.

I felt my legs go weak. "Um, you still won't hurt me, though, right?"

He gave me a reassuring nod. "Eric, I will never do anything but painless things to you. Things you want...or perhaps are begging for."

I felt my cheeks heat. "Oh. Thank you." Thank you? He had to think I was the least sexy person in that moment. "Um, do you like my photography?"

He smiled like a proud papa. "Very impressive. Your work with female models is gorgeous. You make all of them look sultry and alluring. Yet all of them are tasteful. I noticed you had some of them wear unusual outfits and created an atmosphere that enhanced the style of clothing. I liked the one where the model's long hair was blowing behind her, and she was leaning forward with her right hand on her knee and the other on her hip. The fan was blowing the feathers on her sleeves and it was quite artful."

I nodded. "Thanks. I try to create the mood, pose and look to create the right aesthetic."

"You're very good at it," he confirmed. "It makes me wonder why you don't do it full-time."

I shrugged. "You need to be noticed. I can't afford to do it for fun. The insurance job is security."

"I could help you get established," Carrington offered. "I'm sure I could lean on some connections."

"Oh, I wouldn't want something I didn't earn," I told him.

"But you do deserve it," he countered. "I wouldn't have offered if I didn't think so. I believe in promoting great talent."

I nodded. "Thank you. Um, you didn't comment on the photos of the men."

He bit his lip. "Very nice, indeed, though they make me a bit jealous."

"Why?" I whispered.

His eyes were piercing me. "I was picturing you taking photos of them, with some of them in these various stages of undress. It aroused me to think of them turning you on, but it also made me want to stake my claim—though I know it isn't a claim I have a right to stake."

"They didn't turn me on," I said. "Well, not much anyway. None of them were as hot as you—or even Stefan. I just did what they asked unless they asked for nude shots. I refused to do those. It's not that I'm opposed to artistic nudes, but I knew that wasn't what those guys wanted. Sometimes, the supposed models are just looking for a hook-up."

He frowned. "I don't like you putting yourself in dangerous positions. We'll have to think about how to put precautions in place."

I warmed at his inclusion of himself in solving the problem. "I've been able to handle myself so far. I just tell them I have a reputation to protect, and most people are respectful of that. Besides, I get so caught up in the work, thinking about the model in a sexual way doesn't happen."

He crossed his arms and gave me a sly look. "So, when you take pictures of me, you won't be thinking of me in a sexual way?"

I laughed. "Oh, I wasn't planning for this to be a *professional* session. I won't be focusing on making everything flawless. Having the most beautiful model will be enough for me."

He grinned. "Why me and not Stefan, though? He's more attractive than I am. What drew you to me? Whenever girls favored me over him, I assumed it was because I'm the president. You didn't even know I was."

"I think you may have been giving some of the girls too little credit," I hurried. "I know Stefan is the classic handsome man. He may even be the most handsome man I've ever seen." Carrington frowned a bit. "But I'm way more attracted to you. I know this sounds silly, but he's too handsome. I think when someone is perfect, they *aren't* perfect—at least to me. There's nothing interesting about their features. They're pretty, but there's nothing quirky to add an element of cuteness and accessibility. You are almost perfection from a clinical perspective, but I love that one of your bottom teeth is crooked, that you have those little crinkles at the corners of your eyes when you grin and you have a couple of unmanageable waves in your hair. It makes you more…adorable."

He smiled, and it made me wonder if it was to show off two of the features I complimented. "Adorable? Nobody has ever called me that. I must admit, this photo shoot is…arousing, but I fear I may feel foolish. Kind words like that will help me feel less so."

I nodded. "I am happy to point out how nice you look as you pose for me."

He walked over to me and put a hand on my cheek. "I will do the same as I photograph you. It will be easy for me to do so. You, Eric, are the one who is adorable."

I swallowed, aroused and anxious about the reminder that he'd also be studying me under bright lights. "Um, how do you want to start?"

He raised an eyebrow. "You're the professional. I'll rely on your expertise. You take control when you hold the camera. I'll be your muse and do as you wish."

I felt myself straining my boxer briefs. This was *better* than Christmas morning. "Okay. Um, let me just put down this bag."

He smirked. "Wait. Let me see this purple thing of which you spoke." He reached into the bag, extracted the toy and he examined it with curiosity. "It's rather like a very thin, miniature submarine."

I laughed. "I guess. Now I'll be thinking that when I watch it…submerge into the depths."

He grinned and put the toy back in the bag, taking the whole lot of them off my hands and putting the package on a nearby chair. The studio was set up with a backdrop, lighting and a couch, chair and stool for models to use. The way my hands were shaking, I was afraid I would drop my camera when I grabbed it. "Relax, Eric," he soothed. "I'm trying, too. This should be about us having fun, yes? No guilt, no embarrassment, and no worries about judgment. I trust you. Trust me, too."

"You're so thoughtful. I could kiss you," I blurted. "But you had your tongue in my ass."

He gave me a half grin. "I brushed my teeth and gargled when you were changing. Is that not enough?" he asked. "Will I forever be deprived of your kisses now?"

I walked to him and stood on my toes to press my lips on his. "I love kissing you."

He smiled. "Me too. So, what now?"

I tried to calm my excitement. "Um, how about we start with photos of you clothed? It will help you to feel more comfortable. You're so good-looking. Maybe I could keep some of those shots?"

He seemed to consider it, then nodded. "Okay. You may keep the ones of me clothed, but just for your personal viewing."

"Great." I exhaled. "Um, go stand before the backdrop. Maybe just put your hands in the pockets of your jeans and look at the camera. Give me that gorgeous smile of yours."

Carrington did as I asked, but he was stiff and his smile wasn't natural. "Like this?"

"Um, yes, but remember what you said. Relax. It's me, admiring you, remember?" That seemed to work, and his smile became broader and more genuine. His posture relaxed, and I was able to snap off a few shots. "That's it, Carrington. Just be yourself. You are so gorgeous. I love the way that knit shirt clings to your chest and shoulders. I can see the peaks of your nipples against the cotton. It's...erotic."

I could see the intimate talk motivated him more than the pleasantries. The smile vanished and his look became more heated. He puffed out his chest a bit more. "Should I keep standing like this?"

"Um, I have some nice shots of you posing that way," I said. "Would you roll up your sleeves and do the same pose before we proceed to something else? I'd like to get those hairy, muscular forearms highlighted." Carrington followed my directions, then gazed at the lens. "Oh my God, Carrington. That's perfect. You are incredible. So sexy." *Snap, snap, snap.* "Um, can we do a shot with your jeans unbuttoned and your fly down?"

Carrington hesitated for a second before undoing his pants as instructed. "How shall I pose?"

He had put on my white, athletic jock strap and it made my dick fill. "Maybe cross your sexy arms, but have them pull up the hem of your shirt to show some of your belly."

Carrington maneuvered the scene as I choreographed, and I thought I could come looking at him. "That is so hot. I love the happy trail from your stomach to the waistband of the jock."

He smiled, and I took more shots of him showing off his pretty teeth. "I like you directing me," he confessed.

I gurgled. "Uh, can you take your shirt off?"

He gave me a sassy look. "I don't know? Can I? I thought you were in charge."

I swallowed. "Take off your shirt."

Carrington lifted the hem of his shirt and teased me by taking his time pulling it up his incredible torso and over his head. The process messed up his well-coiffed hair, and it made him look even sexier. He tossed the shirt away from the staged area, then put his hands back in his pockets, pushing the jeans down enough to show the full waistband of the jock strap. The way his arms pulled forward pumped out his pecs, and I knew if I died with having seen just that, my life had been worth living. "You're not saying anything, boss," he whispered.

"Um, I'm kind of getting shaky," I confessed. "Carrington, you are the most amazing man I've ever seen. Your face, your body..." I started popping off more shots. "So beautiful. Please push your jeans down a bit more. I want the skin of your legs under the waistband to show." He did, his eyes somewhat glazed. His action also revealed the cloth-covered base of his hard dick. "Jesus. That is going to kill me."

Carrington lightened the mood. "Nah. It will just make you gag some."

I pulled the camera away from my face and gulped. "What? I meant the shot." He laughed. "Asshole," I joked.

"Is it my turn yet?" he asked.

I wanted to procrastinate, but it just would delay the inevitable. "If you're tired of posing. I might need to stop anyway. You are so…smoking. I might pop off just looking at you."

"Mm, such a cum machine," he murmured.

I walked the camera over to him and tried to focus by instructing him on its use. He seemed intent on getting it right, which relieved both of us from the sexual tension for a few moments. Once he felt he had the mechanics down, he told me to pull the stool in front of the backdrop.

Once I did, I looked at him, awaiting further instruction. "What should I do? You want me to sit on it?"

He chuckled. "No, I want you to dance on it. Yes, sit on it, please."

"Smart ass," I muttered, feeling more and more comfortable sassing him for fun, then I took a seat.

"That's it, baby. Mm, those legs are so sexy. Put your feet on the stool's rails. Yes, that's it. I love the slight bend of your limbs. Shows off your calf muscles and your pretty knees." Carrington began to snap photos, and since he didn't tell me to smile, I didn't. I looked at the camera like a rabbit seeing an approaching hawk.

"Relax, baby. Give me the look like the one when you saw me wearing your jock."

I wasn't sure what that look was, but I pictured him again pushing those jeans down a bit. He smiled. "That's it. You are so fucking cute. You have this look of awe and lust, mixed with just a bit of innocent wonder. I can't get enough of you." I didn't know what I was doing, but I was glad it pleased him. I might have even grinned a little at that. He seemed to like it, as he told me to keep the expression as he snapped more photos.

After he took several, I thought I should get him to move on before he got bored. "Should I do anything else?"

He pulled the camera away from his face so I could see him better. "Yeah. I think I'd like very much to see you hike up the legs of those shorts and expose more of your thighs. Also, undo one more button on the shirt. Put your hands on the edge of the stool when you're done."

I started to pull up the hem of the shorts. He encouraged me to go higher and higher. I was feeling quite exposed, but I was encouraged when I saw him appraising me with smoldering eyes. I undid another button, then grabbed the stool for dear life. "Is this what you wanted?"

"And so much more, baby," he replied. "You were right about legs. Yours are exquisite. What are you doing that your thighs are so defined? So smooth and waiting to be licked, right up to that sweet hole of yours."

I squirmed, my erection feeling crammed while I sat in this stiff position. Carrington took some additional photos, then told me to open my shirt altogether. I sighed, but did as I was instructed.

He smiled. "Eric, you are my beautiful angel." More shots. "Take it off, baby." I removed the shirt, trying not to think about how vulnerable I felt. "Don't crouch forward," he chastised. "Sit up straight and cross your arms."

I wasn't sure if I would have thought the pose was sexy, but did what he told me to do. "Better?"

"Oh yes," he breathed. "Shows off your beautiful arms. You can get off the stool, now. Do the pose you had me do. I want you standing with your hands in your pockets. Look at me like I'm going to come over and rip your shorts off and spank your bottom." Once I was posing as he had instructed, he was moaning. "Good, baby. That is so fucking sexy."

Once he took a few more shots, I pointed out that a bead of sweat was dripping down my face. "Maybe we can switch? I didn't realize how hot the lights get."

He smirked. "Starting to have more empathy for your models?"

"I am," I affirmed. "I think I need water." I walked to the mini fridge I had in the studio and retrieved two bottles, tossing one to Carrington. He unscrewed the top, chugging down the liquid in the most erotic way he could muster. I was turned on, but it also made me laugh. "Jerk."

He frowned. "Now Eric, you promised to compliment me. If you want to see more, you'll have to be nicer." His grin was mischievous.

I gulped down half the bottle. "I'll be nice," I squeaked, eliciting more laughter from him. He moved back in front of the backdrop, hands on hips waiting for instruction.

I picked up the camera, afraid it would slip out of my sweating hands. "Oh God. Um, would you lower your pants?" I asked.

Carrington smiled, then pushed his jeans down so that they bunched at the knees. He stood before me, most of his body exposed but for the fine cotton that was encasing his very prominent dick and balls. His legs were as beautiful as I recalled, the light enhancing every muscle and glorious follicle of hair. "Like this?" he asked, batting his eyelashes. I nodded. I couldn't even venture to speak. I was afraid my voice would sound like a high-pitched cartoon animal. "Should I cross my arms, or something?" he asked. I nodded again, which made him smile. He knew what he was doing to me. He flexed and crossed his arms, placing his hands behind his biceps, causing them to pump up even more for the camera. I thought to myself, *Yup, I'm going to cream my pants*. I took more photos, wishing I could keep him here like this forever.

"You're a god," I managed. That made him smile. He was even more beautiful, because now he was showing off all his snow-white teeth.

"Thank you," he answered. "I'm glad you think so anyway."

"Carrington, I don't know how anyone could see you right now and not think it. You're stunning." He nodded a soft thanks my way again. "I think I'd like to see you with the jeans off altogether, if you're comfortable doing that."

He blinked a quiet assent, then he shimmied his way to the stool so he could sit to remove his shoes and socks. As he began to slide the jeans off, I took more photos. "Stay on the stool," I demanded once the jeans were discarded to the corner of the room. "You were right. Your legs look great when you pose, sitting like that."

He let me shoot some photos as he sat. I wanted to rub my hands all over his calves and up those beefy thighs. His dick was still hard and stretching the already too small jock that encased it. I couldn't wait to see him naked. He watched me with hooded eyes, waiting for his next command. I explained that I wanted him on the chair so he could lean back and show me a part of his exposed ass. We dropped the sex toy bag on the floor and moved the chair in front of the backdrop, though he was careful not to let me see his butt when we did so. I told him to take a seat, and lean forward with his forearms resting above his knees. This started him off with preserved modesty, but the teasing pose was flammable. "That's it. Look at me like you want to eat my ass." Carrington smiled at that, recognizing I was mirroring his tactics. Once he did, though, I thought I'd combust.

"Should I lean back into the chair now?" he asked.

"Yes please," I whispered, my face sweating even though I was no longer under the lights. Carrington pushed back a bit, taking a hold of each arm of the chair. I snapped some shots of him like that, his bulge on display, rivaling the beauty of his face, chest, and limbs. Without instruction, he pushed his butt forward more on the chair, reclining his head in a sexy, almost dazed way. He lifted one foot to put on the seat of the cushion, exposing one of the jock's straps and a good portion of his ass. "Oh my God, Carrington. You're…I don't even know what more adjectives to use. Whatever superlatives there are, they apply."

He smiled. "Is my butthole showing? I doubt it's cute like yours."

"It's not," I said. "I mean, it's not showing! Sorry, I didn't mean it's not cute. Um, maybe if you lean back some more, and pull your foot more toward you. Move your other leg so that it's resting over the arm of the chair."

He flushed, but did it to my surprise. His gorgeous butt was on full display. There was some light hair on the crack and the faintest of hairs on his ass cheeks where they met his upper thighs. His small, dark hole was visible, and I realized I had never seen one in real life. Nobody had ever allowed themselves to be so vulnerable just to please me. "Is this what you wanted?" he asked with some nervousness.

I felt a wave of emotion which was more than lust. I was moved that this, until now, straight man was giving so much of himself. "I...I..."

He sat upright. "Are you okay? Is something wrong? Is there a bad flashback or something?" He was now worried and all the sexiness was gone.

I sighed. I feared if I thought about it too much, I'd tear up. "I've never had anyone put my desires before their own. I know this is not something you're comfortable doing, and the fact that you're doing it just to please me is kind of overwhelming. I'm ruining this. I'm sorry."

He shushed me again, pulling me to him and kissing me all over my face. Once I calmed down, he backed up his head to look at me. "Well, thank God. I thought I had hideous hemorrhoids or something." He laughed.

I croaked out one in return before slapping his shoulder. "You're a jerk."

"*You're* a jerk," he returned.

"I'm sorry, Carrington. I don't remember anyone ever doing something so trusting with me. And you're wonderful, and I don't know why I'm still talking because I'm sounding more and more stupid with every word."

Carrington pulled me to the sofa with him and maneuvered me to lie down on top of him. "Let me hold you. I've noticed you relax when you have some compression."

I sighed. "I hate being so messed up when it comes to sex."

He smiled. "That wasn't my impression. You've been the best experience I've had. It's just your first time feeling an emotional pull during intimacy. It can be overwhelming, as you put it. We can stop doing this, if you'd like."

I looked at his face, sure my eyes were pleading for him to reconsider. "Carrington, please no! I'm sorry."

Carrington wiped his thumb across my lips, then onto my cheek. "Baby, I'm not punishing you. I'm trying to make you comfortable."

"No! No, I don't want to be comfortable. I want to feel like this. Like someone might think I'm hot."

He rolled his eyes. "You're still unsure that I see you that way? What more do I need to do to convince you?"

"Keep going with our plan," I begged.

He chuckled. "Are you manipulating me just to get in my pants, Mr. Turner?"

I looked at his bared torso and legs. "I think I already accomplished that."

Carrington swatted my arm. "So fresh. Okay, we'll continue. But just lie here for a minute to cool down. This time, I don't want you to come in your underwear. I want to watch it shoot."

I moaned. His dirty talk wasn't calming me. "This is the best day of my life. I didn't want it to end with me fainting just from seeing a hot guy's ass."

Carrington snickered. "Well, maybe it's not just any hot guy's ass. Maybe I should look at those pictures. I've never seen that...part of me. It must be something."

I smirked at his teasing. "Let's just say, now I get the whole wanting to eat ass thing," I admitted. "If you had pointed out someone walking down the street and asked 'would you like to eat their ass?' I would have gagged, but now that I've seen yours..." He appeared apprehensive. "I'm talking too much again. I'm happy with whatever you like."

He paused, then ran a hand down my back. "This is all so new to me. I'm enjoying it, but..."

"I know," I told him. "It's a lot happening fast. I won't do anything other than what pleases you."

He sighed. "There are those words again. Eric. I am glad you want to please me, but you deserve someone who considers your wants, too. I didn't say no to you. I'll think about it. Okay?"

"Okay," I whispered.

"You're not calming down," he chastised. "Stop thinking about eating my ass."

I laughed. "That sounds funny. I suppose I could think about eating some other person's ass. Like I said, that will cause a total dick deflation."

"If that's what it takes," he quipped. "Think of someone disgusting."

"You didn't have to go that far! Even someone average would have done the trick," I griped. "If I had to think of someone repulsive, though, I'd pick the bitchy next-door neighbor. I know she hates me because I'm gay. She's always snooping and watching me. I try being nice and saying hello to her when she's in her yard or when she walks her dog, but she gives me disapproving glares and looks away. Marietta, nasty old hag."

Carrington laughed. "Wow. I haven't seen you so hostile." He palmed my flaccid penis. "Your nemesis appears to be your erection remedy."

"Yuck, don't say that," I complained. "People will think you mean I have erectile dysfunction and she's the treatment that gets me hard."

He snorted. "Who are these people I'm telling?" He looked toward the doorway and pretended to be speaking to someone else. "Hey, you don't know me, but I'm the president of Yastarus and I'm shagging your neighbor — the guy with erectile dysfunction who has some weird rimming fetish for the hag that lives next door to him."

I fake-punched him on the shoulder. "I do not have erectile dysfunction."

He nodded. "I think you've been hard more than not. I can attest that your equipment is functioning without issue."

I laughed at that. "Well, maybe you need to inspect it to be sure."

Carrington donned a mischievous grin. "Yes, I suppose you're right. Perhaps there's no time like the present."

"But I'm soft," I protested, "thanks to that awful image of eating out Marietta."

"That's okay," he coaxed, touching my chin. "I'm betting it's cute as a bunny when it's soft."

I grimaced. "I don't want you to think my dick is cute. I want you to think it's hot."

He reached down to unbutton and unzip the shorts I was wearing, hooking his thumbs into the waistbands of both the shorts and the boxer briefs. He moved both down an inch, waiting for my reaction. "I want to see you naked, Eric. At some point, I'll see it soft and at some point, I'll see it hard. I want to know your body. Now let me take your clothes off."

I wasn't worried anymore about being soft because I was already coming back to life with just his talk of seeing me naked. I nodded that it was okay. He slid the fabric down my hips with his big hands, and I lifted my butt so the clothes didn't jam up at our crotches. When his reach couldn't push them any further, I rolled to my side and finished the task. He was still looking at my face, waiting for permission to look down. I know I gulped, afraid that seeing a dick would be less thrilling for him than he was anticipating. "It's okay," I assented.

Carrington dropped his gaze to my now semi-erect dick. "Eric, I'm not just saying this. You are beautiful."

I breathed out with relief. "Um, it isn't the biggest."

He surprised me by reaching down to hold it. It made me gasp, but it also made me harder. "It's like the rest of you. It's plenty large, but proportioned to your body. To be honest, I never thought I'd think a dick was a work of art, but yours is."

"I always thought it looked like Darth Vader's white brother," I quipped.

That made Carrington laugh. He held the base of my dick and pretended it was a puppet. "Luke, I am your father."

I swatted his hand away. "Guess Luke's father was a dick."

"Well, yeah. That's the whole plot of *Star Wars*." He shrugged.

"Hmm, when I thought about you playing with my dick, this isn't quite what I imagined," I pouted.

Carrington stroked my chin. "Baby, I'm going to play with it the way you wanted. Trust me. Right now, I'm just admiring it. It's so smooth. Nary a vein to be seen. Such a pretty shade of pink. And your balls are nice too. So little hair on you. Everything is clean and delicious looking."

"So feral." I grinned. "I've found I like that about you. I enjoyed watching you eat. You stuff your mouth, you know. It makes me want to fill it with something else and see what you do with your lips and jaw."

He blushed and cast his eyes down. "I think I'd like that. But, as I said, let's work our way into things, all right?"

"Yes, of course," I agreed, realizing I was pushing him too fast again.

"Back to photos?" he asked. "I want to get some of you in the nude. What do you say?" I groaned with uncertainty, but he chuckled and moved off the sofa. "Turn onto your tummy and press your left knee against the front of the cushion."

I knew the pose would spread my legs, opening me to the camera lens. It was something I decided to block from my mind and just do. I wanted to excite Carrington, if possible. "Um, is that okay?" I asked, once I was positioned as he had instructed.

"Eric, you have the most luscious ass. So incredible," he murmured, snapping shots. "Are you still hard? Would you push your dick so that it's pointing down? I want to see it, your scrotum, and your butt at the same time."

I reached under me, forcing my aching cock in Carrington's direction. I turned my face so that he could see my profile against the sofa pillow.

Carrington approached and stroked my back. "Mm, so sexy, Eric. You are a vision. I don't think I've ever been so hard in my life." He moved his hand down to my buttocks and caressed them, brushing a finger over my hole. I bucked, and I could feel wetness at the tip of my dick. "So hot," he muttered. Before I knew what he was going to do, he bent down and lifted the head of my cock to his tongue, tasting my early emission.

"Oh God!" I jumped a bit, but he put his other hand on my ass to hold me down.

"It's okay," he soothed. "It just looked so inviting. I decided, nothing ventured, nothing gained."

"Oh." I swallowed. "And?"

He went back to massaging my butt. "It doesn't have much taste. I'm relieved. I don't know what I expected, but it's a pleasant surprise. I just taste your clean, warm skin…albeit a little sticky and wet."

"I might need to switch with you now." I panicked, liking too much the friction with the cushion as he pressed my ass.

He chuckled. "I don't know. I think I'd like to see you spray all over that fabric. That would make for a sexy photo."

"Okay. Saves me from the dildo," I pointed out.

He slapped my bottom, which elicited an "ow" from me. "I've waited too long for the dildo act. Get off the sofa. You can take over."

I laughed at his obsession with the dildo. I slid off the couch, reaching for my briefs. "You get on it now," I instructed.

"What are you doing?" he asked as he saw me bend over to put my foot through the leg opening of the brief. "Stay naked."

"While I'm taking pictures?" I asked, somewhat mortified at the idea.

He pulled me up to him and kissed me. "Yes. I've seen everything. Stop being shy. Seeing you hard and leaking will inspire me."

I groaned, then moaned some more when he took his place on the couch, face down. He took the same pose he had instructed me to try. I took some photos, and without direction, he pushed the jock strap down. I helped him by grabbing it from the back of his knees and sliding it off his legs altogether. He pushed his hard dick down between his legs, and it was the sexiest thing I'd ever seen. His cock was long and thick and I found myself wondering if he had a couple of billiard balls in his scrotum. "Holy shit," I whispered.

He lifted his head from the pillow a bit to catch my stare. "Yeah? You like it?"

"Um, yes," I admitted. "I never thought I was a size queen, but maybe I am."

He snickered. "I'm glad. Some girls looked at me like I was brandishing a weapon." He turned onto his back, his big tool flipping up between his hip and his stomach. "Do you think you might fancy sucking it?" He looked worried that I might refuse.

I nodded with enthusiasm. He smiled, and I knew that would have been the best picture of all, had I taken it. Instead, I put the camera down. "Um, do we have to keep taking pictures, or can we do the rest with more body contact?"

Carrington's smile broadened. "I think we have enough photos. Right now, I'd very much like for you to get on this sofa and get those pretty lips on my dick."

I flushed, embarrassed that my cock was too engorged to retreat from its rocket-launch position. Once I was kneeling between his legs, I licked the head, then rubbed it against my lips to get his wetness on me. I looked to his face and was pleased to see his eyes were hooded and his lips were parted. "You taste so good, Carrington."

He grabbed my hair, careful not to pull too hard. "Eric, please…"

I swiped my tongue up his entire length and he shuddered. His sack had tightened, and I licked the now spongy skin before taking each ball in my mouth. Carrington groaned while moving both hands through my hair. I moved my mouth back up his cock, then sucked in the head. Some drool was coming from my mouth, sliding down his dick as I took more of him into me. I pulled off to check Carrington's expression once again, making sure I wasn't doing things wrong. I didn't have much experience, after all. "Carrington, I've never taken in a whole dick before. I want to, but…"

He stroked my face. "Baby, shh. Don't try. You look so beautiful going down on me. God! It's amazing. Just do what you were doing. You can use your hand on the rest of my dick."

I nodded, sucking in as much of him as I could, following his advice to palm what I couldn't. Carrington was squirming and panting, which aroused me even more. I loved the feel of his hot flesh in my mouth and the mild taste of him. I fondled his nuts with my free hand, daring to drift my fingers down to his taint, which I rubbed hard. I pulled off him when his balls pressed up against his body, knowing he was about to blow. "Um, did you want to come now? I can put the submarine in you if you want."

Carrington pulled me up to him. "No, not yet. I don't want to shoot until I've seen you lose it. I want that to put me over the edge," he said through heavy breathing. We lay together for a few moments, just listening to each other exhaling. After a moment, he chuckled. "And don't think I didn't notice your last-minute appeal to insert that ridiculous U-boat in me."

I laughed. "Said the man who is pushing for me to insert something ten times bigger in my own body."

His eyes lit up and he grinned like the villain in a Western. "Hmm, speaking of."

I hesitated. "Carrington, it's been a long time. I will do it for you, but I can't just shove something like that in me without a lot of prepping."

He stroked my hair and cheek. "Baby, I don't want you to hurt yourself. I want to see you experiencing bliss." I nodded, feeling relief to be absolved of his mission. He gave me a sly smile and side eye. "Maybe the vibrator? It's much smaller, right? You had thought my virgin ass could handle it."

Grinning, I shook my head. "Relentless."

His smile broadened. "So, are you saying yes?"

"I'll still need some prep," I cautioned. "I know you don't believe me, but I haven't played with those for months."

His smile just became more devious. "I'll assist." I nodded, but was unable to conceal my nervousness. "Eric, you are so expressive. I can see your apprehension. You don't need to. If you wish to, though, I'll be gentle and try very hard indeed to make you feel wonderful."

"Okay," I whispered, swallowing.

Carrington rubbed his thumb over my chin. "Get back on your tummy, baby. Let me take care of you." I moved into place. It was getting easier to expose myself to him.

Carrington licked the spot on my lower back, right above my buttocks. "I love this little valley." He moved his tongue lower as he pulled my buttocks open, sliding it down my crack until he was circling my entrance.

"Oh," I gasped.

"That's it, baby," he encouraged. "I want to hear you." He resumed his licking and kissing. After a couple of minutes, he ran the tip of his finger around the circumference of my anus, then pushed it in. I clenched around him and he used his other hand to soothe my back. "It's okay. I'm not going to hurt you." He kissed my buttocks until my muscles loosened a bit, then he pushed his finger in further.

"Ooh," I breathed.

"You bring lube downstairs?" he asked.

"In the bag," I replied, motioning my head toward where we had left it, as if he had forgotten. He pulled out of me so he could retrieve the bag and pull it over to the sofa. I heard him pop the top of the lubricant bottle and rub his fingers together to warm it. Then he pushed a finger all the way inside me. "Uh," I gurgled.

"You doing okay, baby?" I nodded yes. Carrington let me adjust to the feel of his finger, then began a probing motion with it. "You are so hot, Eric. That relaxed me, and he started to slide in a second finger. Once he sensed the burn had dissipated, he started to pump me and stretch me. "Still doing okay, baby?"

"Carrington," was all I could whisper.

"I've got you, babe." He continued his motions until I bucked back against his hand. His fingers were grazing my prostate, and I couldn't help myself from writhing beneath him. After a moment, he pulled out his fingers, eliciting a small whimper from me. "Shh. I'm not going to leave you hanging. Turn on your back for me, okay?"

I rolled over, a little embarrassed to have him once again looking at my hard, leaking dick. He reached behind my knees and pushed up my limbs, pressing my knees near my chest. He held them there with one hand while retrieving the vibrator with the other. Before I could think, he was slipping the tip of the toy into me. I was lubed and stretched enough that it didn't sting, which he must have deduced, as he slid the entire length into my cavity.

"Oh God. So hot," he muttered. Carrington started playing with the buttons at the base, causing the tool to vibrate, then pulse, then do who knew what else. Pleasure was overtaking my embarrassment. He started to thrust the vibrator to add more friction, and I found myself once again writhing on the cushions.

"Carrington, I'm going to come," I warned.

He lowered his head and swiped his tongue over my shaft and fondled my balls. "So good, baby," he breathed.

"Uh, I can't hold on," I cried.

With the vibrator inserted, Carrington brought his hand to my ass with a slap, then another, pushing the vibrator hard against my prostate. I squeezed my eyes shut while grimacing, and I spurted cum across my belly and chest.

Carrington was panting, almost as hard as I was. "You are so sexy," he rasped, bringing his tongue to my stomach and tasting some of my semen.

"Carrington..." I said in a feeble attempt to warn him he might not like it.

He licked his lips, then brought his beautiful face to mine, kissing me. I was going to protest that he had been licking my ass, but my mouth seemed to overrule my brain as I let him plunder me with passion. "Whatever puritanical garbage your parents put in your head, ignore it. It would be such a shame for you to withhold this beauty and pleasure from a lucky partner. I've never been so aroused by someone as I have been with you." He resumed kissing my mouth, my chin, my cheeks and my neck. Although I was spent, every touch from his hands and his mouth was electric to my skin. I wrapped my legs around his waist and pulled him tighter to me, basking in his attention.

"Let me take care of you, too," I whispered, realizing after several minutes that he was still hard and waiting for release.

He smiled, then used his strength to roll us over, allowing me to be on top of him. He was already squirming and sighing from the friction. I knew he wouldn't last, so I sped up the teasing sequence, moving my lips and tongue over his beautiful nipples. His strong chest heaved under me, and he pushed my head lower. I gave little pecks to his belly, following the path of hair to his pubes, in which I buried my nose while grabbing his cock. Carrington moaned as I stroked him with my right hand and used my left hand to fondle his balls.

"Lift up, Carrington. I promise, I'll make it good for you," I said, mirroring his earlier promise. His face registered momentary hesitancy, but he nodded, pulling his knees to his chest. "Christ, you're so hot," I gasped. I couldn't believe I was getting erect again after having just ejaculated. I brought my face closer to his ass, glancing up to see if he would welcome the new experience. His expression signaled when he went from uncertainty to lust, and he pulled my head forward with one quick thrust. Once I was in a rhythm of tonguing him, he was thrashing around on the couch, trying to keep his ass in my face.

"Jesus, Eric. Holy shit. I've never felt anything like that," he gasped. "Oh God. I'm going to come if you keep doing that."

I took that as a cue to give him a reprieve while I re-opened the bottle of lubricant. I covered my fingers and took the same, slow approach to stretching Carrington that he had taken with me. I was in awe, watching myself penetrating the man who had turned me into a worshiping, blathering, sex-crazed disciple. He was doing well until I inserted the second finger, which caused him to intake a large gasp of air. "Are you okay?"

"Shit. That stings," he admitted.

I knew if I pulled out, he'd fear trying again. Instead, I stopped moving my hand, and took his dick in my mouth. I licked and sucked until I knew the sensation of pleasure overtook his discomfort. After a while, I was moving the second finger in a fraction at a time, still slurping on his cock. I let it fall from my lips so I could see how he was doing. "I'm all the way in with two fingers, Carrington."

He nodded, but I could tell he had reservations. "Try the submarine. I think it's thinner than your two fingers."

I didn't think that was true, but once I retrieved the toy, I realized he might be right. I lubed it, then began to submerge it in his ass. He continued to take deep breaths, but didn't protest the intrusion. Once it was inserted, I kissed his balls and his cock, getting him back to a firmer erection. "How does that feel?"

He nodded like a man in pain who wanted to convince me he wasn't. "Sure. Good."

"Relax," I whispered. "It will get better. I promise." I resumed blowing him, feeling him swell in my mouth. He was panting now, and he reached for my hand that was holding the sex toy, helping me maneuver it in and out of him. He began to groan and gasp, then he tugged and pushed our combined hands harder with each pass. I realized he had found the joy of his prostate.

"Eric, Eric," he was crying. "It's so fucking intense. I'm going to shoot."

I was ready. I knew what he wanted. I sucked in the head of his penis and let him unleash his load in my mouth. I pulled off before he finished so some of his cum could splatter my lips and cheeks. I relished the heat of his semen in and on me—knowing it was his ecstasy from what I had done for him.

"Was it okay?" I asked with some worry when he hadn't spoken.

Carrington looked down at my cum-soaked face and grinned. "Look at you. How do you still look so sweet, even with spunk all over you?" He brushed a thumb over my face, massaging his cum into my skin.

He reached for the jock strap he had dropped by the couch, then wiped my face with it. "I'm…I don't know what. But that was amazing. It was the most alive I've felt…well, ever."

I hugged him tight with relief, enjoying the sound of his heavy breathing in my ear and feeling his strong arms resting on my back. "I think we have a pool of cum in between our stomachs again." I noted.

"Maybe we should go shower?" he suggested, pulling the purple object from his ass.

I nodded, somewhat reluctant to leave his arms. I wanted to clothe myself when we pulled apart, but I knew he would be insulted by a renewed modesty on my part, so I refrained. I took his hand as he used his other to throw the toys and clothes back in the bag. We walked together to the upstairs bathroom. I knew he was looking me over the entire time, and I feared I was blushing. "Um, you want to shower together?" I wondered.

"Sure," he replied, his gaze intense.

After we finished washing each other under the hot water, Carrington wrapped me in a warm bath towel. He took another from the shelf to dry my hair, chest, arms and legs. I took the towel off me, and used it to dry his own wet form—feeling a need to dry certain places more than was necessary. He chuckled and pulled me into an embrace. "What now, Prince Eric?"

I sighed. I did feel like royalty. "Can we go lie on the bed and cuddle some more?"

"Hmm," he assented. "You go lie down. I'll be but a minute or two. Let me just check in back home, okay? Then we'll nap."

"Maybe afterward, we can eat then go outside for a bit? It looks nice out today. I think the humidity from the storm has passed."

"Sure."

I had opened the bedroom windows, and a soft breeze was blowing the curtains. It felt wonderful against my naked skin. I got into the bed, pulling the sheet up to my stomach. I knew it was false modesty at this point, but I couldn't help myself. Once Carrington re-emerged, still naked, he gave me a side-eye glance to show he didn't approve, though his slight grin signaled he understood me. I enjoyed watching his muscles move as he approached the bed, his maleness swinging with every step. He climbed onto the mattress with me, shimmying his way under the cover as well. I sighed with contentment when he pulled me back into his strong arms, cradling me until we both fell asleep.

Chapter Fifteen

Eric

Once we had awakened and dressed, I made us a salad that we enjoyed for lunch, then we made our way outside to the side porch.

"What's this?" Carrington inquired, pulling a plastic baseball bat from the corner.

"Oh, yeah, that's kind of tacky to leave hanging around in the yard. The storm must have blown it away from the porch. I forgot to put it back in the garage when I was done playing with it."

"But what is it?" he asked again, a slight smile crossing his lips. "Please tell me it's not an even bigger dildo."

My mouth opened in protest. "What? Are you nuts? Give me that!" He handed it to me, and I took a batter's stance on the lawn. "It's a baseball bat. Well, a plastic bat you can use in a neighborhood with a plastic baseball. You can't use a real one or you could break a window."

"Ah, I don't believe I've ever seen a baseball game," he noted. "It's uniquely American."

"No, it's not," I countered. "Japan and Canada have professional baseball. And I think it's popular in the Caribbean and in Central and South America, too."

"Okay. And why do *you* have a bat?" He smirked.

I rolled my eyes at him. "I don't just play with dildos, contrary to your one-track mind. Mateo and I pitch and bat out here sometimes. Just for fun. I used to play hardball when I was a kid in Little League."

"Little League?" Carrington mused. "Sounds adorable."

"Stop it. I wasn't much of an athlete, but I wasn't that bad at baseball. Even my father would come to watch my games. It was one of the few things I did that gave him a sense of pride. I used to wish I was better than I was, but at least he'd clap when I got a hit or made an out."

Carrington frowned for a second, but then smiled. "Show me. I admire your pose with the bat."

I rolled my eyes again. "It's not a pose. It's called a batter's stance." I got into position again to show him what I meant. "It's to help you eye and hit the ball when it's pitched to you."

He shrugged. "I'm sure I don't understand the game, but I think I'd enjoy watching you play. Are there no leagues for amateur adults?"

I nodded. "Sure. But I wasn't *that* good as a kid, so why bother?" I tossed the bat in front of the porch, not wanting to relive how my father had lost interest once he realized I had peaked as an average player. "Let's go sit on the patio."

Carrington looked puzzled. "Are you sure? Perhaps I could pitch this plastic ball to you."

I snickered. "Some other time. Come on." I took his hand, ready to lead him to the backyard, and he pulled me into a soft kiss.

"If you join a league, I'll come to watch you, just to see you take that athletic pose."

I pretended to be inpatient. "Stance. I told you, it's a stance."

"Would you be wearing a sexy uniform?" He grinned.

I laughed in response. "Well, the amateur leagues can be hit or miss when it comes to uniforms, but all of them have tight pants."

"Mm," he murmured, pulling me back into another kiss.

"Disgusting," I heard barked from the street. Carrington and I looked over, and there stood Marietta at the front curb watching us.

"Oh, hi, Marietta," I called out, pretending I hadn't heard her.

She put a hand on her hip and scowled. "There could have been a child walking by while you were doing…that! I don't know why you people can't stay in the cities."

Before I could say anything, she resumed her walk, not giving us another glance.

"She's charming," Carrington deadpanned.

"Told you," I muttered, grabbing his hand and leading him to the enclosed patio.

"You and the boys did a good job cleaning up this place," Carrington commented once I closed the gate behind us.

"It's so nice out. Shall we lie on the chaise longue chairs?" I didn't wait for his response. I pulled the chair cushions from the storage box and laid them on the furniture. I looked over to Carrington, and he was removing his shirt. "What are you doing?"

He cocked his head, indicating I was the strange one for asking. "Getting ready to sunbathe, of course."

"Oh." I gulped. "Um, I guess we could do that. I'll get some sunscreen from the garage."

He chuckled and called out, "If you have the kind that you rub on, I would prefer that." He was going to be the death of me, for sure.

Once I returned from the garage, Carrington was lying on a chaise in his boxer briefs. I put up the sun umbrella to block us from direct rays, then handed him the tube of sunscreen. He looked at me with confusion. "Um, you said you wanted the kind you could rub on."

"No. I said I wanted the kind *you* rub on. Please proceed," he said with a straight face.

I gulped and, under my breath, cursed myself for gulping. "Sure." Even though I now should have been used to touching Carrington, my hand was still quivering when I started rubbing it on his hard shoulders and chest.

"Mm, that feels nice," he whispered. "If the photography thing doesn't work out, you can be my pool boy."

I smirked as I applied more lotion to his arms, then his legs. "Tempting as that sounds, I've started appreciating the finer things in life."

He grinned. "Oh, sweet Eric. I would reward you very well. And I'd pay you well, too." I blushed. "Take your shirt and trousers off," he ordered.

I knew there was no point battling him, as he would win the debate anyway. I removed the garments and placed them at the end of the chaise, then took my seat. "Happy now?" I prodded. "Anything else I can do for your highness?"

He chuckled. "I think you're supposed to address me as 'Mr. President,' though you treating me as a king will suffice." I shot him a pretend look of annoyance, but he kept laughing. He took the tube and started rubbing the lotion into my skin, paying special attention to my chest and belly.

"Um, I think you've got me protected now." I smiled.

"I'll always protect you, Eric." He said it with earnestness, making one of my eyes start to tear. I blinked so he wouldn't notice.

Once he was lying back again, he asked me to tell him more about myself.

"Not much to know," I responded. "No siblings. Grew up in New Jersey. My father was a plant manager at an energy company. My mother was a clerk at a financial firm. Went to college, moved to the city and you kind of know the rest."

"And your parents fought," he reminded me.

I nodded. "Yeah. He drank a lot. Made him mean. She was strict about everything and his alcoholism didn't conform to what she viewed as proper. I guess it wasn't, in retrospect."

"And he was violent toward you," Carrington continued.

I looked over to him. "Why are we going there?"

He glanced back, but there was compassion in his eyes. "I wish to better understand you."

I wanted to push back and tell him that my childhood had nothing to do with the person I had become, but of course, I knew that wasn't true. I had already admitted as much. "Yeah, he was abusive. Lots of parents are. Christ, even my mother got her share in. It's not a big deal. You survive."

"Eric, it is a big deal," he replied. "And I'm sorry they hurt you. From the sound of it, they hurt you for a very long time. They didn't deserve you. You're the kindest, gentlest soul I've met, and they didn't appreciate what a gift they had."

I closed my eyes again, trying not to tear up. "I disappointed them a lot. I wished I could have been...more of what they wanted."

Carrington reached for my hand, and I let him hold it. "I'm going to keep showing you how wonderful you are, and one day, I'm going to rejoice when you realize it's true."

I laughed, then got serious. "What about you? What kind of parents did you have? Your mother seems nice."

He smiled at that observation. "Yes. She's tough, like how she battled her recent illness. She's always had to be strong though, being married to my father and holding the position of First Lady. But she cares about people, and she loves me without conditions. My father put more expectations on me. It's not surprising, I guess. I couldn't embarrass him, considering his career. He wanted me to follow in his footsteps. I've been doing government jobs since graduating from Oxford University. Each one had increasing responsibilities. I knew my fate was to one day be president. It's what he wanted."

"But not what you wanted," I affirmed, recalling our earlier conversation.

He nodded. "Duty calls, and all that. One day, though, I shall be done with it and be able to pursue my own passion."

I paused, then asked in a whisper, "Did he ever hurt you?"

Carrington gave me a questioning look. "You mean physically? No. Neither parent did. My father would be harsher with punishments, but I remember my mother once asked him why he was grounding me for a week—that it seemed excessive. He replied that it was to teach me a lesson. Her response was that she could tell I felt terrible about my transgression—which at the time had been sneaking out at night to attend a party with some friends—and that she felt I had already learned my lesson by him expressing his disappointment in me. She told him that grounding me was revenge to make him feel better, and he should stop pretending he was doing it for my own good." Carrington snickered at the memory.

"He apologized to me and granted me a pardon. That's how she was. She'd let him get his way on things, but if she felt he was doing something wrong or harmful, the toughness kicked in and she'd tell him so. Neither shouted at me. My mother did once, but apologized to me for doing so. She told me that if she could be respectful to people who she didn't care for when they did something that upset her, then she could show the same respect to her own child. I will never forget that, and it will be the way I shall raise my own children one day."

My eyes went wide. "You want to have kids?"

He shrugged. "Yes, of course. Don't you?"

I closed my eyes, thinking any fantasy of a long-distance relationship with Carrington was just that. "Well, it's not in the cards for me—being a gay man."

"Why not? In your country, you can marry another man. You could adopt or even have a child through artificial insemination. Eric, do you *want* to have children one day?"

I sighed. "Yes. I would."

"Then you shall," he concluded. "I'm convinced of it. And you would be the best father."

"Me?" I wondered.

"Yes." He grinned. "Though not perfect."

"Why not?"

He chuckled. "You questioned your paternal skills just a second ago. Now you fancy yourself perfect?" I shook my head to show that I didn't, but he continued laughing. "I think you'd try very hard to please them, which is fine, to an extent. But you can't let your children think they are your friends. You'd need a co-parent who would be willing to take a firmer hand with them—figuratively, of course."

I wondered if Carrington was imagining himself as that co-parent. He would provide that balance, based on how he treated me. A tingle shot through my body as I thought about the possibility. "Yes, I suppose you're right," I conceded.

After a few minutes passed, Carrington's phone buzzed. He reached over, glancing at the text that had been sent. "Stefan and Mateo just crossed back over the Connecticut state line. How long will it take them to get here from the border?"

"One hour," I replied, sorry my time with Carrington would be ending.

It was as if Carrington had sensed my mood change, as he reached over to stroke my arm. "They know about us. We don't have to hide anything from them when they return. We can still be affectionate."

I smiled. "That would make me happy."

"That said," he added, "finding us lounging in our undergarments may be unexpected. Perhaps we should dress and go inside."

I pretended to pout. "Fine. Just when you had me comfortable being naked."

He chuckled. "If you were comfortable being naked, you should have said so. Why were we wearing underwear?"

I chuckled. "Um, to keep your dick from burning?"

He smiled. "It's always burning when you're around."

I barked a laugh. "You're a cornball."

"*You're* a cornball," he replied.

We got up, dressed then went back into the house, unsure what to do with ourselves. "Um, what now?"

He raised his eyebrows and pulled me close. "How about you make one of the fancy feasts you're becoming noted for? I'll catch up with Stefan upon his return, then you can have me back at your disposal. Perhaps there's a movie you and I could watch?"

I hugged him. "That sounds nice."

He winked. "Indeed. And I'll see if I can get rid of our interlopers. I'm sure they'd enjoy a nice night together at Mateo's residence. He must have his electricity back by now."

"That sounds even nicer," I agreed. "For them, I mean...of course."

"Of course," he played along. "And it will also make it less intrusive for us when I take you later this evening."

"Huh?"

"That is, if you'd be okay with me doing so," he whispered.

I was pretty sure what he meant by 'taking me.' I was pleased that my excitement and anticipation were outweighing my usual bouts of fear. "Um, yes. I would."

Carrington smiled, pulling me into a chaste kiss.

Chapter Sixteen

Carrington

Once Stefan and Mateo arrived at Eric's house, Mateo hung back with Eric in the kitchen and Stefan joined me in Eric's living room.

"Has Mateo been asking more questions about us? Has he asked why we're still staying here whilst my mother is going home?" I asked.

"So far, he still believes we're models. I told him that you and I are staying behind because we have a shot at a modeling gig in New York City this week, and your mother played along that she had to get back home to deal with some family issues. He was polite enough not to ask her for details."

I smirked. "Well, I'm not surprised he believes you're a model. I don't think he's paying much attention if he thinks I am. I mean, I have a bottom tooth that's crooked, crinkles around my eyes when I smile, and I can't control this hair."

Stefan looked at me funny. "Since when have those things bothered you? You've never mentioned them before. Trust me, you're model material."

I smiled, thinking about my photo shoot with Eric. "Well, Eric seems to think so."

Stefan studied me. "Your time with him hasn't lessened your infatuation with him, has it?"

My smile broadened. "No. He's wonderful."

My friend looked shocked. "Carrington, what is happening with you? I've never seen you this giddy over a woman, let alone over a person whose gender you've never been interested in."

I ran a hand through my hair. "I don't know! I thought the more I became intimate with him, the more I might pull back. It's been just the opposite."

Stefan's eyes bugged out. "Just how intimate have you been with him?"

I realized I had offered more than I had planned and I felt my face flush. "Stefan, he's very shy. Don't say anything to him or to Mateo about it."

"How intimate?" Stefan pressed.

"I'm not answering that," I snapped. "I'll just say intimate enough to know that I have no reservations about sex with him. I like him very much, and I enjoy being with him."

Stefan ran a hand across his face. "Carrington, you are risking your career."

"I'm willing to take the chance," I argued. "I never wanted to be president. I want him."

"You don't even know him!" Stefan countered.

"That's not true. We've gotten to know each other well these last couple of days. I trust him. Christ. I let him photograph me in…compromising positions."

Stefan's face turned ashen. "Are you out of your fucking mind?"

I refrained from reprimanding him for speaking that way to the president. I knew what I was saying was shocking and concerning. "I told you that I trust him. He told me he's going to delete the photos."

"What? The photos are still in his possession?"

"Relax," I shushed him. "The photos are on his camera downstairs in his studio. It isn't like they're hanging on a wall in New York City. He's going to delete them. I'll remind him right now. Oh, except I told him he could keep the ones of me clothed…and the one where I'm shirtless."

"Shirtless! My God, how revealing are the *other* ones?"

I couldn't help but grin. "Don't ask."

"Carrington, this isn't something to trivialize. You're playing with fire," he warned.

"Stefan, have you paid him any attention? Eric is the sweetest and kindest person I've ever met. He wouldn't hurt me. I don't think he's *capable* of hurting me. If anything, he tries too hard to please me. To please everyone. I'm not worried."

My friend shook his head. "I'm not going to change your mind on this, am I?"

I pursed my lips. "Why would you want to? I haven't been this happy in a long time."

"I don't want you to get hurt," he answered.

"Is that why you don't get attached to anyone? You don't want to get hurt?" He reacted like I had sent a bolt of electricity to his chest. "Why have you never shared with anyone you're gay? Are you avoiding the drama of coming out because you assume you'll never have a partner anyway, figuring they could hurt you?"

He squirmed in the chair. "Are you trying to psychoanalyze me now?"

I pressed forward. "What about Mateo? You like him more than you let on. I can tell. Are you going to keep it going with him, or will you forget about him as soon as we're back in Yastarus?"

"We'd be halfway across the world from each other. What's the point? That's something you should be considering when it comes to Eric."

I nodded. "I have thought about it. It's not ideal, but I'm already thinking I could move here once I finish the presidency."

Stefan was shocked. "You can't be serious! Are you in love with him? How can this be? It's been little more than two days, Carrington."

I sighed. "I know that. I'm not saying I will. I'm saying I *could*, if things work out. We can visit, and there's video chat. If he's the one, then the long distance will be a nuisance, not a deal-breaker. It could be the same for you and Mateo. But that would mean opening your heart to someone, wouldn't it?"

"Fuck you, Carrington. I opened my heart to you for years! What did that get me?"

That stung. It hadn't occurred to me that he'd avoided relationships because he was in love with me for so long. "I'm sorry, Stefan. I swear, I didn't know until you told me the other night. But now that you're no longer in love with me, maybe it's time to give Mateo a chance, yes? He seems like a good chap."

Stefan cast his eyes down and was silent for a while. He whispered, "Yes, maybe I should give him a chance."

I clapped a hand on his shoulder. "Feel free to spend the night at his place. I'll be fine. I'm safer here than anywhere else I could be."

Stefan sneered. "So, do you care about me at all, or was this whole Mateo conversation a means of freeing up the house for you and Eric tonight?"

"Of course, I care about you. You are my best friend, Stefan. I want you to be happy. You and Mateo can stay here tonight, if you prefer. It won't stop my plans with Eric. I just thought it would be a chance for the two of you to spend time together without feeling awkward by our presence."

"What do you mean, your plans with Eric?"

I hesitated. "We've experimented a good deal." I flushed thinking about the deeds we'd already done. "God, I'm not comfortable speaking of this." I looked Stefan in the eye. "I haven't made love to him yet, if you know what I'm saying. I want to this evening."

He frowned. "Are you certain this is wise?"

I raised my chin. "I've never been so sure of anything."

Stefan rose from his chair, slapping his hands against his thighs as he did so. "Fine. After dinner, I'll ask Mateo to show me his apartment and convince him to stay there with me tonight. But I'm returning tomorrow. I don't think you should be left unprotected."

"Very well." I walked over to him and hugged him. "Stefan, I'm sorry about so many things. And I do want you to be happy. Maybe I'm getting carried away, but I think it would be magnificent if you and Mateo were a couple, and we could do things together—the four of us."

Stefan's jaw dropped. "Do you mean that the four of us would have sex together?"

I almost choked out a cough. "My word, no! I meant once I'm no longer the president, we could do normal things that couples do together. I want you in my life, Stefan. But I want Eric in my life, too. At least, right now that's how I feel. I'm falling for him."

Stefan looked doubtful, but nodded and exited to join the others in the kitchen.

Chapter Seventeen

Eric

Once Stefan had left the room to speak with Carrington, I saw that Mateo had a mischievous smile. "So? Have you two done any more together since I last saw you?"

"You know I don't like to talk about that," I answered. "It's kind of disrespectful to the other person, don't you think?"

"You've told me about what you've done with other guys," he noted. "Or more accurately, what you haven't done."

"Ha-ha," I snapped. "Well, I didn't care about those guys."

He beamed. "Ooh, so you care about Carrington, huh? That's a development."

I nodded, afraid that admitting it would jinx me. "Yeah, I do. He's nothing like he was when I first met him. He's so sweet and protective. I can't believe he's interested in me."

Mateo frowned. "Stop it! You're one of the cutest guys I've ever met. I've told you that a million times, but you just refuse to see it."

"You're biased."

"Fuck I am," he retorted. "I thought it from the day I met you."

"I won't age well, remember?" I shot, recalling his comment to me on the patio.

He rubbed a hand across his jaw. "I told you I was sorry for saying that. Hell, what do I know about it? I might be the one who looks like the crypt keeper in ten years. I was just trying to put a sense of urgency in you."

I shrugged. "Well, for whatever reason, Carrington seems to like the way I look, too."

"Of course, he does," Mateo asserted. "He's not blind. Only you have that impairment. Then again, you noticed *he's* hot, so I guess your eyesight isn't that bad."

I grinned, feeling the heat rise to my face. "He is hot, isn't he? God, you should see him naked."

"Okay. Lead the way," he joked, pretending to walk to the room Carrington was in.

I laughed. "You aren't bored with Stefan already, are you?"

"Hell no," he responded. "He's the finest man I've ever been with. Dude, he's a calendar pin-up come to life."

"But do you like him?" I asked, wondering if there was anything between them beyond sexual chemistry.

Mateo's expression softened. "I do. He was a little hard to get to know at first, but he and I seem to have clicked. He doesn't talk much about his modeling or his life back home, but he's told me a lot about places he's been, books he's read, movies he likes and his thoughts on politics. Did you know his home country was once part of the Soviet Union?"

I tried not to roll my eyes. "Yes."

Mateo shrugged. "Well, you always were the smart one. Anyway, he's very kind once you get to know him."

"Do you want to keep it going?"

He nodded. "I would. I don't know what he wants, though. It will be tough with him living so far away and always on the road for modeling assignments."

I felt a wave of guilt that I was complicit in the lies we were telling about Stefan and Carrington. "Um, yeah. I get that."

Mateo sighed. "Yes, I guess you do because you want it to continue with Carrington too, don't you?"

I couldn't help but grin. "Yes."

He clapped my shoulder and pulled me into a hug. "Then I hope it happens for you. It's about time. Listen, don't be so afraid of sex with him that you become like a brother to him—like you did with me. I'm sure you think you've gone full throttle with the guy, but he might think what you've done is foreplay."

I cast my eyes down, biting my lip. "Um, I doubt he thinks that."

Mateo's eyes went wide. "Oh my God. You slut."

I laughed. "I can't help it. He's irresistible. "

"Penetration?"

I shushed him and looked behind me to ensure neither Stefan nor Carrington were nearby. "No. I mean yes, but not with our…dicks."

Mateo started to laugh. "Ooh, you have gone further than I thought you would have. Please tell me you finally swallowed too."

I was mortified. "Jesus. Stop!" He kept his imploring eyes on me. "Okay, yes."

He let out a small scream and hugged me again. "My boy's grown up."

"Shut up!" I laughed, pushing him off me.

Mateo waved a hand through the air to signal I was being a prude. "Just keep in mind, if he still identifies as straight, he's never going to do for you what he wants you to do for him. You catch my meaning?"

I nodded. "He's been pretty open to things so far, though. And he doesn't seem to have regrets about anything we've done. I don't think he's a closet homophobe. It's like he just found out he likes vanilla ice cream as much as he likes chocolate."

"I thought he can't have dairy," Mateo deadpanned.

"You know what I mean," I chastised. "He wants to…go all the way tonight. I told him that I would."

Mateo's eyes bulged. "Eric, you're shocking me here. Okay, be careful. Don't let him hurt you. I'm not going to lie. Your first time will be a bit painful, at least at first. Don't be afraid to tell him to be gentle."

I nodded. "Okay, but I know he will be."

"And make sure you…take care of yourself down there before you get in bed with him. You never know. He may use his tongue to ready you. It's been known to happen, and it's horrifying when you're spending the whole time wondering if you're clean enough. Puts a damper on things. Trust me. I speak from experience."

I laughed. "Um, too late for that."

This time, his jaw dropped. "What in the name of all that's holy? He's really leaning into this gay thing, isn't he? And look at you. You've become a regular porn star. I'm happy for you. You're allowing yourself a good time."

I shrugged a shoulder. "He makes it easy."

At that point, Stefan and Carrington entered the kitchen, silencing both Mateo and me. I was afraid my flushed face revealed to Carrington what we'd been discussing.

Stefan motioned his hand nowhere in particular. "I'm going to do another security check of the home." He looked over to Mateo. "I do that when I'm somewhere unfamiliar. Carrington and I have had stalkers in the past."

Mateo's face was unreadable. "Sure. I guess."

"But then, maybe we can leave this place and I can test your apartment's security," Stefan suggested. "A handsome guy like you — you never know what creeps might be watching you through your windows. I can...protect you."

I almost laughed when Mateo's Adam's apple bobbed, much like mine did when I was excited and nervous. "Um, okay. You sure take this security stuff seriously, huh?"

Stefan grinned. "Very. I've always thought it would be fun to be a TSA agent and give a hot guy like you a full body search."

Mateo's eyes widened. "Uh, you can practice on me if it's a career you're considering..."

Carrington coughed to silence the banter. "Should we just skip dinner?"

Mateo nodded, displaying his eagerness. "I have food at my house, Stefan. Maybe you should move it along. I'm pretty worried about my apartment now. It's not in the nicer part of town like Eric's house is."

Stefan gave Mateo a lascivious grin and left the room to begin his inspection.

I laughed. "You're concerned about the safety of your apartment in *this* town?"

Mateo turned red. "Yes. Watch those crime documentaries on television. The narrator always begins the segment by saying 'murders don't happen in this type of town'."

I laughed louder. "Okay. Well, be safe then."

Mateo gave me a sarcastic, knowing look. "I will. Tonight, you should be…*safe*…too."

* * * *

Carrington and I spent the entirety of dinner speculating about Mateo and Stefan, as well as talking politics. I shared what I knew about current legislative proposals in the United States and at various local levels, and he filled me in on the political and cultural climate of Yastarus. While I knew a little bit about his country, I didn't have any sense of the governmental or judicial structures. He went into significant detail about the history, the country's adversarial relationship with Russia and the culture wars. It became clear that Carrington was viewed as a progressive in his country, though his positions were more aligned with moderates In the United States. He shared a little about how they had learned of the plot against his life, but in so doing, tried to assure me that his country's intelligence and law enforcement agencies had everything under control.

Once we had cleaned and put away the dishes from our meal, he gave me one of his smoldering gazes. He put his hands on my hips and pulled me toward him. "You're very smart," he complimented me.

"I don't know. I worked hard in school, and I watch a lot of news. Maybe more hard-working and educated than smart."

He pulled me a bit closer. "I disagree. I'm sure you do work hard, and you are educated and informed, but you're very intelligent. I'll bet if you had an IQ test done, you'd score quite high."

I shrugged. "Um, they have tested me."

His eyebrows rose. "And?"

I pulled away and started hanging dish towels back on their hooks. "I scored one hundred and forty-five. I guess they consider that..."

"Genius," Carrington finished. He walked over to me and pulled my chin toward him so our eyes could meet. "I knew it. Why are you so humble?"

"It's just a test," I mumbled. "My parents told me that I shouldn't buy into those kinds of things, and that it is important that I keep working hard because that's the real key to success."

Carrington paused, started to open his mouth to say something, but then thought better of it. Instead, he brushed my lips with his fingers. "You promised me a movie."

I smiled. "I did. What do you want to watch?"

He shrugged. "Whatever you want. I'm guessing I'll be watching you more than the film anyway."

I gulped, feeling myself starting to harden. Even I was beginning to be amazed by my raging testosterone. I had never had the inspiration to test it like I had these last few days. "Um, I like superhero movies. Do you like those?"

He grinned. "Why am I not surprised? Eric Turner likes watching cute men in tight outfits hunt the bad guys and make the world a better place? I would never have guessed!"

I flushed. "Well, we could watch something else. Do you want to watch a drama?"

He shook his head no. "I'm not in the mood for anything heavy, are you? I was thinking something that might be a nice prelude to our time together later." His gaze intensified.

"Oh." I swallowed. "Um, maybe a romantic movie?"

"Hmm," he whispered, pulling me back into his arms. Carrington kissed me a couple of times, then took my hand and led me to the family room. "Can you dim the lights?"

"Uh, sure." Once I had, I turned on the television and started skimming through the streaming service movie offerings. "Oh, how about *Moonstruck*?"

He smiled. "Were you even born when that was made?"

I shrugged. "No. But it's a classic. And it stars Cher. She's the one gay icon I like, so watching or listening to her allows me to keep my gay membership card."

Carrington looked confused. "There are gay membership cards in your country?"

I laughed. "No. It's an expression. We can watch something else if you want."

He shook his head. "No, that's fine. I've seen it before, but it's been a long time. I enjoyed it. Besides, I wouldn't want them to revoke your membership."

We both sat on the couch and I started the film. "Um, do you want popcorn?"

He quirked up an eyebrow. "Didn't we just eat?"

I nodded. "Yeah, of course."

Carrington wasn't watching the screen. True to his word, his eyes were on me. "Stop being nervous. And why are you sitting so far away?"

I was two feet from him, so I inferred he wanted to cuddle. I moved up to him and let him wrap an arm over my shoulder. I leaned into his body and sighed. It was a common scenario for many, but one I had never experienced. "This is nice."

"Hmm," he concurred, kissing the top of my head.

We watched the entire movie while Carrington stroked my arm or nuzzled his nose against my hair. During the opera scene when Cher realized she was falling in love with Nicolas Cage and a tear slid down her cheek, a tear fell from my eye as well. I tried a subtle move to wipe it, but Carrington noticed. "Sorry. That's embarrassing. I cry while watching sad movie scenes."

He looked at me with fondness. "It's sweet."

"You don't?" I wondered.

He shook his head no. "I don't cry. Even when my father died, I was composed. Something broken in me, I guess." Carrington huffed a soft laugh at himself.

"I'll try not to," I promised, thinking he might be more comfortable if I was composed, too.

He lifted my chin and pulled me into a kiss. "I like you just as you are, Eric Turner."

What he didn't realize was, though Cher emoting on screen had triggered the tear, the scene had made me realize I was falling in love with Carrington. I doubted he was feeling the same. I had to be content that he liked me.

Once the film ended, I turned off the television and turned to see his reaction. "Did you like watching it a second time?" He nodded. "I guess the criticism of the movie is that people don't fall in love in two days. Maybe they need to be moonstruck—it's a fantasy."

"You don't think it could happen?" he asked, quirking his head.

It was my opportunity to tell him that I thought I was moonstruck the night of the storm, but I was too much of a coward. "Do you?"

He got a funny expression, then broke the tension by starting to talk like Nicolas Cage's character, repeating some of the lines from the movie. It made me laugh until he turned to me and said the line, "Now get into my bed!"

I reached over and pulled him into a deep kiss, licking his lips and tasting his tongue. I know I whimpered as he took control, and it made my cheeks flush. "Sorry. I seem to make dopey noises when you do stuff to me."

His eyes were hooded and his lips were red and full from kissing me. "Don't apologize. Every little noise you make pushes more blood to my dick. Your lovely sounds are like catnip for me."

That made me laugh. "Okay. Descriptive and… weird."

He chuckled. "You're so sweet. And you're such a cheeky devil."

"Are you going to punish me?" I rasped.

He shook his head no. "Eric, I think I know what you want. When you want to play, and when you…don't. I think tonight, you need me to hold you in my arms and make love to you. Not sex. Love-making. Am I correct?"

"Yes," I whispered.

He got a mischievous smile, repeating a line that Cher said in the movie. "You're supposed to say 'okay,

okay — take me to your bed'," he joked, doing a poor job of imitating her movie Brooklyn accent.

I chuckled, but stopped when he lifted me from the couch, carrying me in his arms — replicating the actions of the movie characters. "That's right, baby. I'm going to take you and make you feel so good," he promised.

Carrington didn't put me down, so I didn't bother turning off the downstairs light. He carried me up the stairs like I weighed nothing, entering my bedroom and laying me on my bed. "Um, that was…nice. Are your arms aching now?"

He laughed and nodded. "Yes."

"Oh. You shouldn't have carried me," I worried.

Carrington looked at me with affection. "My arms are aching because you're no longer in them." He sat on the side of the bed and took off his socks. "I suppose we should wash before we do this, huh? I mean, we were sweating outside before dinner."

Darned practicality, but I remembered Mateo's advice and nodded in agreement. "Um, yes. I don't want you to think I smell bad."

He smiled and reached for my hand. "Come on. But no fooling around in the shower. I'll take care of you once we're dried off and in bed."

Chapter Eighteen

Carrington

Once I had toweled off my beautiful guy, I took his hand and led him to his bed. "Leave the nightstand lamp on. I want to see you, okay?"

He nodded, getting on the bed, acting like it was a coincidence that his right hand was covering his privates. I smiled at my shy Eric. I climbed on top of him, kissing him, eliciting a little squeak that went right to my groin. "You smell good," he whispered.

"I had the loveliest person make me nice and clean," I reminded him. He hummed. I kissed him again. After a few moments of soft pecks over his lips, cheeks, neck and ears, he was pushing his hips against me. "Slow and sweet, baby," I coaxed. He was the most responsive lover I had ever had, so excited and happy for every touch.

"Please," he said, or I thought he did—it was muffled and buried against my throat.

I moved my hands down his silky chest and stomach, marveling at how soft his skin was, and yet how hard his muscles were. "So beautiful," I praised. I grazed my fingers over his scrotum, making him try to push his aching dick into my hand. "Patience, Eric."

"I need you, though," he pleaded.

His eyes were full of wonder and desire. I couldn't refuse him. "Baby, I've been celibate for several months. Being the president, I need to have check-ups every four months. I get tested, and I'm negative." He nodded, seeming to understand what I was suggesting. "You're a virgin—at least as far as intercourse is concerned. I don't think we need to use a condom, unless you want me to."

He bit his lip. "I don't want you to. I trust you."

I kissed him again, stroking his taint and crack. "I'm just going to get you ready, okay?"

Eric nodded, dropping the side of his face to the pillow and running a hand through his own hair. It was like he didn't know what to do with his energy and want. I kissed my way down his body until I reached his pulsing dick, licking it a few times to get him wet. He moaned and made soft cries. I lowered my head more, pushing up the backs of his thighs to give me access to his entrance. I drooled out some saliva onto his hole and began to lick. It was hard keeping his legs elevated, as he was thrashing with every press on his nerves. "God, Carrington."

I knew he wouldn't last if I kept rimming him. He'd shown me already that his youth came with a hair-trigger libido. I reached for the bottle of lubricant he had left on the nightstand, popping the top and warming some of the liquid between my fingers.

I kissed his thighs. "Keep your hand on mine. You guide me in." That was what Eric did over the next minute until I had three fingers inside him. I was so aroused looking at how I was penetrating my man. He pulled up his legs more so I could hit his prostate.

"Carrington, please. Want you in me," he managed through his writhing.

I pulled out of him and squeezed lubricant over my dick. "Okay, promise me you'll tell me if I'm hurting you." He bit his lower lip, nodding yes. I lined the head of my dick to his loosened hole, pushing in. His eyes rolled back and I wasn't sure if he was liking it or dying. "Eric, please let me know if this is good for you."

"Yes," he whispered. "Please, Carrington. Keep going."

I pushed in further, causing him to bite harder on his lower lip. I paused, letting him get used to the intrusion. I knew from my earlier experience that there was a ring of nerves or muscle that I had to get past before he would start feeling pleasure. He looked to me, giving me a slight smile and a nod. I pushed in until the base of my dick was encased by his tight channel. "Eric, I'm inside you. Baby, it's…thank you," I gasped, bending down to kiss his panting mouth.

"So full," he breathed.

"Okay?"

"Yeah," he answered. "Just getting used to it. But I like it. I like having you inside me, Carrington." He gazed into my eyes as I remained within him, then he touched my cheek. "You're so handsome. And you're so wonderful. I'm glad you're the one…"

I assumed he meant that I was the one to take his virginity. I found myself wishing he meant that I was the one to be with him from now on. I ran my hand through his damp hair. "Want me to start moving?"

Eric blinked his eyes in assent and, for several minutes, I pumped in and out whilst kissing him. It was the first time in a very long while that I felt strong emotion as I was making love to someone.

"I'm ready," he whispered.

I angled his hips a bit higher and drove my own a bit harder. Eric started uttering an 'ah' with every thrust. When it felt like I was going to shoot, I pulled all the way out, spewed over his hole, and pushed the cum and my dick back inside of his warmth. He blew his own load within seconds, crying out my name whilst babbling nonsensical words. I caught his face with both hands to steady him, staying buried in him and pressing my shoulders down to his. Eric was still eliciting a soft cry with each exhale of breath, his expression one of disbelief about what had just happened.

Once his breathing slowed, I kissed him again, petting his hair and caressing one of his ears. "You were wonderful, Eric."

He still had the look of wonder on his face. "Carrington, that was the best experience of my life." I smiled. He was so cute. "Thank you. You knew just what to do to make me feel...special."

"Baby, you *are* special," I reminded him. "So special."

The slight nervousness was etched on his face once more. "Um, that was your first time too."

I kissed him to assure him that I was fine. "Eric, stop worrying. It's clear that I'm not straight. I'm enjoying being with you way too much for there to be a question about that. I want it all with you."

He looked at me with a questioning gaze. "What?"

I feared Eric would be spooked if he knew just how fast I was falling for him, and I decided to backpedal. "I mean, there's nothing I wouldn't do with you. I think it's fair to say I fancy you."

He giggled. "You fancy me? Shall we begin courting?"

"Ah, so you are back to mocking me, I see. Just because I refrained from spanking you tonight doesn't mean you're off-limits tomorrow." I grinned and gave him another peck.

"Um, that was so hot the way you came on me, then pushed it in me," he said, face flushing. "Does that turn you on?"

"Hmm, indeed," I confirmed. "I'm afraid I'm becoming quite possessive of you. It felt like I was marking you as mine."

"I want to be yours," he blurted.

I paused, unsure of whether he meant sexually or more. "Eric, I'm beginning to have real feelings for you. This isn't just sexual experimentation for me."

He gulped. "Me either."

"As much as I wish to continue cuddling, we should clean up."

He sighed. "I know. I'll get a washcloth."

I pushed him back flat. "Babe, I told you, I'm taking care of you tonight. I'll get it. Just lay there. I'll return straight away." I went to the ensuite and dampened the cloth with hot water, walking back to Eric, where he remained uncovered—not even hiding his now flaccid dick from me. It made me feel trusted, and that made me elated. I climbed back on the mattress and wiped him clean.

"Carrington?"

"Yes?"

He bit his lower lip. "Will I sound too needy if I ask to sleep on your chest again?"

I smiled. "Will there be a repeat drooling incident?"

He nodded. "Probably."

My smile broadened. "Okay. I think I can endure it." I rolled us so that I was on my back, and he moved his body down so that he could rest his head on me.

"I can hear your heart beating. It's…comforting," he murmured.

I stroked his hair, thinking it was soothing for me too, having my guy sleeping on me. "Did you have a nice day, Eric?"

He hummed, which I took as a yes. Within moments, his breathing slowed and became deeper, signaling he was asleep. I closed my eyes, content and grateful our driver had brought us to Connecticut — brought me to Eric.

* * * *

"Good morning, sweet prince," I murmured when Eric opened his eyes.

Sometime during the night, he had turned, moving off my body. I had spooned him instead, basking in his warmth and the coconut smell of his shampoo. Now, he had rolled on his back, forcing his eyes to open for longer intervals after each attempt. He started to yawn, bringing a fist to his mouth before completing the action with a small whimper and jerky motions of his arms. I couldn't help but grin.

"What?" he asked.

"You. You're so adorable," I explained.

He sighed. "Glad *you* think so." He appraised me and frowned. "It's not fair. How do you look so good in the morning?" Eric leaned closer and sniffed me. "And smell so good?" He pretended to be annoyed. "You got up and brushed your teeth, didn't you?"

I shrugged. "Guilty. You were just sleeping the day away. I figured I might as well do something productive."

"And you brushed your hair," he accused.

"And showered, and still you slept. As I said, I saw no point in lollygagging just because you're a man of leisure."

"Ha! Carrington said to the man who's been doing all the cooking and cleaning since he arrived. And tomorrow, my company expects all employees returned to work since the area has its power back. So much for a life of leisure."

I frowned a bit. "I don't like to think about us going back to work."

He frowned too. "Me either. I wish this could go on forever."

I was thinking the same. "Perhaps you should rise and shower. Let's make the most of our last day together."

Eric's lips upturned into a mischievous grin. "We're already in bed. Want to start the day off with a bang?"

I shot him a smile. "You are insatiable. How can you still have fuel in the tank?"

He licked his upper lip. "Uh, I don't know. Just much younger than you, I guess."

I chuckled. "You little devil." I pounced on him and started to tickle him, causing him to scream with laughter, trying to squirm away from my attacks.

"Okay! Okay! I'm sorry," he screeched.

I ceased my torture, smirking at his shaking form. "There are consequences to naughtiness, Eric."

His expression indicated he had no intention of behaving. "Consequences like being forced to suck your dick?" He licked his lips again, then looked down at my rising staff.

"Incorrigible," I remarked.

Once he finished blessing me with sweet attention and letting me orgasm down his throat, he looked at me with big, brown puppy-dog eyes—my softening dick still wedged between his lips. I gasped. "How is it you look like such an angel, and yet you are so dirty at the same time?"

He let me fall from his mouth. "It's a gift, I guess."

I paused, rubbing the side of his face. "Hmm, that it is. Thank you for that lovely morning greeting."

He wiped his lips with the back of his hand. "Oh, it was my pleasure. Fellatio gagging is so much better than…lollygagging."

I snickered. "You best get your butt into that shower before it ends up over my knee."

Eric saluted, which made me laugh. Then he jumped off the bed and scampered away.

After we were both dressed, I spent the morning outside with Eric teaching me the rules of baseball. I had convinced him that I wanted to learn, and he started to warm to the idea. Before long, I was pitching the ball to him, proud of him for hitting it quite well. Of course, that meant me continuing to fetch the plastic toy wherever he knocked it. When he allowed me to take the bat, I wiggled my jean-clad ass whilst taking the batting position. That made him laugh, so I decided to do it every time he was ready to pitch me a ball. As Eric thought—maybe even feared—my natural athleticism did allow me to become quite proficient at batting. At first, he was surprised and complimentary, but he soon started to bemoan that I would be too good to play with him. I assured him that I would always want to play with him—baseball or otherwise.

"We've been out here for a couple of hours," he announced, not realizing it had been that long.

"The time flew. I was having fun, indeed. I like this game," I told him. "But I suppose the boys will be coming by soon and I need to check in back home."

Eric nodded, somewhat disappointed. "Maybe we can play some more the next time you visit."

I smiled—glad he wanted a next time. "I would like that. In fact, I may buy and ship some equipment to Yastarus so you and I can play there. There's enough acreage at the residence to play the hardball version you spoke of. Would you like that?"

He nodded, turning his face a bit to hide how he was beaming at the idea. "Um, I'll get the ball. You can just throw the bat by the porch. Mateo might want to play with me at some point."

I felt a stab of jealousy, but nodded and placed the bat by the steps. "Eric, I'll make that phone call now. It will be a short while, yes?"

"Okay," he shouted back to me, as he had crossed the length of the yard to retrieve the ball I had hit. "I'll just go into my studio while you're checking in. I have some pictures to delete."

"Good man," I yelled back, relieved that he had remembered. I went into the house, deciding to take the call from Eric's room so there would be no distractions.

Once I was connected to my office, I was told the vice president wished to speak with me. I was patched through. "Joseph," I greeted. "I trust all is going well."

"Mr. President, there is an issue," he responded, ignoring my greeting, worrying me that the concern was significant. "I just ended a call with Stefan. Has he already told you? I assume he's in a nearby room?" I was too embarrassed to tell the vice president that Stefan might still be cleaning up from being balls deep in another man across town.

"Uh, perhaps. He may be speaking with our host," I lied.

Joseph continued. "The individual who escaped capture — we've been able to make his accomplices talk. Mr. President, the individual at large was a member of our intelligence agency. Boris Smirnoff. He has been spying for Russia."

"What? How did they not vet him? They're intelligence!"

"Mr. President, there was nothing about his background to suggest an issue. He's been with intelligence for years and he was born in Yastarus. It seems he's had financial difficulties, making him vulnerable to nefarious solicitation from Russian intelligence. A once loyal citizen was turned against our country, sir."

"Joseph, since they know his identity, they can track him down," I reasoned.

"Yes, Mr. President. The thing is, since he was working with our intelligence team, he might be aware of where you are, as well as the alias you've been using. We've been sharing your whereabouts, the identity of Mr. Eric Turner and your travel arrangements with intelligence, thinking it was keeping you safe."

I groaned, feeling sweat over my upper lip. "Do they know if he's still in Yastarus?"

There was a pause on the other end of the line. "Mr. President, we don't. What we know is that he wasn't at his residence when law enforcement raided it. He's vanished. Smirnoff could be traveling using an alias, and he could be anywhere, including the United States. He's had a day to get away."

I felt a surge of panic and it wasn't for myself. My first thought was Eric, unguarded somewhere else on the property. "I must return home as soon as possible. I cannot put Mr. Turner in jeopardy, and I'm here with no security."

"Except for Stefan," Joseph stated. "He's a good man and he knows how to do his job, but you should have more than one person protecting you. So yes, you should both come home. Whilst speaking with Stefan, he agreed and said he will look for flights. In the meantime, I don't think I need to tell you that you should leave your current location. For his safety, Mr. Turner should go somewhere else until we can track and apprehend Smirnoff."

I wiped a hand over my now sweating face. "Yes, yes. Of course. I'll get to Eric — Mr. Turner — right now."

We disconnected, and I felt like someone had punched me in the stomach. It was then I heard a ruckus outside.

Chapter Nineteen

Eric

I had just finished deleting the 'naughty' photos of me and Carrington, leaving just the pictures of him clothed and the one of him shirtless. I put my camera in a locked cabinet when I heard a vehicle pulling up outside. Mateo and Stefan must have been returning from their all-night escapade, and though I was sorry to lose my alone time with Carrington, I was eager to learn how things were progressing for my friend.

I raced upstairs and out to the side porch by the driveway, surprised to see a parked car with a pizza delivery sign on its roof. A beefy, blond man emerged from the vehicle, opened the rear door and pulled out a large pizza box. He smiled, but it was one that looked forced or perhaps the type I might have seen on a sadist when they were hurting someone.

"Good day," he greeted in an indistinguishable accent.

"Hello," I responded. "Um, I didn't call for a pizza."

"No? Are you Mr. Howard?" he inquired, seeming perturbed. "This is the address he gave to me."

Carrington was using the alias of Carrington Howard, so it was possible he had put in the order. I was surprised he would have done so without first checking to see if I had started lunch. I didn't want to be paranoid, but I thought it best not to acknowledge a Mr. Howard being present. "I'm not Mr. Howard. I think you may have the wrong address."

He appeared impatient. "You are Mr. Turner, yes? Mr. Howard left instruction that you might accept pizza."

I squinted, trying to fathom how else this man would know my name unless Carrington had called in the pizza. Maybe he thought it would be a nice gesture to save me from cooking again? But a pizza? Carrington was dairy intolerant and didn't eat meat. Unless it was a Neapolitan pizza, it didn't make sense. "What kind did he order?"

The man's smile broadened. "Ah, so you are Mr. Turner. Yes, he ordered pizza. I'll bring it in and put on table for you."

Without waiting to hear my response, he walked past me and up to the screen door, ready to open it to enter. As he passed me, there was a strong smell of sausage or hamburger, or both. As he was reaching for the door handle, I raced for the plastic bat Carrington had dropped at the foot of the porch and raised it in a threatening a manner. "Who are you? Do not go into the house!"

The man looked surprised for a moment, then his face hardened as he shoved the pizza box at me. I almost toppled off the steps that rose to the screen door, but saved my balance at the last second. I swung the bat, but it hit the man's shoulder instead of the aimed-for head. He looked at me like I was an annoying mosquito, nothing to be feared but necessary to snuff. He dove at me, hurling both of us to the ground, my back hitting the sidewalk and the back of my head slamming into the pizza pie that had fallen out of the box. Before I could stop him, he was straddling me. The breath rushed out of me, and he kept any air from re-entering by squeezing my throat with his hands. I tried to squirm away from him, but he was much larger and I was beginning to weaken.

With what strength I could muster, I raised my knee up into his groin while using both hands to poke him in his eyes. He let out a cry, reaching for his eyes, allowing my lungs to refill. I was gasping, trying to roll him off me, but he was too heavy. I tried connecting to his groin again, but he anticipated that, moving up my body so my knee hit open air. He pushed my hands to the ground so I couldn't attack his now puffy red eyes—then brought his forehead down to mine with a loud cracking noise. I screamed in pain, dizzy from the blow and lack of oxygen.

"Eric!" It was Carrington, but I didn't know from where the voice sounded. I tried to yell back, but the goon's hands were back around my throat as he lifted and slammed my skull against the ground. Although the upper part of my body had shifted off the sidewalk to the grass, the force to my head was enough to make my teeth clatter.

My attacker must have sensed Carrington approaching behind him, as he released me and tried to vault to an erect position. He wasn't fast enough, as Carrington lifted the bat and connected it with the goon's head. It knocked him off balance, and Carrington used the moment to his advantage to continue driving blows to the man's skull. The pizza guy from Hell dropped to the ground, giving Carrington a chance to sit on his throat. Carrington turned to me. "Get something to tie him up!"

I knew I had rope in the garage, which was a few feet away. I struggled to my feet and sprinted to the building, pulling rope from a shelf before running back to Carrington. The intruder was trying to punch or kick Carrington, but he was short of breath from the pressure on his neck, his legs were kicking at air and Carrington was able to hold back his hands.

I raced over to tie rope around one of the man's wrists that Carrington was holding, then pulled his hand toward his other wrist so I could bind them together. "Make sure that's tight enough while I get his feet," I gasped out to Carrington.

I maneuvered to where the attacker's legs were flailing, trying to grab one of his ankles. He still had enough strength to use one of them to kick me in the ribs.

"Are you okay?" Carrington shouted.

"Yeah," I managed to breathe out. I grabbed the offending foot and wrapped rope around it — bringing it to his other foot and binding the ankles. I tied triple knots, worried that this walking weapon would still find a way to break free. I fell to the ground on my knees, panting, sweating and feeling like I'd collapse. The pizza guy started cursing and yelling something at Carrington in a foreign language. Carrington lifted the plastic bat and crashed it down once more on the guy's head.

"Shut up!" Carrington ordered.

It was then that I turned to survey my surroundings to ensure there were no other threats, and saw my neighbor Marietta standing by the curb. I imagined she might have watched the whole incident with horror. "Oh, hi, Marietta," I struggled to say.

Carrington shot me an incredulous expression, then looked at the still mortified Marietta. "He forgot the pepperoni!" he called to her, a snarl on his face. Marietta gasped, then hurried on her way. Carrington turned back to me and smirked. "You're right. She's annoying."

* * * *

While the police were at the house, Stefan returned alone. I wasn't sure if something bad had happened between him and Mateo, but with the cops milling about, it wasn't the time to ask. The detective in charge, after a long line of questioning and connecting with an American-based Yastarusian diplomat, was convinced that Carrington and Stefan were who they claimed to be. My small-town police department had not been expecting to respond to the attempted assassination of a foreign president.

Carrington let the officers sit in on a conference call with other U.S. and Yastarusian politicians, formulating a plan of next steps and sharing with the local law enforcement what they could. They made it clear that it was in the best interests of Yastarus that the details were not made public, and that the police report identified the incident as a home invasion. The town's detectives committed to taking the pizza guy into custody until he could be turned over to federal authorities, who would extradite him to Yastarus to stand trial.

The law enforcement officers shared with us that the delivery vehicle had been carjacked by our assailant, and the unsuspecting pizza employee had been knocked upside the head and left in the parking lot. We were glad to hear that he was going to be okay. Although the attacker refused to reveal his identity, Carrington explained to us that he was an individual named Boris Smirnoff who had infiltrated the Yastarus Intelligence Agency, and had eluded capture once his co-conspirators had been discovered.

After spending time with us, the police officers relaxed and even became a bit jovial, joking that this was going to be the highlight of their careers. One laughed about Marietta calling in the incident, reporting her 'sicko neighbor' had beaten and tied up a pizza delivery man for failing to put pepperoni on the pie. "What the hell gave her that crazy idea?" he snickered, causing the others to laugh as well. I shot Carrington a chastising look, but he just shrugged with the corner of his mouth uplifted.

Once everyone but Carrington and Stefan were gone, Carrington rushed to my side on the sofa. "Baby, are you okay? I wanted to check your injuries, but with them here…"

"I'm okay," I promised. He kissed the side of my head and touched my side where he had seen the spy kick me.

"I knew I shouldn't have left you," Stefan spat. "God, you could have been killed, Carrington." I guessed he didn't care if I had been.

Carrington chuckled. "Not with this tough guy here. Eric was wrestling that traitor to the ground."

My eyes went wide. Had he not seen that I was the one on my back with the guy's hands around my throat? I had been about a minute away from death. At least I had held him off long enough that he couldn't take Carrington by surprise. "Trust me, I would have been happy to have you here, Stefan," I muttered.

"How did you know he wasn't a legitimate pizza delivery driver?" Stefan wondered.

"Well, there were lots of warning signs, but once I smelled the cheese and meat, I knew there was no way Carrington had ordered it," I reasoned.

"So smart," Carrington murmured, pulling the side of my head to his lips again.

Stefan seemed uncomfortable watching the display of affection, so I did nothing to encourage it. "Uh, Stefan? Where's Mateo? Didn't he want to come?"

Stefan snorted. "Trust me, he wanted to—many times in the last twelve hours. I don't think he has any left in him."

Carrington moaned. "Okay, too much information."

Stefan snarled. "Complained the man who's been pawing his lover boy ever since the authorities left. At least I wasn't giving you a live performance."

Carrington's mood darkened. "What is wrong with you? Eric just took a beating because of me. After all he's done for us, can you not find it in you to be nice for just a minute?"

Stefan blanched, then softened. "Eric, my apologies, and thank you on behalf of the people of Yastarus for helping protect our president."

I nodded. "Thanks. Um, so why didn't Mateo come over? You didn't answer my question."

Stefan shifted from one foot to the next. "I had spoken with Yastarus authorities before coming here. I became aware of the threat. I didn't want to reveal our identities to Mateo and put him in danger. I told him that Carrington and I were successful in securing the modeling gig in the city and that we would be leaving this evening."

"This evening?" I squeaked.

Stefan turned to Carrington. "When I spoke with the vice president and with the head of intelligence, everyone felt it would be safer for you to return to Yastarus now, so I booked a flight from LaGuardia Airport at nine-forty this evening. I see no reason to change those plans just because the threat has been eliminated. You are needed back home, Mr. President."

I looked over to Carrington, hoping against hope there was a compelling reason for him to stay. I saw resignation in his eyes, though, and he nodded his head in agreement. "We don't have much time. That's in Queens, New York, yes?"

Stefan nodded. "We'll have to find a way into the city. If we leave within the hour, we should be able to get there in time for dinner before heading to the airport. I'll line up a drive on Uber."

I gulped, realizing that the remaining moments would entail them packing, then bidding me farewell. "Um, I can take you there."

Carrington seemed relieved. "Would you? That would be wonderful. Perhaps you'd join us for dinner before we depart."

Stefan wasn't enthused, but I was concerned with pleasing Carrington. And I wanted to spend more time with him. "Yes, I'll look up a place to eat and make reservations. You guys go pack."

Carrington gave me a sad smile, then pulled me into a kiss. "Eric, you'll come visit soon, yes? We'll make this work."

Those were the words I needed to hear in that moment.

Chapter Twenty

Carrington

Eric had been playing pop music whilst we were driving through Connecticut, which seemed to annoy Stefan. Each time I glanced back at him, he rolled his eyes or frowned. If it wasn't the music, it might have been Stefan being irritated by the looks of affection I continued to shower on Eric.

"Um, the traffic isn't as heavy as usual," Eric spoke. "I think we'll make our reservations all right."

"Thank you again for driving us," I offered, reaching over the console to place my hand on his thigh. Eric swallowed, taking a quick glance at me, smiling. I turned to look at Stefan in the back seat, and he either didn't notice or decided it was a good time to check his phone.

"Do you mind the music?" Eric asked Stefan, eyeing him in the rear-view mirror.

Stefan shrugged. "It's your car. Your choice to play what you fancy." He didn't lift his head from the screen.

Eric glanced at me, biting his lip. "Is it okay? I can put on something else."

I chuckled. "It's fine. I'm not familiar with most of the songs, but I've liked some of them."

Eric nodded, but turned down the radio a bit, allowing for us to tune it out if that was our preference. "It's my current playlist," he explained.

"Once I'm back in Yastarus, you can send me a list of songs that remind you of me," I smiled. "I'd like to listen to what you'd choose."

Stefan pretended to vomit, and I chose to ignore him.

Eric was too polite, however. I could tell he was compelled to draw Stefan into the conversation. "Um, Stefan, are you going to see Mateo again?"

I saw Stefan grimace. "Well, that will be quite difficult. Yastarus isn't right around the corner. It's not conducive to dating someone in Connecticut, is it?"

I was tiring of my friend's attitude and his blatant attempt to discourage Eric from maintaining a relationship with me was infuriating. "Maybe when you care about someone enough, you'll make the effort," I snapped.

Stefan clicked his tongue. "People say that, but then life and the many responsibilities interfere. Before long, good intentions become poorly executed actions until they cease altogether."

Eric looked miserable, and it made my head hurt. "Stefan, what happens between you and Mateo is your business. However, I will thank you not to project your negativity on me and Eric."

I massaged Eric's thigh, trying to reassure him that I was serious about us. He gave me a weak smile, but his eyes were dimmer than usual.

"How much longer?" Stefan whined like the impatient child on a long car journey.

I was thankful for the change of subject. Eric looked at the GPS before responding. "We should be at the restaurant in about twenty minutes."

"I hope it's not an establishment that plays ear candy," Stefan mumbled, getting in a jab about Eric's musical taste.

Eric reached over to turn off the radio. "For God's sake, I asked you enough times if it was bothering you. You could have just said yes."

We sat in silence until we reached our destination, but I continued to massage Eric's leg, hoping it would calm him.

I had been to New York City a few times before, and I gave Eric credit that he was brave enough to navigate his vehicle around its busy streets. It wasn't just the weaving of cars in various lanes, but also the people who thought crosswalks and pedestrian signs were suggestions. The noise was overwhelming. Horns were blaring as drivers vented their frustrations. Large trucks would come alongside our vehicle within millimeters, and the racket of their engines made me jump more than once. I was relieved once Eric pulled into a parking garage, handing his keys to a valet.

We walked through the bustling crowds of people, most of them sweaty, determined, and miserable. Once we found the restaurant, it was like an oasis with its air-conditioning and quieter din.

Stefan's mood was better once he was eating. I guessed the stress of the day, the ride and leaving

Mateo had all contributed to his earlier bout of unpleasantness. He even laughed at a joke Eric had made about the water, which I hadn't quite heard. It made me happy to see my friend starting to get along with my man.

Once the bill arrived, I insisted on paying it. I couldn't believe that Eric reached for his wallet considering all he had already done for us. I was relieved that he didn't argue when I pushed his hand back on the table. I didn't think he understood yet that I also liked to take care of him.

I was beginning to feel angst that the night was coming to an end, and I would be saying goodbye to Eric. I had meant what I had said about trying to maintain the relationship, but I knew being thousands of miles apart and both of us returning to work would be less than optimal. I was already fantasizing about the things Eric and I could do once he came for a visit.

With the bill paid, the three of us put our napkins on the table, readying to leave. Stefan took one more look at his phone, I assumed to check the flight status. "Shit," he muttered.

I felt a bit of hope, thinking the flight may have been canceled. "What is it?"

Stefan's face was pained. "We have a problem."

We all sat ourselves again, awaiting the news. "What?" Eric prodded.

"Mateo posted a picture of Carrington on Facebook. A shirtless photo," Stefan whispered.

"What?" I exclaimed. "You must be mistaken. There are no shirtless photos of me on the internet for him to have posted." I grabbed Stefan's phone to see what he was looking at. My mouth opened in horror. It was one of the pictures Eric had taken of me, evidenced by the background and furniture from his studio. I was reminded that I had posed shirtless, my jeans had been unbuttoned and unzipped, and I had been showing the waistband of a jockstrap. My hands shook as I scrolled to see what Mateo had typed.

Here's a great photo of a model, newcomer Carrington Howard. I had the pleasure of meeting him and his hot-as-you-know-what model friend, Stefan. What do you think of the picture? This was taken by my buddy, photographer Eric Turner. How about you all show him some love? He's so talented. If you're a model, reach out to Eric. He'll make sure you look good — not that Carrington needed much help. He and Stefan are going to set the world ablaze. So proud of my friends! — Mateo

I turned to Eric, and he could tell from my shocked expression that it was bad. He grabbed the phone from me and groaned. "What the fuck!"

"Fuck indeed! What have you done, Eric?" I accused, my voice rising enough that fellow diners looked over.

Eric swallowed and looked like a lost child. "I didn't give him this. I don't know how he got it."

I grabbed the phone back from Eric's shaking hand, reading more of the thread to see if people were commenting. That was when the nightmare became reality. One of the people replied to Mateo's post, writing *"Carrington Howard? That's Carrington Von Dorran — he's the president of Yastarus. Is this a doctored pic?"* Others started commenting, saying they had looked up photos of me online, and there was no question of the identity of the man in the photo. Several respondents were writing explicit remarks or innuendo, but the question kept popping up through the thread as to whether the photo was a fake.

"Give me the phone, I'll tell Mateo to take down the post," Stefan suggested.

"It's too late," I replied, somewhat dazed that this was happening to me. "It's been up for over an hour, and people have been re-posting it." I wiped a hand over my face, feeling sweat despite the air-conditioned room. "Shit! Fucking shit!"

"Carrington, I..." Eric began.

"Shut up, Eric," I spat, cutting him off. "Stefan, call Mateo. Maybe get him to post that it's a fake and an ill-conceived hoax."

Stefan nodded with uncertainty. "Okay. But Carrington, you belonged to the Pennington Knights football team. All the players saw you without your shirt many times. Past girlfriends have seen you, as well. Some of them are bound to tell people that they know the picture is real."

I closed my eyes, trying to block the voices shouting at me that I was stupid to have indulged in the photography, and even more idiotic to have trusted Eric. My anger toward him returned. "Eric, you knew the picture was private, didn't you?" He knew. I had stressed it several times. I was flailing.

Eric looked back and forth between the hostile faces of Stefan's and mine, his eyes welling with tears. "Carrington, I don't know how Mateo got the picture. I swear. It doesn't make sense."

I shook my head in disbelief. It was bad enough that he had betrayed my trust, but now he was sitting there lying to me. Even though I knew he was scared, I thought he was honest and strong enough to take accountability. Stefan had been right all along. I didn't know this man well. Before I could say anything, my own cell phone buzzed. It was my mother. As much as I hoped it was a social call, the timing led me to believe otherwise. I debated answering, but gave in. "Mother?"

"Carrington, the internet is blowing up. Everyone in our political party has been asking me if I know anything about that picture. Please tell me it's Photoshopped."

I sighed. When I didn't answer, she started ranting in our native language. "I'm sorry, Mother."

"What were you thinking? Did he goad you into posing shirtless—and unbuttoning the top of your trousers, no less? Did you know he was going to have Mateo promote his photography with it? Carrington, this is an utter mess. You're the President of Yastarus!" I didn't know that there was a good response, so I sat silent, suffering her punishing words. "I'm glad your father isn't alive to see this. He'd be devastated and humiliated. Everyone is asking me what I'm going to do—as if this is my burden to bear. You tell me what *you're* going to do."

"I don't know, Mother. I just learned of the leak a couple of moments ago," I explained. "Eric was driving me and Stefan to the airport."

"Do not even mention that man's name to me. I regret encouraging you to figure out what you wanted with him. Didn't I tell you to be discreet? This is the *furthest* thing from discretion—unless some photos of you naked pop up next."

I felt my cheeks heat. She was being sarcastic and not suspecting I had been *that* foolish. I glanced at Eric and prayed he wouldn't have shared the explicit photos. He was staring back at me, forlorn, a tear rolling down his cheek. I looked back at Stefan, too angry and disappointed to lock eyes with Eric. "Mother, maybe I could tell people I did it because we agreed it would be private — wanting a picture for myself only — to be able to look at it in the future and remember my days as a youthful man."

She paused. "I'm not sure you have much choice. But it *didn't* stay private. You'll have to tell them you bonded with Eric Turner when he sheltered us during the storm, and regretfully, you showed a serious lack of judgment by trusting him to take the photo. It will be scandalous, but survivable."

At this point, a salacious story about my vanity, wanting a shirtless picture keepsake, seemed like a gift. Providing the other photos and my indiscretions with Eric stayed buried, I could ride out the embarrassment. "Very well. Mother, have our public relations team put together and release a statement from me to that effect. Please review it before its release to ensure it minimizes the damage as much as possible."

"Carrington, I don't need to tell you — you can't have another bombshell follow this one. Ensure Eric Turner's silence regarding anything you two did together. You need to convince him that we will bring the full weight of the Yastarus government against him if he tries to profit off your...whatever it was."

I choked back a cry, thinking it was love. How had everything gone to shit so fast? "Yes. I will. Mother, Stefan and I must depart or we'll miss our flight."

"Be prepared," she warned. "Once reporters sniff out the flight you'll be on, you'll be landing into a press orgy. Just keep repeating that you released a statement and you have nothing to add. Agreed?"

"Yes. Yes, I understand." I leaned my forehead into my open hand. "Mother, I'm so sorry."

There was another pause, then her voice softened. "I know you are. We've all made mistakes, Carrington. Try not to make future ones as asinine as this one. You'll get through it. I'll see you in a few hours."

"Thank you, Mother. Bye," I said before disconnecting. I looked over to Stefan, who was frowning, awaiting the plan. "They'll be releasing a statement on my behalf, stating that in a foolish moment of vanity, I asked Mr. Turner to take the photo of me, wanting it for the future to remember my youth. We had an agreement that it was for me alone, but he had released it—much to my embarrassment. It will say that I hope the people of Yastarus will forgive my serious error in judgment."

Stefan nodded. "It's not like other political leaders haven't been caught shirtless—or worse. It will blow over."

I glanced at Eric, who was fidgeting with his cell phone. "I think it's best Stefan and I leave from here in a taxi cab. Thank you for driving us this far."

Eric's eyes went wide, his mouth quivering. "But I've been trying to contact Mateo to find out how he got the picture. He hasn't responded."

"I don't care," I mumbled without emotion. "What difference does it make now?"

Another tear ran down his face. "Because his explanation might prove I'm telling you the truth. You're telling the world I betrayed you. I didn't."

I looked past him, not wanting to feel empathy for his pitiful state. "Eric, I was at your house, remember? Mateo never went down to your basement when I was there. There's only one way the photo could have made its way to him."

"I've been trying to figure that out," he cut in. "I was wondering if I had a setting on the camera that would have sent him photos as I took them. I've had the camera for a couple of years, and he helped me set it up. I don't think it can do that. I don't remember us doing that, and I don't know why I would have done that, but nothing is making sense."

"For your sake, you had better hope you didn't do something so fucking stupid," I snarled. "That would mean he has all the photos. All of them. Are you that incompetent that you'd set up something like that and not remember it? Why would you do that?"

He started inaudible crying. "I wouldn't! I mean, I'm sure I didn't. I don't know."

His explanation was implausible—downright ridiculous, in fact, for someone with an alleged genius IQ. If he was so desperate that he would spin a tale that made him sound like an imbecile, he had to be covering a lie. "Let me be clear, if anything else comes out that embarrasses me in any way, I will use my power to ruin you."

Eric was gasping, trying to stop himself from crying. He shot Stefan a pleading look, which was met with more iciness than I was projecting. "Carrington... please..."

"Goodbye, Eric," I responded in a clipped tone. I motioned to Stefan that it was time for us to leave. I didn't look back at Eric. Despite my anger, there was a small part of me that wanted to console him. I guessed I couldn't just flip a switch to turn off what I had begun to feel for him, but returning to Yastarus was a start.

Once we were out of the restaurant, I experienced a mild panic attack. Alarmed, Stefan grabbed my arm and was rubbing my back as I began gasping for air. He sat me down on the sidewalk, and true to New York City's reputation, nobody paid attention to us.

"It will be okay, Carrington," Stefan soothed, hand on my shoulder.

"Will it, though?" I rasped. I knew I would make it through the scandal, but I had lost so much more. I had been in love for the first time in my life, and like so many times in the past, the partner in my relationship had used me for their own gain. Maybe it was the universe's payback for breaking Stefan's heart.

"Come on," Stefan urged once my breathing had normalized, putting an arm under my armpit to lift me from the pavement. "Let's get out of this place. Time to go home."

* * * *

Stefan and I were in the airline's private lounge, awaiting the announcement to begin boarding the plane. Neither he nor I had said much since hailing the taxi. Anything we had to say would have been redundant and unhelpful.

I tried to focus on how I'd respond to questions from reporters and fellow countrymen, but thoughts of Eric continued creeping into my head. I tried to think of any possible explanation for how Mateo could have secured the photo without Eric's assistance, but nothing made sense. It was obvious Eric was guilty.

However, I was beginning to believe he hadn't pushed Mateo to release the photo to bolster his photography career. His shock at seeing the photo on Mateo's Facebook page seemed real enough. He might have showed off to Mateo, asking him to keep the picture to himself, thinking he could trust him — just as

I had trusted Eric. His naïveté regarding the difficulty for a sitting president to explain a leaked shirtless photo was surprising. I wasn't a pop celebrity. I blamed myself for thinking a twenty-six-year-old would be mature enough to comprehend the consequences. It made me reassess, concluding Eric wasn't selfish—he just needed to grow up. I wished I had realized that in the moment and parted more amicably. A relationship would be a mistake, but believing I could stop caring about him was wishful thinking.

Stefan's cell phone began to buzz. He looked at it, then mouthed to me that it was Mateo. I leaned in closer so I could hear the conversation.

"Where have you been? I've been trying to reach you," Stefan shouted.

"I've been talking to Eric. Dude, why the hell didn't you tell me the truth? You said you were models. Now I find out Carrington is the president of Belarus!"

"Yastarus," Stefan corrected with irritation.

"Whatever! Jesus, it's a shit storm. I've had people from your government calling me to tell me to remove the photo. They've been asking if I doctored the picture. What the fuck, man?"

"How did you get the photo?" Stefan snapped.

There was a pause on the other end of the line. "From you."

Stefan looked at me, his face draining of color. "What are you talking about? I didn't give you that photo."

"Last night, when you told me to order us take-out. I went to call the local Chinese place, but my phone was dead. It died during the power outage, and I forgot to charge it at Eric's house. I figured I would use your phone. I was going to ask you for the password, but then I saw you didn't have one, and the picture of Carrington was your screensaver."

Stefan started to turn his face and the phone away from me, but I pulled his chin back in my direction. His cheeks were flushed, fear in his eyes. "Mateo…"

"Dude, I'm sorry. I thought you two were struggling models. You both seemed to have no clue how to ignite your careers. I figured there was no harm in sending myself the photo of Carrington. It was just a shirtless picture that every male model has in their portfolio. I knew Eric took the photo because I recognized the background studio. It was a great picture and I thought I could help you all. How was I to know Carrington's the fucking president of Belarus?"

"Jesus," Stefan muttered, putting his face in his free hand. I wondered if he did so to hide from my death glare.

"I told Eric how I got the photo, and he wanted to know how you got it. He told me he didn't give it to you," Mateo continued.

"Shit," Stefan answered.

"Never mind. You know what, I don't care," Mateo cut in. "I know you guys are all pissed about the scandal and all that bullshit, but what I care about is Eric. He's a mess, man."

I lurched forward and pulled the phone from Stefan's hand. "Mateo, it's Carrington. Where's Eric?"

"Dude, he's going to do something stupid. You need to help him," Mateo pleaded.

"Mateo, where is he?" I pressed, growing worried.

"He's hurt, Carrington. He was crying and I couldn't understand everything he was saying. It was something about how you wouldn't believe him, even though he was telling you the truth about everything.

Then he started going on about how you had left him just like his mother did, abandoning him in the city with nothing but a look of hatred."

"Oh God." I swallowed. Acid rose in my chest.

"Carrington, what the fuck man? How could you re-traumatize him like that? He kept sobbing, saying he loved you but he realized that he's not somebody worth loving back."

I wanted to beg Mateo to stop. Every word was ripping me like an eagle with its prey. "Mateo, where is he?" I pushed.

"He's still in the city," he answered. "I'm on my way down there to try to find him. He told me he's going to Manny's."

"Who is that?" I asked, ready to rush there as soon as I disconnected from Mateo.

"It's a gay bar. More like a nightclub, I guess. He and I used to go there a lot, until Eric started getting a reputation as the guy who wouldn't put out. People started harassing him, calling him a cock tease and shit. They didn't get that he's kind of broken, you know? He's been waiting for some knight in shining armor, and I tried telling him that those are characters in fairy tales for a reason — they don't exist."

"Mateo, focus," I pleaded.

"Eric told me that what I used to say was right, that white knights don't exist. He said he's going to do what he should have done a long time ago. He said he was going to Manny's to, as he put it, get hammered and nailed by everyone who gives him a second look because there's no such thing as love — just men who want to use him, and he was going to let them. I was like, dude, what are you talking about? You'll let guys—plural—have you? This is Eric we're talking about. He's screwed up bad."

"God." The word came out strangled.

"Carrington, I asked him to please not do this. I reminded him that he's upset and not thinking straight. I told him he could get hurt, and he replied that's what he wants. Can you believe that? He said he's hoping they will hurt him because he'd rather feel the physical pain than what he's feeling now. Carrington, you need to go to Manny's to stop him. I'm driving down, but I'm still a long way away."

"Give me his number, Mateo!" I had intended to ask Eric for his phone number before we had parted, but with the way things had ended, I never had. "I'll call him."

"I'll text you the number, but, dude, it won't do any good. He told me to leave him alone and that he was shutting off the phone. I've been trying to call him back, but it just keeps rolling to voicemail."

I put my thumb and forefinger to the bridge of my nose, trying to stop the pain that was now coursing through. "Text me anyway. I'll keep trying. In the meantime, we'll head over to Manny's. Where is it?"

"It's in the Village. I'll text you the address," he rushed. I heard a beeping horn followed by a stream of swears.

"Mateo? What's going on? Are you okay?" I panicked.

"Yeah," he mumbled. "There's a reason they tell you not to text and drive. Shit. I almost drove into an oncoming car. Okay, you should have the address on Stefan's phone now. I'm hanging up. Go get him!"

I looked down at the 'messages' icon, pressed it and saw the text come through from Mateo. I threw the phone back at Stefan. "Get us to that address now!"

"Carrington, I can explain…"

I held up a hand to silence him. "Stefan, right now, my priority is getting Eric safe. Did you hear any of what Mateo said?"

Stefan nodded with a frown. "Carrington, I'm so sorry. I swear, I thought Eric shared the photo with Mateo. I shouldn't have gone into the studio to look at the pictures. It's just that when you told me that you and Eric had done that risqué photo shoot, I was jealous. The old feelings came back and I was upset that he was getting so much of you after just two days, and I was miserable for so many years. I saw the picture, and I just wanted a little bit of you for myself."

I looked at him like he had lost his mind. "Stefan, I can't even…talk with you right now. I need to get Eric. Do you understand? If anything happens to him, I'll never forgive you. I'll never forgive myself."

He nodded. Having a mission seemed to steady him, and he pulled me through the airport, leading me to where a sign indicated taxi cabs were waiting. "Our luggage," he reminded me. "We checked it. All we have are our overnight bags."

"I don't give a fuck," I snapped. "Just get me to the address on your phone now."

Chapter Twenty-One

Carrington

We hadn't talked in the taxi. Stefan tried dialing Eric's number a few times, but each attempt ended with Stefan giving me a defeated look.

I was busy wringing my hands and trying to calm myself through slow, steady breathing. For his part, Stefan looked crestfallen. Except for when he dialed Eric, he kept his eyes on the passing view, seeming as though he wasn't seeing it.

I knew the Village was quite a ride from the airport, and we still had several minutes before we would reach our destination. I blew out a breath, staring down at my lap. "Stefan, I just don't understand how you could have invaded my privacy like that."

I didn't look to him, but I felt his sad eyes on me. "I know I shouldn't have. I went downstairs at his house to make sure everything was secure, and the camera was lying out on the table and I thought, I'll just look at one picture. I felt horrible about it, telling myself that I was a better man than that. You need to understand, I've idolized you for years. I thought that seeing a picture of you naked would...I don't know, give me closure or something."

I shook my head, still not making eye contact with him. "They weren't your pictures to see."

"I know," he whispered. "I have no excuse. The temptation was overwhelming. I saw the pictures of you clothed, and you looked so happy. Carrington, you were looking at the camera — at Eric — with love in your eyes. It made me cry. I don't know why. I thought I was over you. I think I am over you. It's just that it hurt me that I spent so much time hoping for you to look at me like that. I kept scrolling and saw...well, a lot. I'm not proud of it, but I couldn't stop looking. Seeing you naked and doing things I fantasized about. It was like telling a starving person to look away from a banquet. I thought if I could just burn the images in my head, I would never need anything more from you than the fantasies."

I sighed. "You realize you sound like a sick stalker right now, don't you?"

His voice cracked. "Yes. I felt even more disgusted with myself that I resented the photos of Eric. I could see he was looking at you with the same sense of awe, and it made me feel like something was stolen from me. The fact that he looked so...amazing and hot just made me feel worse — like the old guy who'd been tossed aside for a newer, sexier version."

I glared at him. "You can't be tossed aside if I never had you. It's all been in your head." He nodded. "How did you get the picture to your phone? Please tell me it's the only one you stole."

He bowed his head in embarrassment. "I wanted the ones of your ass in the jock strap, but I knew that it would be risky for you if I put those on my phone. I settled for the one of you shirtless, thinking I could explain it away if anyone ever saw it. Once I realized there was a USB cable near the camera, I connected it to my phone and transferred the photo."

I wiped my sweaty upper lip. "And made it a screensaver? And what kind of security person doesn't password-protect their phone?"

He grimaced. "One who deserves to be chastised?"

I looked out through the window and saw the hundreds of lights shining from windows, wondering how so many people could be packed into one small area. "You realize you cost me everything?"

I heard him whimper. "Carrington, you can stick to your public statement and the scandal will blow over."

I was too tired to be angry. I shook my head. "No. The statement impugns Eric's integrity. I'm going to tell people the truth—about everything."

"What? You can't do that. Carrington, they'll want you to resign," Stefan protested.

"I know," I replied in a dead tone.

"Eric may not even take you back. You're willing to give up the presidency even if he rejects you?"

I resumed looking at the many windows of the city. I reminded myself that there were hundreds of people behind those curtains who were dealing with worse than losing a job they didn't even want. I had the means to start over. "Yes, even if he rejects me. I won't lie to the people of Yastarus. I shouldn't have allowed the statement to go out." I rested my elbow on the door's armrest, leaning my mouth against my fist, feeling more disappointment with myself than with Stefan. "I shouldn't have doubted Eric, either. I should have listened to him. I'm as much to blame for the way things turned out as you are."

We were silent for a few more minutes before Stefan cleared his throat. "Carrington, do you think you can ever forgive me?"

I didn't answer for a long while. I didn't know. I wasn't trying to be cruel. I just couldn't think and I didn't want to say yes, then spurn him later. I didn't want to say no, because I wasn't sure that was true either. My head hurt and my heart ached, and I was frightened about what Eric might be doing, or who might be hurting him. "Let's just find Eric, okay? I don't feel like talking anymore."

* * * *

When we arrived at Manny's, my energy had returned and I was eager to run into the club to find Eric. There was a line of patrons waiting to enter the establishment. All I could think was that every passing moment was another where Eric could be doing something he'd regret.

"Stefan, we cannot wait in this queue. Talk to the doorman. Tell him I'm the president of Yastarus," I instructed.

Stefan looked back at me like I had been whacked in the head. "A president wanting entrance to a gay bar? Oh, that won't add to the scandals."

"I don't care," I replied. "I need to get to Eric." Stefan shook his head no. "Fine, I'll go tell him myself."

Stefan stopped me with a hand to my chest. "Let me talk to him." He went to the doorman and I saw them both look back at me. Stefan leaned in close to the guard, whispering something in his ear. After what seemed like eternity, Stefan turned to me and waved for me to join them at the door. I anticipated protests from the waiting crowd, but they remained silent. Perhaps they were used to some people receiving special treatment. The doorman motioned for the two of us to enter the club.

"Scandal avoided," Stefan muttered to me.

"How's that?" I asked.

"I used one hand to slip him a hundred, and I used the other hand to grope him," Stefan explained. "Let me just remind you — bald, tattooed daddies are *not* my type."

"Thank you," I offered in response to his sacrifice. I started scanning the club, looking for Eric. The place was packed. It wouldn't be easy to find him in the crowd, as Eric was a head shorter than most of the clientele.

"Let's split up," Stefan suggested. "If I find him first, I'll text you. You do the same if you locate him."

"Okay," I agreed. Stefan cut to the right-side of the club, so I went to the left side. It was the part of the room that was nearest the bar. There were several tables and chairs with a view of the dance floor. After pushing my way through the throngs of people, I found Eric sitting in a corner booth with a young, muscular, striking man of Asian descent. As I moved closer, the man put his hand on Eric's arm, which Eric pulled away. The man started laughing, putting his hand back on the arm. Eric shot him a look that made it obvious the gesture was unwanted. Nevertheless, the man reached his other hand beneath the table, causing Eric to jump a bit.

I bounded toward their table, pushing annoyed people out of my way. "Get the fuck off him," I demanded of Eric's companion.

The music was so loud, I wasn't sure if they had even heard what I said. The man looked up at me with a questioning glance. "What was that?"

"I said, get your hands off him."

The guy laughed. "I was here first."

I looked over at Eric. Close up, I could see his eyes were glazed and his body was wobbling. "How much have you had to drink?"

Eric gave me a confused look. "Carrington?"

"Come, Eric. I'm taking you out of here."

"Like hell you are," the companion shot. "Eric and I were getting to know each other, and I'm looking forward to getting to know him *even better*. So why don't you run along and find someone more...your own age."

"How about you run along before I rearrange your face?" I spat.

Eric emitted a drunken giggle, staring at nothing in particular. "Rearrange your face," he repeated like it was the punchline in a comedy.

The companion did not find it amusing. He stood and I realized he was taller and more muscular than me. "Ass wipe, if you don't get away from me, what will be rearranged is your gender when I cut off your dick and feed it to the rats outside."

I saw the next scandal happening within seconds. The headline would read that the president of Yastarus was beaten up by a rival for his male lover in a NYC gay club. My mother would have a coronary. I figured before going there, I should try to dial back the hostility I had created. "Look, I don't want trouble. Eric is...my boyfriend. He and I had an unfortunate misunderstanding. He's incapacitated and I wish to get him home."

The rival smirked. "Aw, sweet. So, I'm supposed to just walk away after investing six drinks into your puppy? Don't think so. It isn't like he's been protesting, and he didn't tell me he had a boyfriend. So, either you're full of shit, or he's not interested in a reconciliation. But since I'm a nice guy, if you apologize, you can join us at my place. I'll let you watch me fuck his little ass."

I clenched my fists. Just as I was about to raise my arm, it was restrained and a hand was placed on my left shoulder. "Hi, buddy. Who's your friend?" Stefan asked.

"What?" I asked, confused.

Eric started snickering, his head lolling a bit. "Popular place."

"Now who the fuck are you?" my rival asked Stefan.

"He'll be the guy who helps me rearrange your face." I smiled.

That had Eric laughing some more. "Rearrange your face." His hands were resting on the table, and he dropped his face onto them.

"Fuck this," the guy snarled. "I guess you two girls need to gang up to win a fight. I'll make Eric my little bitch the next time he comes here, and I'm sure he will. He could do better than an old guy like you." With that, he pulled Eric's head up by his hair, and leaned into his face. "Until we meet again, sugar tits." He forced an obscene kiss on Eric's mouth whilst pawing one of Eric's nipples through his cotton pullover. I tried to bolt over to the creep so I could punch him upside the head. Stefan was holding me back, causing my tormentor to bellow a laugh. "Until I can collect the balance, that's the down payment on what he owes me."

I flipped out my wallet and threw a hundred-dollar note at him. "Paid off. How about you roll the bill and shove it up your ass?"

The guy barked a laugh, leaving the money on the table. "No thanks. I prefer my debts paid off in other ways." He turned back to Eric. "I'll keep an eye out for you." The man glared at me and Stefan, then brushed by me with enough force to knock me into my friend. I was about to follow him, but Stefan restrained me once more.

"Let it go," Stefan commanded. "You and Eric won't be back here, so it's moot."

I *hoped* Eric wouldn't be back here. I looked over to him, and it was clear to me that he was in an alcoholic fog. He was muttering to himself. "Don't grab me. Don't like being grabbed."

"Jesus!" Mateo's voice boomed behind me and Stefan. "You found him." Stefan and Mateo exchanged uneasy glances, then hugged.

"Just in the nick of time," Stefan said. "Carrington was about to…get his ass kicked by a suitor of Eric's."

"Was not," I protested. "If you hadn't stopped me…"

"Rearrange your face." Eric chuckled, head still down on the table.

"What's up with him?" Mateo asked.

"Drunk as a skunk," Stefan responded. "How are we getting him out of here?"

Now that the adrenaline rush was over, I looked at Eric and felt immense remorse. My poor broken guy — broken because of me.

"Carrington, focus!" Mateo barked, mirroring what I had said to him earlier on the phone.

"What?"

"Come on, help us guide Eric out of here," Mateo demanded.

I nodded and the three of us were trying to prop up Eric to his feet. He was alternating between chuckles and complaints. "Sleepy. Just let me lie down on the couch over there."

"No can do, buddy," Mateo told him. "Once you're asleep, you'll be out for hours. We're taking you out of here."

"Where's your car?" I asked Mateo.

"In a parking garage a couple of blocks down."

Stefan was applying a lot of strength to keep Eric upright. "Christ, I don't know if we'll make it. He's dead weight."

"We can't drive back to Connecticut with him like this," I reasoned. "What if he gets sick on the drive?"

Mateo nodded. "He will, too. He gets carsick when he's not driving, and that's when he's sober. I don't think there are many places we could pull over until we're out of the metro area. Plus, he parked his car somewhere here in the Village. We can't just leave it."

"Stefan, can you get us hotel rooms?" I asked.

We sat Eric down, watching him fall into a lifeless pile. He wasn't even muttering anymore, and I was beginning to worry that he might need medical attention.

After a couple of minutes, Stefan turned to us with a grimace. "There's just one available room in the city, unless we wish to stay in a fleabag. Should I grab it? It has two double beds."

"Yes," I responded. "Let's get him somewhere comfortable."

Once Stefan confirmed the room, the three of us lifted Eric again, making our way out of the club — more dragging than walking him. There were several patrons watching with expressions that signaled disgust or amusement. It wasn't until we reached the doorman that someone seemed empathetic.

"Rough night for this one, huh?" he asked Stefan, maybe remembering the tip and the one-second hand job.

"I think he overdosed on ear candy today," Stefan quipped. "That club music is God-awful, dude."

Dude? Stefan was already picking up the Mateo and Eric lingo. The doorman just laughed and shrugged. We spent several minutes pulling Eric down the street, his tennis shoes skimming the pavement as he made a few attempts to take steps on his own. The three of us were sweating and panting once we had Eric secured and strapped in the back seat of Mateo's car. "Don't let him puke on my seats," Mateo commanded, implying I should sit in the back with Eric. I was happy to.

As Mateo drove uptown, I used the opportunity to take Eric's hand in mine. He looked so fragile, lying with his head falling to the side, a noticeable bruise where the assassin had pounded him earlier in the day. "I'm so sorry, baby," I whispered to him.

Getting Eric into the hotel from its parking garage was the latest challenge. It would have been easier to lift him and carry him, but I knew that would draw more scrutiny and could bar us from entering. Mateo and I lingered in the back of the lobby, propping up Eric as Stefan carried our overnight bags and checked us in at the front desk. When it appeared the desk clerk was distracted helping another customer, Mateo and I dragged Eric down the hall to the elevator banks.

"You need to check in at home, Carrington. There's going to be a lot of worry as to why you're not on the flight you said you'd be on and most of your luggage is," Stefan reminded me.

I nodded. "When we get in the room, I'll call Mother to tell her. It will be early morning there, so I'm sure to get another earful for waking her."

"If you end up resigning, maybe you should just stay in the United States." Stefan grinned. "You may not want to face the people of Yastarus."

"You're resigning?" Mateo asked wide-eyed.

I cocked my head toward Eric. "Let's handle one crisis at a time, shall we?"

The elevator pinged and the door opened. There were no others in the car and we were able to rest Eric against a rail as we rode to the twenty-third floor. As the elevator door opened, Mateo and I struggled to get our arms under Eric's armpits to help him along. The door began to close since our progress was slow, and Stefan had to push it back open for us.

"To hell with it," I stated to neither of them. I lifted Eric into my arms. "Eric, baby, put your arms around my neck. Will you do that for me? It will be easier to carry you."

Eric seemed to have enough mental functioning to comprehend, as he clasped the back of my neck. With one forearm under his back and another under his buttocks, I walked him to our door. A couple emerged from a nearby room just as Stefan was inserting the card key.

"Oh, just married?" the man asked, though I could tell from his expression that he was skeptical. His female partner tried to smile, uncertain if he had guessed right.

"Um, sure," I replied.

"Then what are the other two guys doing with you?" the woman asked.

"Uh...well, in my country, the bridal bed has to have witnesses to ensure you consummated the marriage." I pushed Eric through the open door before they could throw us additional questions.

Once the door closed, Mateo burst out laughing. "That was the first thought that came to your head? Oh my God. You should have seen their faces. They'll be telling people that story for the next year."

I lowered Eric's limp body onto the bed closest to the bathroom, figuring he might want quick access. I hovered over him, stroking his hair and brushing my thumb over his cheek. "My sweet Eric."

"Uh, not to be a killjoy, but I wouldn't go assuming he's your anything," Mateo warned. "You wounded him, Carrington."

I nodded, feeling like all my muscles were being twisted by some strange force. "Of course. I'll refrain from such comments."

Mateo put a hand on my back to show support. "Come on, let's get him undressed. If he pukes on those clothes, he won't have anything clean to wear for the drive home tomorrow."

Stefan took a seat on the opposite bed. Mateo and I pulled the shirt over Eric's head. Mateo started to fold it as I undid Eric's belt buckle and lowered his zipper. "I'll hold up his bum. You pull off his jeans," I told Mateo.

Once Eric was down to his undergarments, Mateo let out a gasp, taking a long look at him. "What the hell happened?" He was pointing at the large bruise under Eric's rib cage as well as a couple of others near his throat that were visible once his shirt was removed. "I noticed earlier his forehead was bruised, too. Carrington, so help me God, if you abused him…"

I held up my hand in protest. "I most certainly did not, nor would I ever. It's a long story. Suffice it to say, we encountered a potential assassin, and Eric brought him to the ground whilst I subdued him. Eric was very courageous, indeed."

Mateo looked at me with horror. "Are you fucking kidding me?"

"I can assure you I'm not."

Mateo looked over at Stefan, who nodded that it was true. "I should have been there," Stefan said. "It's a good thing your friend is quite the soldier."

At this point, Eric, upon hearing the word 'soldier,' started mumbling. "Gonna rearrange your face," he muttered in an affected tough-guy tone, punching his fists at the air despite his closed eyes. "Gonna rearrange it."

I couldn't help but smile. I put his hands back down to his sides and kissed his forehead. "Okay, Tiger. You got him. Good job. Get some well-earned sleep now."

Mateo still had a look of incredulity. "You treated him like shit after he put his life in danger for you?"

Mateo might as well have punched me in the face. The blow was as harsh. "I…"

"You don't deserve him," Mateo spat. "He's too good for you."

I nodded, feeling great sadness. "Indeed. He is."

Mateo took off his shirt, his eyes still shooting darts at me. "I will sleep in bed with Eric tonight. When he wakes, I want him seeing somebody he trusts and knows will take care of him."

What could I say? His comment was more than fair. I hadn't proven myself trustworthy and, as much as I liked to think I would be the one who would take care of Eric, I had failed when a challenge had arisen. "Yes, I think that's wise," was all I could manage.

I watched as Mateo climbed into bed with Eric, pulling him into an enviable embrace. Instead, after a bruising call with my mother, I undressed and shared a bed with Stefan. Whilst he was awake, there was an awkwardness and tension lingering. I had made everyone in the room miserable and if there had been any other accommodations, I would have taken them. Instead, I lay on my back, staring at the blackness of the darkened room, wondering if there would ever be light in my life again.

Chapter Twenty-Two

Eric

I awoke to the noise of nearby chatting. The room was too bright, hurting my eyes when I struggled to open them. Everything but the people was unfamiliar. Mateo was sitting on the bed next to me. He was engaged in conversation with Stefan, who sat across from him on another bed. Someone was in the bathroom, as I heard water running into a sink or tub.

"Where are we?" I groaned. My head was pounding and though they had been whispering, it all seemed too loud.

"You're awake?" Mateo smiled. "I was worried about you."

I could tell from the room configuration and the furnishings we were in a hotel, but I didn't remember checking into it. I couldn't remember much about last night, other than going to Manny's after the terrible incident with Carrington. "What are you doing here? What is this place?" I managed.

"We came to get you," Mateo explained. "You were pretty wasted last night. We're at the Marriott Marquis in Times Square."

"Oh," was all I could muster. I dropped my head back onto the pillow, closing my eyes to block the glare.

I heard the bathroom door open, followed by Carrington's voice. "He's still out?"

I wondered why he was here. I didn't want to re-open my eyes. I didn't think I could look at him. Maybe I could pretend I had fallen back to sleep.

"He's up," Mateo, the traitor, announced. Mateo reached over to shake my leg. "Come on, Eric. We need to check out by eleven. We've let you sleep as long as we could."

I pushed his hand off my leg. "Don't grab me. I don't like being grabbed," I mumbled, still refusing to open my eyes.

I could feel Mateo's breath as he leaned closer to my face. "So grouchy in the morning. Listen, Stefan and I are going down to the lobby for their free coffee. When we return, you need to be dressed and ready to leave, okay? We'll get your car where you parked it, then you can follow me back to Connecticut."

I opened my eyes. Carrington was looking down at me from the foot of the bed. I tried to discern his expression. It looked like concern, but I reminded myself that I was good at misreading him. "Take him with you," I told Mateo. Carrington reacted like I had twisted his heart with my bare hand, then frowned and nodded.

"No," Mateo declared. He put a hand on my chest, applying the slightest of pressure. "He's staying because you two need to talk."

I rubbed my eyes, the mortification starting to set in that the three men were looking at my half-naked body. I grabbed the sheet and pulled it up to my shoulders. "Why are we here again? I didn't ask to come."

"Half hour," was Mateo's response. "You talk, brush your teeth, wash, get dressed. And hurl if you need to. There isn't a lot of time. Clock's ticking."

"I think Carrington said everything he needed to tell me yesterday," I mumbled.

Carrington remained quiet. Mateo piped up instead. "I'm not sure he did. I know *you* didn't tell him everything you needed to say, and here's your chance before he leaves for Belarus."

I looked over at Carrington. "Why are you going to Belarus?"

Carrington was about to answer, but Mateo cut him off. "Eric, you had way too much to drink last night. Your synapses are haywire. He needs to go home...Belarus? Duh. Now, have your talk. Stefan and I will be back in..." — he looked at his watch — "twenty-seven minutes."

After Stefan and Mateo left the room, Carrington stood motionless, looking fearful. I was relieved that he wasn't angry or ready to attack me some more. I figured by now Stefan and Mateo must have told him what had happened with the photograph, so maybe Carrington wanted to apologize before he left. If it was an apology, we could be done in a minute.

"Is it okay if I sit on the other bed?" Carrington asked.

I shrugged. "I assume you paid for the room. Who am I to stop you?"

He grimaced, but made his way to the edge of the other bed, sitting so he could face me. I hoisted my body up on the bed so I was sitting, leaning back against the headboard and crossing my arms. My body ached from the beating from the day before, or maybe from the booze or from both. I sighed, waiting for the apology or more tongue-lashing, hoping he'd make it quick.

"Eric, Mateo explained everything," Carrington whispered. "I am so sorry."

I looked away from him, casting my eyes on the bathroom door as if it was the most interesting piece of architecture I'd ever seen. "Okay."

I heard him swallow. I felt a bit of satisfaction that he was picking up my embarrassing habits. "Eric, I don't blame you if you don't forgive me. I have no right to ask you to do so. But I'm going to anyway. I was cruel and selfish. Despite the memories you've given me, I fear last night's will be the one that remains most prominent. I'm...ashamed."

I turned to face him, and I was surprised how defeated and sad he appeared. I realized he meant it. "Okay. I forgive you."

He smiled a bit. "Does that mean..."

I felt a bit of anger rise. "Mean what, Carrington? That I want to jump on your lap? No, that's not what it means."

It was the second time it appeared Carrington had just been given a wallop upside the head. "I wasn't suggesting..."

"I trusted you. You told me I could. You told me you trusted me! It was all bullshit, Carrington. As soon as something got a little rough for you, you turned on me. You wouldn't even listen to me!"

He shook his head. "Yes, true..."

"I should have realized when you lied to me right from the beginning about who you are, *that you lie about who you are!*"

He nodded, then looked down at his hands. "Yes, all very fair. Mateo told me I don't deserve you. He was correct, of course." He looked back up, a tear rolling down his cheek. "I'm very sorry, Eric. I am sorry for myself, but even more sorry I hurt you."

Carrington rose from the bed, grabbed his overnight bag then started for the door. I heard him sniff, accompanied by a soft whimper. He paused, maybe hoping something else would pop into his head to say, or maybe trying to regain his composure before exiting. Then he opened the door and left.

It was then that it hit me. I had seen the tear, and what I had heard was him crying...the man who had told me he did not cry. Nobody had ever cared that much about losing me. I recognized that if I didn't act quickly, Carrington would be out of my life for good. Deep down, I knew that wasn't the outcome I wanted. Before I could overthink it, I jumped out of the bed, ignoring the hungover queasiness that came with the action, then I bolted to the door. When I opened it, Carrington was just about to enter the elevator. I shouted his name, running down the hall.

His expression was hard to read because his face was red and puffy. But he didn't enter the elevator. I ran up to him and hugged him. "Don't go."

Carrington's cries became louder, and he pulled me into a tighter embrace, getting the side of my face and shoulder wet. "I made such a miserable mess of things," he croaked, pulling away and moving his hands in the air like he didn't know what to do with them. "I'm ruining my life. Your life. Stefan's life.

You're better off without me, and that kills me because I want you so much."

I pulled him back to me. "Shh. I'm sorry I was being a prick. It's just, I was hurt."

He nodded. "Of course. You had a right to be angry with me."

I reached up to wipe his tears with my hands. He was getting the sobs under control. "Don't cry. I don't want to be the reason you're sad."

He barked out a laugh, though his face still showed pain. "Always wanting to please."

I touched his chin. "I guess I'll always want to please *you*."

"Eric, you were right to reject me..." he started.

I moved my fingers up to his lips to silence him. "No, I wasn't. You're the best thing that ever happened to me. Carrington, I'm not going to lie and say that I can go right back to trusting you again. I'm not there yet." He nodded with regret. "But my heart wants you anyway."

At this point, the elevator doors opened and two women walked out, both eyeing the unusual scene. When they had walked a little distance away from us, I heard one say to the other, "Only in New York."

Carrington sniffled, wiped his eyes then chuckled. "Um, you're not dressed."

I grinned. "To think that just a couple of days ago, I was nervous about you seeing me in my underwear. Now, I'm showing all of New York."

He smiled back. "Come. Let's finish talking in the hotel room."

We walked back down the hall to our door. I looked at him. "Well, I'm not carrying the card key in my boxer briefs. Use yours."

He stared back at me with alarm, but a bit of amusement as well. "I don't have one."

"Oh," I gulped. "Well, that's...embarrassing."

Carrington shrugged. "No problem, I'll text Stefan now to tell him of our predicament. He can use his key to let us back in."

"Give me your shirt," I demanded.

"What? I'm not removing my shirt. I don't have an undershirt on," he protested.

I rolled my eyes. "So what? You're all over the internet shirtless. At least you'd have pants on, which is still more than I'm wearing."

He chuckled again. "I think it would look worse if we were both half-dressed, don't you?"

"Said the man who's dressed."

Carrington sighed. "If I give you my shirt, will it help move you toward trusting me again?"

I thought about it for a second. I nodded. Carrington began unbuttoning his shirt, unaware that another couple had opened their door and were entering the hallway, watching the whole scene. "Good Lord!" the woman exclaimed to the presumed husband. "Perverts," the man added as they rushed down the hall.

I should have been mortified, but I started laughing, finding the situation ridiculous. It was also a release of the hurt and tension I had been carrying for hours. Within seconds, Carrington was laughing, too.

"You don't have to give me your shirt," I told him. "You're right. I'll look just as silly whether I have your shirt or not. No need to create another scandal for yourself."

Carrington held up a finger. "Hold that thought." He pulled out his phone and texted Stefan of our plight.

"About that…I'm going to resign today. It doesn't matter how many scandals I have now." He continued unbuttoning his shirt.

I put a hand over his to stop him. "It's okay. As much as I like looking at your chest, I don't want you embarrassed just because I am. That's not what a partnership is about." He smiled with appreciation. "Besides, the fact that you were willing to give me your shirt means a lot to me."

He winked. "The proverbial giving you the shirt off my back."

"Hmm, you can do that literally when we're in private," I whispered. "But about that resignation thing…"

"I was going to whether you agreed to keep seeing me or not," he explained. "I'm not going to lie to my countrymen. I'm not going to make up tales about the photo. And since you're willing to give me another chance, I will not hide you. It was wrong for me to have thought it acceptable. I won't miss the presidency. I realized last night, the one thing I worried about losing was you."

"What will you do?" I asked.

He grinned. "Concerned I'll become a man of leisure, relying on your income to keep me housed and clothed?"

I laughed, looking down at my half-naked form. "Um, you may not want to bet on this horse, considering I can't keep *myself* clothed."

"Mm," he murmured. "I don't want you in clothes anyway." He pulled me into a chaste kiss.

"But I don't want you to be bored and unhappy," I lamented.

"I won't be. First off, I was being facetious about the money. I have an abundance, as you know. We'll be fine. I will pursue my ambition in sports medicine and training. In fact, I was contemplating finishing my education here in the United States, if you would like that..."

I beamed. "I would *love* that. Will you be able to get citizenship here?"

"As a full-time student, along with my connections, I can call in some favors," he assured me.

"Hmm, well, this won't be the time I criticize the rich and powerful for getting special treatment," I mused.

The elevator doors opened and Carrington reacted by standing in front of me, shielding me from the view of whomever came out. Peeking around Carrington's body, I saw that it was Stefan. He snickered when he spotted us. "Looking to start another salacious news story, Mr. President?"

Carrington pretended to be annoyed. "Just open the door."

Stefan snorted, but did as commanded. The three of us rushed back inside the room, then Carrington pulled me into his arms, crashing his mouth against mine. When he pulled back for air, he muttered, "I've been wanting to do that since I saw you at Manny's last night."

Stefan rolled his eyes. "Get a room."

Carrington looked at him with surprise. "Uh, I believe we do have a room."

I ignored their banter. "You were at Manny's last night?"

Carrington stroked my cheek. "Wow, you were really out of it."

Stefan jumped in. "He was there to save you from yourself. Carrington was ready to take a beating from a bigger chap to keep him off you."

Carrington shot him a look of annoyance. "You don't know that he would have won the fight."

Stefan barked a laugh. "Yes, I'm quite sure he would have."

"Fuck you," Carrington shot, though there was no venom with the bite. "You're not inspiring me to forgive you for your role in the photo travesty."

Stefan didn't laugh. He became quite somber.

I stroked Carrington's arm. "I don't purport to know everything behind what happened or why Stefan did what he did." I looked to Stefan, and he dropped his head. He appeared to be ashamed about the incident. "But Carrington, I forgave *you*. And as a wise man once told me, if you punish someone, it should be to teach them a lesson. When they've already learned their lesson, punishing them further is just revenge."

Carrington lifted my chin and kissed my nose. "I believe it isn't the man that is wise—but he is smart enough to respect advice from his mother. And now, from his boyfriend."

I was elated. He hadn't used that term before. "Boyfriend?"

His face softened and became loving. "If you're all right with that."

I gulped. "Yes, I would like that."

Carrington smiled. "Good, because I love you, Eric. I know it's quick, but...I love you."

"I love you too," I blurted, pulling him back to me. I wanted his mouth back on mine.

After a few moments of kissing, I remembered that Stefan was still in the room.

"I'm sorry," I told him when we broke for air.

Stefan grinned. "Congratulations, Carrington. You found the person who is right for you. I mean that."

Carrington rushed to Stefan and pulled him into a hug. "Thank you." He then whispered in his ear. "I forgive you, even if you and Mateo kept me awake all night, snoring at me in stereo. But Stefan, can you forgive me? I was too self-absorbed to see you for who you are. I hate that I was hurting you."

Stefan hugged him back. "It's okay, mate. Your friendship means the world to me. I won't betray it again." He then glanced at me. "I'm sorry, Eric. I was unfair to you because of my jealousy and insecurity. You've been kind and generous from the day I met you. I hope you can forgive me and that we can be friends as well."

I crossed the room and pulled Stefan into an embrace. I pulled away, flushing, realizing I was still half dressed. "Uh, I forgot I don't have clothes."

Stefan laughed. "Trust me. I don't mind. You might have made me a little stiff there."

Carrington feigned anger. "Hey! Don't make me regret forgiving you."

Stefan laughed louder. "Sorry, mate. I saw the photos, remember? I know what's under his briefs. My body's going to react when he's half-naked and hugging me."

My cheeks heated more, and I wanted to change the subject. "So, speaking of looking at other men, where's Mateo? You can't leave him alone too long, you know."

Stefan smirked. "Oh, I have that lion tamed. I told him I would be right back down. I figured you two would want some private time together."

"But we have to check out," I reminded him.

Stefan waved a hand through the air. "Nah, I figured you two would kiss and make up. I went to the check-out desk and secured a second night. There was another empty room available. Guess who'll be next door?"

Carrington smiled, then turned to me with alarm. "Eric, you're supposed to be at work today!"

"Ugh," I groaned. "I'd better call in sick. They must be wondering where I am. Since I've never faked an illness before, they shouldn't suspect I'm lying."

"But you aren't lying. You're lovesick," Stefan reasoned.

Carrington pulled me back into his arms. "Lovesick? In that case, I hope there's no cure. Sorry, babe." He kissed my cheek and stroked my back. "Eric, consider moving back to this wretched city."

"What?"

"I don't love New York, but I have learned there is a good sports medicine training program at NYU. You could follow your passion and resume your photography full-time. I have the resources to make it work for us," he urged. He turned to Stefan. "You and Mateo should move here too. Mateo could restart his hair-styling business, and you could continue being my security and protect Eric from any would-be creeps that come into his studio."

I patted Carrington's chest. "It's a lot for us to consider. We don't have to decide right now. You make your calls back home and I'll call my office to tell them I'll be out today."

Stefan rose from his chair. "And I'll head back down to bring Mateo to our hotel room. Carrington, I'll text you when we're ready to hook up again. Plan on something like twenty-four hours from now." Stefan shot us a mischievous grin, then hugged each of us one more time. He put a hand on one of my pectoral muscles as he pulled away from me. "Hmm. Make Carrington work for it. He has no problem punishing others."

"Get out!" Carrington laughed.

Once Stefan exited, Carrington put the 'don't disturb' sign on the outside of our door. "Even though I'm resigning, I guess we don't need to *invite* another scandal by having the housekeeper walk in on us and snapping pictures on her phone."

"Eh. People will just look at the internet and say, 'him again—can't that guy keep his clothes on?'" I snickered.

Carrington grinned. "Perhaps. Nevertheless, I would suggest we limit the photography to your models henceforth. Besides, you don't need pictures to view me naked. But I think we should make our calls before we get into other activities."

I rolled my eyes. "Okay, okay. But if anyone in Yastarus insists you go back today, I swear, I'm flying there with you. Point me at the culprit, and I'll rearrange their face."

He looked at me with an odd expression. "What did you say?"

"Um, I don't know. Rearrange their face? Don't worry, I didn't mean it. Of course, I wouldn't hit someone. For some reason, that phrase popped into my head," I answered. Carrington began cackling. "What? It's not even funny." He kept guffawing. "Okay, you're weird."

He calmed down. "*You're* weird," he replied. "But you're also adorable. And you know what else you are?"

I crossed my arms, waiting for a barb. "What?"

"Mine." He smiled.

I grinned in return. "My favorite adjective you've used to describe me so far."

Carrington uncrossed my arms and pulled me into a kiss. When he broke away, his expression was playful. "You do know that 'mine' isn't an adjective, right?"

I slapped his shoulder. "Yes! God, just get back to kissing me, Professor."

He laughed again. "Hmm, another role-play scenario. We have so much fun in our future."

Chapter Twenty-Three

Carrington
December 24th

Eric and I had been together for a few months, me attending NYU whilst he flourished as a full-time photographer in the West Village. He'd quit his job at the insurance company and, with a bit of sadness, sold his charming home in Connecticut. I had purchased a one-bedroom apartment in the city, and was thrilled when Eric agreed to move in with me.

Mateo, who had never enjoyed the suburbs anyway, was quick to follow us to the Big Apple, re-establishing his hair-styling practice and renting an apartment on the booming Lower East Side. As I had hoped, Stefan was able to secure a Green Card to continue providing me security. An ex-president still had top-secret knowledge, and Yastarus didn't want me kidnapped and compromised. Since the reality of a threat was low, Stefan also assisted Eric during his photo shoots with the real intention of preventing unwelcome advances toward my boyfriend. Although Eric would tell me that there was nothing to worry about, Stefan clued me in that there were many times he had to intervene to stop inappropriate behavior from models. I couldn't blame them. Had I been one of his models, I would have flirted with Eric as well.

Whilst back in Yastarus, I had prepared my mother and the vice president for my planned resignation. The vice president was gracious, never showing glee that my decision would make him the most powerful man in the country. My mother was stoic, but expressed her support. Once she knew of Eric's innocence in the scandal and learned of his heroics against my assailant, her previous fondness for him returned.

The resignation itself, as well as its reasons, elicited shock from many of the prudish, disapproving people of Yastarus. In the months that followed, however, the country slipped into a slight recession and my replacement's popularity dipped. A survey conducted in late-November showed Yastarusians were having an attitude shift, with the majority indicating they were unconcerned about my relationship with a man, and an even bigger majority signaling they would welcome my return to the presidency if I were to run again. I assured Eric that I wouldn't be tempted to do so.

Although I had encouraged my mother to consider a move to America, she made it clear that she wouldn't leave the land where her husband was buried. I spoke with her or FaceTimed her often, though not as much as Eric did. He and my mother had become good mates, chatting about cooking, books, movies and me. My mother complained that were it not for her conversations with Eric, she'd have no idea what I was up to, sharing that he gave her the *real* scoop. I guessed that meant Eric didn't always sugar-coat what happened in my life, but it didn't bother me. I was happy to see my mother and my boyfriend develop a bond, as it filled a void left by Eric's own mother. I was eager to fly Eric to Yastarus after Christmas. It would be the first time I could show him my country, and Eric was looking forward to holiday time with my mother.

Eric and I had joined a softball league in the city, playing until the weather turned cold. My boyfriend was a decent shortstop, though perhaps more beloved by our team members for his ability to lift everyone's spirits and encourage their efforts. I had become quite good at batting, holding the team's highest average. To Eric's chagrin, I continued to wiggle my butt when assuming the batter's position. He told me he was certain that the ladies in the stands came just to watch me. That encouraged me to give them what they came for, eliciting whoops and catcalls from the bystanders when I shimmied what God gave me. Some of the women flirted and I enjoyed flirting back, whilst making it clear Eric would be the one in my bed that evening. They knew our story but would exaggerate their disappointment, causing Eric to roll his eyes and smirk at our behavior. I knew he didn't mind, as he had once joked *"guess you should enjoy it before gravity has your ass cheeks sliding into home plate before the rest of you does."* Such insolence! That had earned him a bare-bottomed spanking that evening, which he had panted for the entire ride home from the ballfield.

As we had prepared for the holiday season, Eric had insisted on decorating our home. Though I would have preferred a small tree with simple white lights, he was set on an oversized tree with multi-colored lights, stockings on the mantel, candles in the windows and various other Christmas frills. It was a bit gauche for my taste, but he had slipped and said that it reminded him of the one day each year he had felt joy when growing up. Had I known when he first started buying the decorations, I would have given him my credit card and suggested he spend whatever necessary to replicate his cherished holidays.

With it being the day before Christmas, Eric was in a spirited mood, playing holiday music performed by the same pop artists he favored throughout the year. I walked into our kitchen to the aroma of fresh-baked cookies and Eric humming to the Christmas tunes. He had become an expert at making delicious foods that excluded dairy, and many of those cookies were already on cooling racks on our kitchen counters. Eric was using some contraption to dust powdered sugar on them, causing me to laugh when some of it blew back on his face. That was when he noticed me and gave me his endearing puppy-dog look. But this time, he had a dusting of white sweetness on his nose and cheeks.

"What?" he wondered.

I walked over to pull him into an embrace. "Nothing. You're just so cute."

Eric shook his head like I was always saying strange things, but the corners of his mouth upturned to reveal his fondness for the affection. He saw me grab one of the cookies and shot me a warning look. "Don't!"

I took a bite and let out a little moan of delight. "So good."

"They would taste better if you'd let them cool. Besides, you're going to ruin your appetite for dinner." He sighed.

"You know what would make you look even more adorable right now?" I asked, ignoring his chastising, and popping the rest of the cookie in my mouth. He tried to pretend he was annoyed, but I could also see he was aroused by my full, chewing mouth and the look of ecstasy on my face.

"What?"

"You baking those cookies with nothing on but an apron," I replied once I had swallowed his confection.

Eric smirked. "It's Christmas. It's not the annual 'celebrate a porn star' day."

"They have one of those in this country?" I wondered.

He chuckled. "No. Dope. I'm saying, it's Christmas—you shouldn't be thinking dirty thoughts."

"Why not? You're not religious."

He shrugged. "It's a day for Santa, and Rudolph and Frosty. Not Stormy Daniels."

"Hmm. I see. Well, I guess I'll have to rethink the gift I planned to give you when we're in bed tonight," I remarked.

Eric laughed. "Okay, that is wrong on so many levels. First off, we open gifts on Christmas morning, not on Christmas Eve. Secondly, you better not have bought me sex toys. I'd like to think you bought stuff that made you think of me."

"Oh, baby, you know I think of you when I see a sex toy." I winked.

He rolled his eyes. "Thanks for the heads-up that I won't be showing off my presents to my friends."

I pretended to be serious. "Well, I believe Stefan already saw photos of you with your sex toys, so it would be redundant."

Eric looked mortified. "God, don't remind me that he looked at those photos. And we didn't take any when we were using the sex toys, remember? Still, he must think I'm such a slut."

I couldn't help but laugh. "Oh, since seeing the photos, he's come up with quite a few sexy adjectives to describe you, but slut wasn't one of them."

Eric grimaced, then walked over and tapped his fist against my forehead. "You do know that 'slut' isn't an adjective, right?"

"Touché," I responded. It was a grammar game to which we had become accustomed. "Well, back to your earlier concern, there will be no sex toys under the tree for you."

He appeared a bit surprised. "No?" I nodded. He looked skeptical. "So, what was this gift you had planned for tonight? Oh, you mean, *that one* won't be under the tree."

I shook my head no. "Incorrect. There are no sex toys being offered as gifts this Christmas. I hope you didn't have your heart set on receiving one."

He held back a laugh. "Um, I think I can make do with the ones I have. Maybe you could buy some to donate to needy gay boys who can't afford them. So, what did you have to give me this evening?"

"You know I can't tell you before you unwrap it," I teased. "Besides, I won't be sharing it if you object to anything sexual on Christmas."

I could tell his curiosity and his healthy sexual appetite were overpowering his celebration principles. "Um, I guess if it's once we're in bed it would be okay."

"Hmm. I'm glad. I've been...preparing this gift for some time now." He cocked an eyebrow, unable to hide his interest. "I think it may make tomorrow morning's festivities feel anticlimactic."

Eric crossed his arms over his chest. "Ha! I doubt that. I don't think you realize how much I've been looking forward to Christmas." But of course, I did. He hadn't had cause to celebrate the holiday for several years. It was why I was determined to make the day as special as possible for him.

"We'll see," I challenged, grabbing another cookie from the cooling rack and shoving it in my mouth, earning a playful smack on my arm.

"Get out of my kitchen," he gasped, feigned outrage at my unruliness. "Don't come back until I tell you dinner is ready."

Chapter Twenty-Four

Eric

We enjoyed an intimate Christmas Eve dinner. I had prepared most of the food in advance for this sitting, as well as for Christmas Day, so all I had to do was heat and serve. Carrington had shaken his mood for teasing me once he left the kitchen, as he had been almost romantic since returning. He was sharing with me stories of his childhood holidays, the plans he was making for us when I joined him in Yastarus and his appreciation for the fine cuisine before him. Carrington had indulged in three glasses of wine, which was unusual, but I chalked it up to celebrating the holiday.

As dinner progressed, however, he became quieter and were it not for the heated glances he cast my way, I would have worried that he was becoming somber. He also started to seem nervous, fidgeting with his napkin and glancing down at his plate—all of which was very unlike him.

"Everything okay, Carrington?" I asked.

His face flushed. "Pardon? Oh, yes. Everything was delicious, as always. Thank you, Eric."

I nodded. "I meant you seem to have gotten…lost in your head somewhere."

He gave me a small smile. "Have I? I apologize. You have my attention, I assure you. You look exquisite tonight. Thank you for changing into those beautiful clothes. You're enchanting."

Right before dinner, I had put on an off-white cashmere turtleneck sweater that clung to my shoulders, arms and chest. It was tucked into a pair of high-waisted, butt-hugging wool slacks that emphasized my flat stomach and Carrington's favorite asset. "Um, thanks. You're sure you're not upset about something? Is it what I said about the sex toys? If you bought me a sex toy, I won't be mad."

I couldn't tell if he sighed or laughed. "I'm not upset, and I didn't buy you a sex toy."

"Oh, okay. Well, I'll clean up the kitchen. Why don't you go into the living room, look at the tree and relax?" I suggested.

He raised his eyes to me as I rose from the chair. "Are you sure? You did all the cooking. I can take over now."

I leaned over and kissed his beautiful hair. "I'm sure. Go on."

If I wasn't mistaken, his heated glance hit me again. "Eric? Would you mind if I go take a shower instead? I was thinking that maybe after you clean up, you could join me in bed? I'd like to snuggle with you."

"Um, sure. That would be nice. I might be a while though."

"Take your time," he jumped in. "It's fine."

I smiled. "Okay. Don't fall asleep on me before I get into bed. You promised me cuddles."

Carrington stood from his chair and pulled me into a chaste kiss. "I promise. I'll be awake and waiting for you."

* * * *

Once I had stacked the dishwasher, hand-washed the pots and pans and cleaned away crumbs from the table and counters, I went to the hall closet to pull out Carrington's Christmas presents. Though they had been hidden under blankets, and I had warned him not to peek, I wasn't sure if he had or not. I placed them under the tree, noticing he had not put anything there for me yet. It made me guess he might have just one present hidden somewhere, and while I didn't mind there weren't more, I hoped my six for him wouldn't worry him that he had disappointed me. I was more excited to watch him open the presents from me than I was to receive something.

As was the tradition when I was growing up, I didn't turn off the Christmas lights since it was Christmas Eve. It was a terrible waste of electricity, but I wanted the magic of waking Christmas morning with everything aglow.

Carrington had been so quiet after the shower turned off, I feared he had struggled to stay awake and I would have to settle for curling up against his sleeping body. I smiled, though, thinking even that was a pleasure I never tired of. If he fell asleep first, I couldn't work my way back into his arms, so I would spoon him. It would be a rare treat since I was his 'little spoon' most nights.

I padded my way into the bedroom, surprised the lights were on. When I looked over to the bed, I gasped out loud. Carrington was lying on his back with his hands behind his head. He was naked, save for a large Christmas bow covering his private area. He smiled when he saw my reaction. "I hope you like your first present."

I composed myself, then grinned. "Mm, I do. You're a gift I never tire of unwrapping."

His smile broadened, but there was that lingering nervousness that had me worried. "Baby, the gift is a bit more than just…removing the bow."

I couldn't imagine what he was talking about, and I was fearful he had done something that I would find off-putting, like getting a tattoo on his butt. I gulped at the thought, preparing myself to pretend I loved whatever he was going to present to me. "Uh, okay. Not sure what you mean."

Carrington pursed his lips, then got a look of determination on his face. He scooted back against the headboard, then pulled his feet toward his butt, exposing enough of his ass for me to see there was an inserted butt plug. "I've been practicing."

I knew I looked confused, though I was sure I looked horny too. "Um, practicing what, baby?"

He lowered his legs to get himself back into a comfortable position. "I know when I first tried that submarine thing you have, I had a bit of trouble when we first put it in. Do you remember?" I nodded, dazed by the oddity of the conversation. "Well, even though it felt good at the end, I didn't love the beginning. I kind of shied away from playing with it after that."

I nodded. "I know. I sensed that, and I'm okay with it. Carrington, you don't need to be doing this to make me happy."

He shook his head no. "Eric, this isn't about me playing with a toy to give you a show. I wanted to get used to it so I could give you *me*."

I scrunched my face from bewilderment. "I don't understand. You always give me you... What are you saying?"

"Eric, I want you to make love to me tonight. I want you inside of me," he explained.

I gulped. "Oh." I swallowed again. "Are you sure? Carrington, I love you topping me, you know. You don't have to do this."

"Baby, please come over to the bed. I feel kind of vulnerable talking to you whilst I'm lying here on the bed naked with a butt plug up my ass — and you're standing there looking like you just walked off the cover of *GQ* magazine." He sighed.

To make him more comfortable, I whipped off my sweater and chucked off my pants, throwing them over a nearby chair. Then I climbed onto the bed with him and stroked his hair. "Better?"

He smiled. "Yes. Thank you."

"Carrington, I know you're a top. I am so happy every time I'm with you and I don't feel like I'm missing anything," I assured him. "We don't need to do what you're proposing. I don't want something hurting you when we're making love."

He nodded. "I know. That's why I've been practicing with the plug. I started with the submarine and worked my way up to the vibrator. I even tried the dildo a couple of times. I won't lie, that was a total no-go on the first effort. I thought I was going to end up bleeding." I gave him a look of horror. "No. It's okay. My point is, I found that it was getting easier. I just needed some experience and a little…stretching."

"But again, I didn't ask you to do this."

He put a finger to my lips. "I know. I wanted to. Eric, I want to know what it feels like to have you inside me, to have you come inside me. You're my guy. I want you to be the only one who ever has me that way."

They weren't the words my mother had taught me were romantic things to say to a lover, but they brought a tear to my eye.

"Eric, I knew if you started to enter me and I felt pain, you'd want to stop. Hell, maybe I would have wanted you to stop. I knew I had to get myself ready in my head and for the bed. And tonight, whilst you were cleaning up, I took a hot shower and lubed myself up, stretching myself with this stupid butt plug. But Eric, now you can enter me and it won't hurt. I'll just enjoy the experience of having the man I love inside me. I want that."

I didn't say anything, overwhelmed. He mistook that as doubt on my part. "God, did I misread things? Do you not want me like that?"

I pounced on his mouth, thrilled by his wet tongue darting against my own. He pulled my body on top of his, and my hardness was crushing his pretty bow. "Oops. I forgot to unwrap you first."

He laughed. "Please. It's not the softest of material. I don't want to end up explaining to a doctor how I got a ribbon cut on my dick."

I untied the bow and pulled it away, salivating at the sight of his engorged dick and hefty nut sack. "You are so hot. I don't think I'll ever cease being amazed at how perfect you are, Carrington."

"So, you didn't tell me. Do you want to top me tonight? You don't have to if you don't want to. I'm always happy to make love to you, baby," he promised.

My eyes went wide. "I love it when you top me, but I want to get inside you."

He was shaking a bit under me, his smile a bit uncertain. "Good. I've been thinking about it for a while." He grabbed both sides of my face and pulled me into another kiss. "Until a few months ago, I would never have contemplated doing this, but I want this now. You and I will only have had each other this way. It makes me feel like — we belong to each other."

I nodded. "We do, though, don't we? I want to belong to you, Carrington."

He smiled. "Yes. And I'm yours too, baby."

I reached down to pull the intrusion from Carrington's ass. That elicited a slight hiss from him. I soothed him by rubbing his pecs and kissing his neck. I worked my way down his sexy torso, licking and kissing until I reached his aching shaft. I didn't know if I could ever be enthusiastic about fellatio with someone else, but I thought about satisfying Carrington all the time. Having him in my mouth felt so intimate, and his warmth and taste were intoxicating. I had learned to take all of him without gagging, and knowing that entire beautiful cock was in my mouth and throat was a major turn-on for both of us.

This night, I slurped and sucked with lots of saliva, just as he liked it. When I pulled off him, the spit mixed with his own leaking liquid was drooling out of my mouth and down my chin. I knew it was a sight that sent Carrington into a daze, and tonight was no exception. His eyes clouded and his mouth opened like he just saw a vision. He grabbed me by my neck and pulled me back up to him so he could kiss me once more, licking at my messy lips.

"I'm going to start to get you ready, okay?" I whispered when he parted for air. He nodded, though I wasn't sure if he was even comprehending. He was lost in lust. When he pulled my mouth back to his, I slipped a finger into his already slicked hole. Carrington moaned. Like an acrobat, I kept kissing him, fingering him, then used my right hand to grab the lubricant from the nightstand. I pulled away from him long enough to coat two more fingers. "Ready for more, baby?"

He nodded. I slid another digit into him, and he bit down, closing his eyes. I was relieved when he reopened them, giving me a small smile. "I'm good. It feels good."

After stretching and probing him, I inched in the third finger, eliciting an 'ooh' from him while he wrapped his arms around my shoulders. "Tell me if it's too much," I coaxed.

"Not too much," he breathed. "Pump me."

I started to push my fingers in and out, which didn't seem to cause him discomfort. His eyes were rolling and he was gasping, so I figured he was past feelings of discomfort. I placed one of the pillows under his bottom so I could angle my fingers better, hitting his prostate with every thrust. His cries told me I was striking the mark. "Jesus, Carrington. You could make me cry just from looking at you," I gasped.

"I'm ready," he almost yelled.

I ripped off my shorts, lubed my shaft then pressed the head of it against his loosened hole. When I started to enter him, he emitted a groan of pleasure. Before I could ask if he was okay, he put his strong hands on my hips and pulled me into him. He cried out from the entry, and I was afraid I had hurt him. I stilled, waiting for a signal from him on what I should do. He looked at me with a puzzled expression.

"I was trying to go slow," I panicked. "I didn't mean to…"

"Fuck me!" he demanded. "God, Eric. What are you waiting for?"

I started to grind into his hard ass. I had never experienced anything that felt so tight, warm and wet. Knowing I was inside Carrington had me heady, and I was basking in his sounds, his smell and the sexy contortions of his face each time I thrust against his prostate. "Are you doing okay, Care?"

"I didn't know it could be like this. It's…amazing. It's so intense. Yes, keep doing that. Please, Eric."

After I had been pumping at a steady pace for about a minute, he looked into my eyes and smiled. "Good?" I asked.

"So good," he whispered back. "Faster, Eric. Pump those sexy little hips, baby. I want to feel your balls slapping my ass."

I lifted his legs higher, no longer worried that I would be hurting him. I was pounding him like I was driving a stubborn nail. He was gripping the sheets and crying out nonsense words, mixed with F-bombs and various other swears. I knew we'd crest soon, so I watched as I fucked him. I wanted to etch into memory his beautiful face and body, taking me, loving me and being undone by me. It was leading to one of the most intense orgasms I would ever have. I was sweating from the workout, and I was hot inside from the intense pleasure. "Oh, Care, I'm going to come!"

He stopped his cries long enough to grab his cock and begin pumping. "Do it, Eric. Come in me. Fill me with your load."

He knew dirty talk put me over the edge. I cried out. My dick jerked inside his tight channel. My ejaculation was so intense it almost felt like razors touching my skin as every nerve in my cock became electrified. "Uh, fuck. Care, Care…."

"Pull out. Get the last of it on my hole, then go back in," he panted.

Even with my dick still twitching, I suppressed a laugh. I had learned this was his fetish since being with him. I slipped out, smeared his hole then pushed back in him. I pumped my dick while it was still hard enough, bumping up against his prostate a couple of more times, triggering his orgasm. He was writhing beneath me, manhandling his needy shaft as we both watched him spray load after load of beautiful white cream all over his belly, chest and even his chin.

I leaned over to lick the cum off his face, then kissed him open-mouthed, letting him taste himself. He held my head with both hands, devouring my mouth despite mutual gasping. When I pulled out, he lowered his legs so I could lie flat against his body, mushing his seed between our chests and abdomens. Still, we kissed and slid our bodies against each other.

When I released his face, he looked like he was drugged. "Carrington, are you okay?"

He sighed. "Jesus. No wonder you like me topping you. I can just imagine how great *my big dick* feels." With that, he let out a mischievous chuckle and pulled me back into a kiss to let me know it was in jest. "Eric, you are…amazing."

I wasn't feeling very pretty, knowing there was spit and cum all over my face, and my hair was wild from his hands raking my head. "Um, what you're seeing is a little rough right now, I'm sure."

His gaze softened. "Sweet Eric. You're beautiful. You know what you look like right now?" I shook my head no. "Mine."

"Yeah?" I smiled.

"Mm," he approved. "You once said you needed to see the real me to trust me again. This is the real me — the man who loves Eric Turner, first and foremost. I'm his. I'll always be his."

My eyes welled up. "Carrington, I *do* trust you. I have for a long time now." I stroked his cheek. "And you were right. I can't imagine any gift tomorrow being better than this one."

He laughed. "Ah, you never know. I just may have gotten you that dragon-shaped lamp you were eyeing at the store the other day."

I had been eyeing it all right — with horror. I chuckled. "Well, okay then. I guess it will get better."

"You're a brat." He smirked.

"*You're* a brat," I countered.

"And you're messy," he added. "Uh, I guess I'm even messier. Come on. Let's take a shower. I'll be a prune after washing up again, but I wouldn't want Santa to see us all cum-covered. He might skip our house and you'd miss your big day."

I knew that I appeared mortified at the notion. "Santa wouldn't do that."

He chuckled. "No, I guess he wouldn't. You've been naughty sometimes, but Santa sees I keep you in line with a firm hand."

I looked out the window. The snowstorm they had been predicting was upon us. "Look. It's going to be a white Christmas."

"Hmm," he observed. Then he kissed me. "Who says storms don't bring good things?"

Chapter Twenty-Five

Carrington

I woke from a light shaft of winter light poking through the bedroom window. I blinked a couple of times, then jumped when I turned to see if Eric was still asleep. He was on his side, leaning his chin on the palm of his hand, staring at me like a horror movie stalker.

"Jesus! What are you doing?"

He sighed with contentment. "You're up. I was wondering if you were going to sleep Christmas morning away," he answered.

"What time is it?" I griped.

"It's already seven. Merry Christmas." He bent over and gave me a peck on the lips. "Come on. You need to see what Santa brought."

I was still trying to clear the grogginess from my head. "Huh? What are you, five?"

Eric's smile disappeared as he flinched. "Oh...sorry. You can sleep if you want."

I hated that I killed his joy. I reached up and messed up his hair even more than it already was. "No, I'm sorry. I love your holiday enthusiasm. I'll get up, but would you be my best mate and start some coffee while I brush my teeth?"

"You sure?" he asked, unable to hide his hope.

I smiled to reassure him. "Yes, I'm sure. You exorcised the Grinch from me. Go out to see the presents Santa left you, but don't start opening them until I get out there."

He looked insulted. "Of course, I wouldn't! If I was going to do that, why would I have waited an hour for you to wake up?"

"An hour?" I shook my head. This guy was a serious Christmas junkie. "Just go make the coffee, you nut."

He jumped off the bed, already dressed in pajamas, and scooted into the living room. I hoped he was enjoying the sight of the presents I had put there once he had fallen asleep the night before. I took his cue to put on pajamas and, after brushing my teeth and taking a morning piss, I walked into the living room. He was sitting on the couch enjoying the lights, gifts and still-falling snow outside the window. I could understand why he thought it was magical.

He gave me a small smile. "Coffee is ready."

Once we were both cuddled close on the sofa, he emitted a slight hum of contentment. "Are we going to open the presents, or are we just going to admire the wrapping?"

He tapped my arm. "I don't want to rush."

I laughed. "Said the man who was up before dawn to start the festivities."

Eric rolled his eyes. "Okay. I just don't want Christmas to end. I'll get a present for each of us to open." He then looked back at me with a furrowed brow. "Where did you hide all these presents anyway? It's not like the apartment is that big."

I snickered. "Promise not to peek next year if I use the same hiding place?" He nodded. I had my feet resting on the trunk we used as a coffee table, but lowered one of them to undo the latch and pop up the lid.

Eric made an "oh" expression. "I emptied that out a while ago to use the blankets to cover *your* presents."

We both laughed, then took our time opening gifts. He and I examined each, sharing thanks and sweet kisses. I had bought Eric several camera and studio accessories he had been wanting, a new parka for these windy, cold New York City days and evenings and a couple of sexy bathing suits I wanted him to wear on the Greek island vacation we had planned for the new year. He had bought me some beautiful sweaters, some antique books I had admired when we were shopping at the Cape and a framed article from a Yastarus newspaper that outlined my accomplishments as president and overstated credit for preventing the country's drift to communism. The frame was exquisite and must have cost Eric a small fortune. It was such a thoughtful gift — something he had done some research to find.

"Last one." Eric sighed, looking at the wrapped jewelry box on his lap. I realized from his expression that he was hoping it was an engagement ring. It wasn't, and I felt apprehension about the disappointment he'd feel upon opening the box.

"Baby, it's not what you might be thinking," I warned. "I hope you'll still think it's special, though."

His eyes clouded for a moment before he forced a smile. "I wasn't expecting anything. I'm sure I'll love it." He opened the box and pulled out the chain that had a coin-like medallion. I knew he wouldn't be able to make out what it said without his contact lenses in, and he was too vain to put on his glasses. I reached over to the end table, pulled them out of its drawer, and insisted he put them on. He sighed, but did so.

"I don't know why you hate your glasses so much," I wondered. "The black frames make you so...what's the expression? Adorkable."

He rolled his eyes, but then put the coin in his mouth and bit down. "Hmm."

"What are you doing?" I asked, wondering if he lost his mind. "It isn't candy."

"The box says it's fourteen 'carrot' white gold. I wanted to make sure you didn't get rooked when you bought this," he joked.

"Just read the inscription," I barked, pretending to be impatient.

He looked at the face of the coin, which had an engraving of a tree blowing in the wind. The words around the perimeter read 'brought by the storm.' The flipside read 'and by your side through all future ones.' I could tell from his eyes moistening that he understood the sentiment. "Carrington, I love it. I will treasure it always."

I brushed my thumb over a tear that was trickling down his cheek. I began to unbutton his pajama top until his lovely chest was exposed. Taking the chain from his hand, I slipped it over his head and pressed the medallion against his breastbone. "Beautiful," I murmured.

He wrapped his arms around me and we stayed in an embrace for a couple of minutes. When he pulled away, he melted my heart with his innocent-looking face staring at me. "Thank you, Carrington. This was the best Christmas ever."

"What? You're talking like it's done," I protested.

He seemed surprised. "But it is, isn't it?"

I put his face in my hands. "I have a whole Christmas day planned for us."

Eric looked at me with wonder. "You do?"

I nodded. "Providing you want to. I thought we'd start by having breakfast. I'll even make it whilst you play with your new toys." He rolled his eyes, but grinned like an excited child who wanted to do just that. "Then, after we clean up, I thought we could go over to Washington Square and play in the snow. I'm quite good at snowball fighting, I should warn you." He laughed. His excitement was evident. "And I want you to make a snow angel."

"What? People will think I'm crazy," he laughed.

"No. They'll all take pictures of the impression left by a real, live angel," I insisted. He rolled his eyes again, but he smiled despite himself. "After we're done frolicking, I thought we could come back here and enjoy that feast you were planning to heat up for us. Then, we can cuddle on the sofa and watch Christmas movies."

"I thought you said they're corny," he reminded me.

I shrugged. "I didn't say I *hate* corny." He smiled. "When those are over, and it's dark outside, I thought I could light a fire in the fireplace."

He laughed. "You mean turn the switch to the gas line on."

"Mmhmm," I responded, ignoring the snark. "I think we should put some blankets and pillows on the floor, then I'm going to take off your clothes and worship every part of you with kisses, enjoying how your beautiful skin glows from the fire and Christmas lights."

"Oh," he whispered, as was his habit when he was too overwhelmed to respond. Then he gulped and it took everything in me to avoid skipping to the love-making right then and there.

"Uh, that's if my plans meet your approval, of course."

He nodded, swallowing once again. "Yes. I like your plans."

* * * *

The day had gone as I had hoped, right down to gentle, caring love-making. Eric exceeded any work of art, lying naked on white fur blankets in the darkened room, lit by the fireplace and holiday lights. His expression said everything—a man who was sated, awed and in love. I had cleaned him up after we had climaxed, and I was enjoying holding him, smelling him and kissing him.

"Baby, come sit on the sofa with me. We can wrap the fur around us," I coaxed.

I could tell he was reluctant to leave his spot on the floor, but he took my hand and let me lead him to the seating. Once we were under the coverlet, I kissed his cheek.

"Did you get everything you wanted?" I asked him.

"Yes." I knew he had been hoping I would propose to him, but I let his fib slide.

"Hmm," I acknowledged. "I'm glad. I received most of what I wanted."

He picked up on my qualifier and looked at me with worry. "Most? Was there something you wanted that I didn't get? I didn't know…"

I nodded. I knew I was a tease, but watching him get worked up was always comical. "I guess *you didn't* know. I thought you would have."

"What?" he pressed. "I'm sorry, Carrington. What did you want?"

I looked at him side-eyed, unable to hide my mischievous grin. "I thought, since the day is so special to you, you might have proposed to me."

I could hear his intake of air. "Me? You wanted *me* to propose?"

I sat looking at him, pretending to be disappointed. "Why not? Oh, did you think I should propose just because I'm older, bigger and more extroverted. That's a bit cliché, isn't it?"

He looked heartbroken. "I…I didn't know you wanted me to. So, you're saying you'd marry me?"

"I don't know. It depends on the quality of the proposal," I responded.

His anxiety turned to annoyance. "Are you serious?"

I shrugged. "Sure. It must be something I'd be proud to share with my children one day. But it seems that you're not ready to take that step. Oh well, maybe next year."

He panicked. "No. I can propose to you. I mean, I want to marry you. I'd love to marry you."

I shook my head with a frown. "Is that the proposal? It's not very memorable."

By now, Eric was wising up to my teasing and his expression registered both irritation and amusement. "You're a jerk."

I looked down at my lap like I felt defeated. "Wow, worst proposal ever."

Eric lifted my chin and pointed it in his direction. "You aren't being fair. I'm not prepared."

"If it's from the heart, you shouldn't have to prepare," I goaded.

He narrowed his eyes. I was seconds away from a proposal or a beating. "Fine." He took in a breath, readying himself to take on the challenge. After closing his eyes for a couple of seconds, he opened them with a determined expression. "Carrington, I thought I was happy before I met you. I convinced myself that I didn't need anyone, that people just disappoint you in the end. Then you came along, and I think I started to crush on you even when you were being a total ass in the grocery store."

I was about to object to the quality of the proposal again, but he put a hand over my mouth to shush me. "I could see you were just a guy who was overwhelmed by the situation, not wanting to let down your mother and that there was no bite in your bark. In a matter of hours, I was wishing you'd notice me the way I saw you. When you did, I was overjoyed. It was like a fantasy that I never dared dream, and it's been that way since." At this point, Eric swallowed hard, bowed his head for a moment then picked it back up with a tear running down his face. He croaked out the rest. "Carrington, every day I spend loving you, I spend it fearing I'll lose you. I don't think I could handle it if you left me. I love you with all my heart, and I want to spend the rest of my life showing you just how much.

Please say you'll marry me, Carrington. I promise I'll try to make you happy."

I couldn't tell if he wanted to say more, but he couldn't even if he had wanted to. He was trying too hard to keep from crying.

"Shh, Eric," I soothed. "You won't lose me. Yes, I will marry you. And you *always* make me happy. Since meeting you, it's like I'm reborn into the life I should always have been living. I'm so grateful to you, and I love you with all my heart, too." I pulled him into a kiss whilst brushing my fingers over his tears.

He parted from me and stared at me with wet eyes. "I admit, I was hoping you would ask me to marry you. I can't believe we're going to get married. This is the best day ever."

I looked at my watch. "And see? It's twelve-thirty, December twenty-sixth." He looked bewildered. "You were worried about Christmas being over, thinking nothing could top it. Eric, we have lots of special days ahead, as long as we're together and loving each other." He smiled, gasping out one more sob. "Hey, even though the holiday has passed, I think there is one more gift I forgot to give you."

Eric stared back with surprise. "There is?"

I reached my hand between the cushions of the sofa, pulling out another jewelry box. "Yeah. These darned small boxes. So hard not to lose them."

He looked down at the gift I extended to him, suspecting what it was. He flipped the box top, revealing the two gold rings within. "You're a jerk," he pretended to snarl, but his tears and laughter betrayed his true feelings.

"*You're* a jerk," I replied.

He chuckled. "You will not be sharing with our children how you teased me into a proposal when you already had this planned. I'll tell them you dropped to one knee and begged me to marry you."

I smiled and kissed his forehead. "As you should. If you hadn't proposed, I was prepared to beg. You own my heart. It is yours to do with as you wish."

He hugged me and whispered. "I wish to cherish it for the rest of my days." He pulled back and looked at the tear running down my cheek. "You've become a crier since you met me."

"Indeed. You fixed me. Maybe that's what we can tell our children one day."

He pondered that. "Nah, they'll never believe you weren't perfect. Besides, we already have a wonderful story to tell them."

"What's that?"

He kissed my temple. "How you came into my life. Brought by the storm."

I pressed my lips to his, grateful that the forces of nature had brought me life's greatest gift. "Indeed."

Want to see more from this author? Here's a taster for you to enjoy!

All on the Line: Saved by the Pitcher
Gareth Chris

Excerpt

James sat in the window-facing café booth, awaiting his brother Billy and Billy's girlfriend, Nadia. He had missed them for the three weeks they had been overseas on a charity mission. Although James had kept busy with his starring role in a successful Broadway musical, the downtime between performances had reminded him of the companionship dependency he had on his sibling.

James had casual friendships with the cast and crew of the show, but his colleagues were more like neighbors who chatted in passing without ever inviting each other to visit. He assumed they were wary of him because of his right-wing senator father, Charles Vicksburg. The senator's wealth and extreme views didn't sit well with the diversity of artists who made up the Broadway community, most of whom struggled to reach their positions. James thought they might not trust his proclaimed liberal views, but he had his own reasons for remaining quiet about his father's politics.

He knew that to those around him, his silence made him appear like a coward at best—and complicit at worst. They didn't understand his father's reach or connections, nor the willingness of so many to do the senator's bidding, even when nefarious. James had been a target himself on more than one occasion, and he had learned discretion equaled survival. James did his best to offset negative perceptions by being a supportive, dedicated team-player in the workplace.

During her marriage, James' mother had been miserable, contradicting his father on almost everything. While in boarding school, James learned of his mother's fatal car accident via a text from his father. The notification was brief, followed by a command to pack in preparation for the funeral. James had longed to read that his father shared his grief or was thinking about his love for his family. Instead, the text had closed with a message to be strong.

After a few years of living as a widower, Charles Vicksburg met the woman who became Billy's mother when James was nine years old. It was ironic that it was the second time James' father was smitten by a woman from a left-leaning family which deplored Charles' politics. Undeterred by pressure from her parents and siblings, Billy's mother married Charles, believing he must be a good man to have been raising James on his own.

Not having taken time to acquaint herself with her fiancé proved fatal for her marriage, as she disagreed with him on every culture-war issue. The bigger wedge was their different opinions regarding child-rearing. Billy's mother abhorred Charles' support of corporal punishment, emphasis on masculine sports for his boys and his compulsion to see his children match his career success at any cost. The couple divorced after two years, sharing custody of their then-one-year-old son. Once he was grown, Billy often complained to James about his childhood and how he had been bounced between two households with different expectations. Like James, Billy grew up to be sensitive, gravitating to his mother's more liberal views of the world, much to his father's chagrin. Charles blamed the adult versions of his sons on soft mothers and the influence of their New York City friends. The senator had hoped his sons' circles would be comprised of citizens from the more conservative districts of New York—the areas that had voted Vicksburg into office.

When Billy had begun dating Nadia, the daughter of a white man and an African-American woman, James' father couldn't conceal his contempt. In public, he didn't criticize the union, recognizing it would be frowned upon by most—even in more conservative circles. In private, he bemoaned white Americans losing their identity, heritage and more powerful positions in society. Billy was shocked when his father told him that Nadia was the type of girl he could experiment with, but to use protection so there wasn't an undesirable consequence which would 'tarnish' the Vicksburg lineage.

While James and Billy were expected, and sometimes coerced, to appear at their father's campaign rallies, Senator Vicksburg made it clear that the platform was for family members only. That sidelined Nadia, despite her two-year relationship with Billy.

James broke into a broad smile when the five-foot-six Billy and his taller girlfriend enter the café. Unlike the stoic and constipated-looking Vicksburg clan, Billy and his girlfriend were cute and exuded fun and affection. Upon seeing James, Billy returned the joyous expression and rushed to him with arms outstretched.

After a couple of pats on each other's backs, James kissed Billy's forehead. James adored his little brother, and he didn't care if them being affectionate seemed odd to others. He knew it was distasteful to their father, for sure. But James wanted Billy to experience how much he meant to him. It was something he never had himself when growing up.

Nadia laughed and rolled her eyes, pushing Billy away from his brother so she could wrap her own arms around James. She pulled the man in for a quick peck. When she backed away, she was still beaming, brushing aside a lock of James' thick, shiny mane.

"It's so good to see you guys," James said, pointing to the booth for them to sit. "How was the trip? It killed me that we couldn't connect much."

Billy and Nadia shuffled into the booth, and James sat opposite them.

"Oh my God, dude, the devastation from the earthquake was awful," Billy began.

"But it was really rewarding to be there to help," Nadia finished. "We weren't able to participate in recovery missions, of course, but they let us help care for the injured, find places for displaced pets…"

"Oh man, that was so sad, James. You should have seen all the poor animals that were wandering, lost and looking for their owners. It broke my heart," Billy added, his eyes watering at the memory.

Nadia placed her hand on Billy's thigh, nodding in agreement. "It was sad, but going there helped, and I'd do it again in a minute."

"Yeah," Billy concurred, then he turned to face James. "I wished you could have been there with us, bro."

"Me too," James admitted. "But you know, the show must go on, as they say."

"Still filling the house?" Nadia asked.

James tapped his fist on the table for good luck. "So far, so good. I'm afraid I'll jinx it by saying this, but box office receipts are holding up. *Variety* magazine called the show an 'official smash.' I knew it was possible when we prepped this show for the last two years, but to see it happening is wild."

"I'm happy for you." Billy smiled. "You deserve it. And the show is super good. So much better than some of the other crap you've performed in." He snickered, then gulped some water from the glass before him.

"Stop it," Nadia chastised. "Be nice. You haven't seen James in weeks."

"It's okay." James laughed. "He's right, and I'm glad he's honest. At least when he says something is good, I can believe that he means it."

"Dude, I always praise *your* work," Billy reminded him. "It's just some of the shows you've been in weren't worthy of your performances."

A blonde, large-busted server approached the table to take their orders, directing most of her attention to James. When she walked away, Billy gave James a leering look.

"What?" James inquired.

"She's hot, and I think she has an eye for you," Billy responded. "I'll bet she saw you sitting on the other side of the booth all by your lonesome, thinking how she'd like to make us a quartet."

"She was being polite. She wants a good tip," James dismissed him.

"Nah, she took one look at you and thought, 'I know the other guy is much cuter, but he seems to be taken. Fortunately, the loner isn't too hard on the eyes,'" Billy quipped.

"Ha! I doubt it. I think she's wondering why Nadia isn't sitting with me instead of you. She's worried she fell into some upside-down parallel universe," James retorted.

"Guys, stop! Do we have to go through this all the time?" Nadia snapped, though unable to hide her amusement. "I wish you each had a dose of humility to go with your handsome features."

"Ask her out," Billy prodded, ignoring Nadia.

"What? I don't know the first thing about her. She could be taken," James reasoned.

Billy glanced around the café to see if he could spot the server. "Hmm. I don't see her. Bet you ten dollars she's in the ladies' room primping to make a better impression with you."

"You don't have ten dollars to bet," James rebuked. "If it hadn't been for the government aid to pay for your trip, you two would never be able to afford to leave your apartment."

"That's the truth," Nadia said. "We might not have had to pay for the trip, but it was also three weeks where neither Billy nor I made money. I'll be glad to get back to my own server job so I can pay this month's bills."

James knew both his brother and Nadia spent most of their spare hours working. Billy tended bar at a busy club while his girlfriend was a diner-counter waitress. Together, they had to earn enough to cover the rent of an East Village walk-up apartment and pay their living expenses. Nadia's parents were of modest means, and it was with some hardship they were helping her with college expenses. Despite his wealth, Charles Vicksburg was willing to cover only the cost of Billy's NYU tuition and books as he continued his education to become a veterinarian.

"You could tell Father that you've had an epiphany, and you're joining the Proud Boys or some other white supremacist group." James laughed. "He'd pay for everything then."

Nadia rolled her eyes. "A Proud Boy dating a biracial girl? I think there's a big hole in that plan."

"Yeah, the big hole being Father," James sniped.

"I'll bet Lilah will have all expenses paid for anything she wants when she gets out of high school." Billy pouted.

Lilah was the last child of Charles Vicksburg, courtesy of third wife Victoria. Unlike his first two marriages, Charles was pleased with the stuffy, proper Victoria Kent-Vicksburg—a woman with an abundance of money, cosmetic surgeries and blood-red lipstick. Lilah was the precocious offspring Charles had always craved—besotted with Daddy, agreeing with his every word and looking down on anyone from another social class. She was eleven. James shuddered to think of the monster she'd be once she hit adulthood.

"Hmm, Lilah the Pariah." James smiled. "But can we be sure she's Father's child? Some speculate she's the devil's seed."

"Same thing," Nadia added.

The server brought the customers their food, and James admitted to himself that she was making overtures with her eyes and smiles. He grinned at her in return, but looked away quickly enough to discourage a connection.

Once the three were alone, Billy laughed. "Told you."

"If I ever start flirting like that on my job, please rip out my tampon and use it to wipe up my leaking dignity." Nadia gagged.

James paused mid-squeeze of the catchup on his veggie burger. "Um, bad timing for that image, thank you."

"And why would you be flirting with the customers?" Billy asked.

"Maybe because my boyfriend hogs all the French Fries," she replied, pointing at how he'd dumped the 'shared' platter of potatoes next to his hamburger.

"Oh, sorry," he said, looking down at his plate with embarrassment. "You know you're welcome to pick food off my plate."

"And I will," she responded, taking a napkin to grab a handful of fries and relocate them to her dish.

"So, are you guys still coming to the show tonight?" James asked once their mouths were chewing instead of bickering.

"Of course," Billy replied upon swallowing. "I told you. We're bringing Maria. She can't wait to see you, dude."

James smiled. Maria was the woman who had helped care for him and Billy when they were being raised in their father's house. She had been brought illegally to the United States by her husband several years earlier when much of their family had been executed by a Mexican cartel in a case of mistaken identity. Maria's husband had crossed back to meet with the gang leader, hoping to secure safe passage home, but had ended up losing his head instead. Maria had performed cleaning services in progressively wealthier homes, working the last several years in the residence of Charles Vicksburg. The irony of him employing an illegal was never lost on James or Billy, considering his campaign slogans about closing the Mexican border to everyone, including asylum-seekers.

Nevertheless, James and Billy never called out his hypocrisy for fear he'd fire or deport Maria in response.

"I can't wait to see her," Nadia said. "She's the only one in that Vicksburg house that's normal."

"She's wonderful." James grinned. "I love that woman."

Billy chuckled, turning to Nadia. "One of Father's favorite things to do was to challenge me or James as we started eating dinner. He'd ask about our grades or our political positions on something, and if he didn't like the answer, he'd tell us we were dismissed from the table. It was his way of sending us to bed without supper."

James laughed. "What he didn't know was Maria would sneak food to us, and as kids, we always thought it was better than the fancy shit he made us eat."

Billy smiled. "It was the only time we ate grilled cheese sandwiches, burgers or chips."

"Or French fries," James added, grabbing one from Billy's plate.

"Hey!" Billy protested. "Nadia can do that because she sleeps with me."

"Charming," Nadia said.

"Oh Billy, you're not going to get me to sleep with you by offering me French fries," James snickered.

Billy scrunched his face. "Dude! So gross. I told you a thousand times that brother-on-brother jokes are nasty."

James hooted out loud. "I just had to see that expression on your face. You crack me up when you get that look like you just ate poop."

Billy rolled his eyes. "You're one twisted, sick man, James. Anyway, since Maria never gets to go out, we figured we'd take her to dinner after the show."

James nodded. "That's nice. But you guys just said you're having money problems."

Nadia nodded. "By 'we,' Billy meant 'you.' Can you spring for it tonight? We'll try to pay you back in a couple of weeks."

James was paid quite well for his theater work, but his swankier West Village apartment sucked up most of those earnings. He did a mental calculation and surmised he had enough in his account to cover both the café lunch and dinner for all of them. He gave Nadia his assent with a smirk and a nod. "Fine, but it needs to be healthier than this place. I can't keep eating like this if I want to fit into my stage costumes. And make sure the restaurant isn't too expensive. I don't have Father's money."

Nadia laughed. "Not yet. I keep telling you to knock him off already so you and Billy can inherit."

Billy narrowed his eyes at her. "I'm sure Father's cut us from his will since the thing from Victoria's womb emerged."

James grimaced. "She *is* our half-sister. We should try to be nice."

Billy huffed. "You mean like when I saved and saved to buy her an American Girl doll for her spawn-day, only to discover later from Father that she used it for target practice when he took her to the shooting range?"

Nadia gasped. "Your father took an eleven-year-old to a gun range? And they let him use a life-like doll for shooting practice?"

"Never too early to learn how to handle a gun, Father would say," James answered. "And people tend to do what the senator tells them to do. I'll bet Lilah is already capable with a gun."

"Great. Another school mass-shooter in the making," Nadia grumbled.

Billy snarled. "She'd be an efficient one, too. Father confirmed her aim is excellent. She blew a hole through the doll's head."

"Why would he even tell you that?" Nadia snapped, disgusted.

"He said, 'William, it's time to get her a new doll'," Billy recalled. "Well, fuck that."

"Now that's the brotherly love I was talking about," James deadpanned.

"Whatever, dude," Billy replied. "So, the server is a no-go?"

"Um, that would be correct," James concurred.

"Why not?" Nadia pressed. "She seems to be your type. Slutty and desperate."

James shrugged, ignoring the jab. "Not in the mood."

Billy's countenance became serious. "Maybe you should stop messing around and look for something meaningful. Bro, it's been a couple of years since..."

"Don't," James warned.

There was uncomfortable silence for a couple of moments, then James signaled the server for the check.

About the Author

Gareth Chris has a degree in English and a minor in Theater / Playwriting. When he isn't writing stories about dashing men overcoming challenging situations, he provides consultative organizational design and executive coaching to international clients. He volunteers his time to local charitable organizations that focus on helping the less fortunate—particularly those needing food and shelter.

Gareth makes his home in the lovely New England area of the United States, where he, family, and friends enjoy the proximity to beaches, mountains, and numerous historical cities and sites.

Gareth loves to hear from readers. You can find his contact information, website details and author profile page at https://www.firstforromance.com/

Sign up for our newsletter and find out about all our romance book releases, eBook sales and promotions, sneak peeks and FREE romance books!

Printed in Great Britain
by Amazon

40393589R00172